Astoria

Prose Series 26

Robert Viscusi

Astoria

A Novel

WINNER OF THE AMERICAN BOOK AWARD 1996

Guernica

Toronto / New York / Lancaster
1996

Second printing.
Copyright © 1995, 1996 Robert Viscusi
and Guernica Editions Inc.
All rights reserved.

Antonio D'Alfonso, Editor.
Guernica Editions, Inc.
P.O. Box 117, Station P, Toronto (Ontario), Canada M5S 2S6
250 Sonwil Drive, Buffalo, New York 14225 U.S.A.
Gazelle, Falcon House, Queen Square, Lancaster LA1 1RN U.K.

Legal Deposit — Second Quarter
National Library of Canada

Library of Congress Catalog Card Number: 93-77803

Canadian Cataloguing in Publication Data
Viscusi, Robert
Astoria
(Prose series; 26)
ISBN 0-920717-93-4
I. Titre. II. Series.
PS3572.I73A78 1993 813'.54 C93-090049-9

To Robert and Victoria

A Note
from the Author

This is a woman's book written by a man. The writer is totally dominated by his mother's imagination. He struggles to escape, but keeps falling back. Think of an ambitious dolphin trying to climb onto dry land.

The man in question is myself from early 1986 to mid spring of 1987, which is when I principally wrote this book: that is a long time ago, and I must confess that the me of 1992 finds this 1987 fellow even stranger than he expected I would.

He is still attached to a woman who calls him a greater poet than Shakespeare and greater prose stylist than Henry James. He returns the compliment, too: to him, she is Napoléon.

You might imagine them playing Mutual Exaggeration and other tickle games when he is a baby of two and she a young wife of twenty-seven.

But now he is forty-five and she is dead. He is married, has children, responsibilities, a successful career as a professor at Brooklyn

College. He is invited to teach in Paris. While he is there, he walks around looking at everything, but all he can see is this imaginary and incestuous world. He calls it many things — *The Stendhal Syndrome* is the name he uses when trying to introduce it in his professor voice. But its real name is *Astoria*. *L'Astoria*, he calls it (for reasons he explains), when he falls entirely into it and tries to make sense of it from there.

Watching him try is sometimes dizzying. At his most intense, he writes a kind of sentence that reads like the autobiography of a pinball. It begins in one direction, rolls down a ways, strikes a bumper, bounces up and across, and so forth. This can go on, in his case, for pages, before he finally slides into the hole. It is a pretentious, a demanding, way of writing — though far less so than one might expect from the son of a woman called Napoléon.

By the time he sits down to write, the pretence has grown weak and threadbare, anyway. The more bloated the rhetoric the more suspicious. Astoria, in real life, is the name of an immigrant neighborhood in North Queens. Its faded glories don't amount to much and never did, especially when you see them against the strict laws of immigrant life — the narrow doorways, the pinched purses, the carefully graduated ambitions. So the professor's pretences have a wistful music about them. He is like a child who announces that some broken water pipe is a miraculous fountain. He makes Paris and Rome colonies of Astoria, as if his mother's childhood, bloody and bitter as it was, had really been an empire, as if he had actually been its heir.

Manhattan Terrace (Brooklyn),
June 12, 1992

Prologue

The Stendhal Syndrome

Rome, February 23, 1987. The weekly *L'Espresso* reports that Florentine psychiatrists have baptized a new condition, *sindrome di Stendhal*. A young foreigner, twenty to forty years old, arrives alone in Florence. He walks into the Uffizi Gallery. In front of Leonardo's *Annunciation*, suddenly he feels faint. When they revive him, he cannot remember who or where he is. The psychiatrists deal with him in unspecified ways (*neuroelectric* is a word they use), after which he finds he has a powerful desire to go home. Since 1979, more than a hundred cases of this new condition have turned up in the city of the Medici. Stendhal once in 1817, after visiting the spectacular church of Santa Croce, wrote in his diary that his heart was pounding from the sensations and that he walked with fear of falling. The psychiatrists find the similarities important. So do I. But most of the professional art critics consulted by *L'Espresso* sniffed at the idea that these mere industrialized tourists could experience the delicate passions of the great Italophile novelist. There is no snob like an Italian snob.

It is pleasant to be able to report, however, that the philosopher Gianni Vattimo takes these cases seriously enough to suggest that our epoch is attributing too much cultural value to works of art. This seems closer to the truth. Thinking about this disagreement among experts, I felt they were touching an area where there was surely a great deal more to be said. What was really going on in these strange episodes? Suddenly, with that uneasy sensation you get whenever you find your innermost suspicions cheerfully discussed in the newspapers, I realized that they had explained for me the nature of the book I was in the midst of finishing. I too have experienced this syndrome.

A year ago today I landed in Paris for the first time in my life. I had been offered the chance to give some lectures there and had accepted gladly. French books and movies had made Paris a part of my experience that, unaccountably, I had never visited. While I cannot say that the beauties of the city made me feel faint or lose my sense of space and time or forget my name, it is true that I was intensely puzzled. Rather than myself, however, it was Paris that did not seem to know where it was. Nothing was as it should be. For one thing it was snowing. It was snowing great sheets of grey chalk down the steep gables of the Hôtel de Ville when I came out of the Métro for the first time. The Parisians made believe it wasn't snowing. They walked about in good shoes and did not shovel the walks. But it was snowing, nonetheless, and it kept on snowing in fits for days on end. I must go back to Paris and see it again. I stayed only two weeks. True, I walked tirelessly about with a guidebook in my hand, but I saw something else, which I have written down in this book. I am glad I did not know about the Stendhal syndrome before I had begun, because that might have kept me from writing and from making what I now realize is a contribution to psychiatric literature. I have discovered a new profile of the syndrome, not reported before. A middle-aged professor arrives alone in Paris. One day he walks into Les Invalides. In front of the tomb of Napoléon, he starts to think like Stendhal. This is not the classic Florentine version, admittedly, which no doubt requires Florence and greater youth. What happened to me was that I looked at works of art and I saw Napoléon. More, I saw the people who made Napoléon what he was. And, like Stendhal, I saw myself.

Let me be more precise. I did not exactly see myself. Rather, I looked for myself and found instead an indistinct, milling crowd, not really like a single person at all, more like a collection of friends and relatives in the lobby of a funeral parlor. My journey no longer seemed to me my own expedition but rather the node or nerve-ending of what I knew to be a vast movement of people. Suddenly, the improbability, the startling leap, that had made the Italian migration to the United States that afterwards had made me, the famous convulsion in our collective fortunes which had in the fullness of time sent me to Paris to lecture in the university — suddenly this seemed very pressing. The psychiatrists say that social mobility causes the Stendhal syndrome. You feel guilty seeing what your parents couldn't and you want to go home. That makes sense to me. Rather than fainting, however, I assuaged my guilt by pointing out to myself that I was seeing it on their behalf. And, as I began explaining what this meant, I found that there was much to discover. What do you think of when you look at something breathtakingly beautiful? That is not an easy question to answer. If you own it, that's one thing. If you feel sure that some ancestors of yours were forced to live like slaves so that this thing could exist, that's another thing. And neither thing is simple. To take the second case, which is mine: knowing how we had been excluded from all this does not make me hate the beauties of Europe. But it does make me embrace them a little differently from the way that Florentine art critics (all of them, no doubt, lineal descendants of Palla Strozzi and Poggio Bracciolini) do so. It seemed worthwhile to investigate this problem, because clearly, now that tens of millions of us, grandchildren of shepherds and pushcart-vendors, come to Europe with a little money in our pockets and a lot of books in our valises, the difficulty was not mine alone. And yet not much had been written about it. Henry James and the other great American expatriates did not feel nearly so rapidly elevated as we do. Their humble antecedents, whoever they may have been, seemed already decently distant in time. This is not true for us, and I thought our predicament deserved a book of its own.

It was not, as I worked on it, an easy book to describe. Often, when people asked me what I was up to, I did feel some of the classic symptoms of disorientation and palpitations. 'It's sort of a novel in the form of a poem in the form of three essays about the meaning of history,' I would stammer. When you say things like this, people generally decide that there is no point in asking you further questions. And yet I never had any doubt of what I meant to do. I merely did not know what to call it. Not, that is, until I opened *L'Espresso* at lunchtime and saw it there, just at the right moment, all at once, in this glistening new fragment of psychiatric nosology. At that moment I realized that I was writing a book that was a new version of that familiar thing, a travel book.

Syndrome is a Greek word which means *running together*. The taxonomists of mental (and physical) disorders use it to mean a group of signs that ordinarily appear in company. But when the doctor at l'Ospedale di Santa Maria Nuova coupled this word with the name of the

17

author of *La Chartreuse de Parme*, she coined the name of a literary form which has, in fact, existed a long time. You can find its first foreshadowings in the famous battle scenes of that masterpiece. Bits of it also are to be found scattered throughout later modernist writings, right down to the *Three Poems* of John Ashbery. What is it? It is the attempt to represent in literature something you yourself know very well: when you experience this syndrome — whether in its pure youthful state like Stendhal at Santa Croce or like the Belgian *au pair* who starts perspiring at the sight of the Birth of Venus, or in the more leisurely and articulate form it took with me in Paris — you encounter an enormous number of things all at once moving at considerable speed, mostly in the same direction, but colliding nonetheless, like horses in one of those riderless races they used to love in Florence, hanging spiked balls at the animals' flanks to keep them running, or like art critics on stilts at the Carnevale all making for the punchbowl at the same moment, tripping sometimes, falling, but all in a great rush to get where they want to get. That is, this syndrome is the instantaneous recognition of all the travels it took to get you where you are.

What brings it on? The psychiatrist says it is a result of crazed and uncontrolled tourism. That, perhaps, justifies the force of her interventions (just what does *neuroelectric* mean in this context?). One art critic says that it is persecution-mania pure and simple and that the work of art has nothing to do with it at all. Vattimo, again, gets closer to the truth. 'It is not possible to concentrate centuries of history, history of art, history of culture, in half an afternoon.' And he very sensibly cites the Frankfurt-School aesthetician Theodor Adorno to the effect that of course some people are going to be terrorized by Caravaggio. In fact, this condition is brought on by the sudden recognition of something your entire life has prepared you to know on sight. It should hardly come as a surprise that the great rush of things running to hail this culminating perception should take a little time to subside. It seems to me altogether an error to regard such a moment as pathological. Why should a French graduate student be punished with drugs and neuroelectricity for feeling things Stendhal once felt? Why should he not instead be hailed, as Stendhal so often has been, as a precursor of a new age?

Probably half the people on jet planes these days are suffering from various forms of Stendhal syndrome. Stendhal, like his hero Napoléon, is everybody's father now. Even Florentine art critics must sometimes, despite their years of exquisite preparation, be stunned to the point of incoherence by their first experience of a modern city like Rio or New York. (Perhaps this sort of speeding forward in time is something so different that it should

19

have its own name — say, the Tarzan syndrome. A good example of this one in action is Jean Baudrillard's book *L'Amérique*, which I read a day or two after arriving in Paris: I was glad to have done so, as it relieved me in advance of any little hesitation I might later have felt about my capacity to do justice to a place I knew perfectly well I could not understand.) No doubt many such cases are misdiagnosed as jet lag. That is a safer disease to have, as doctors generally do not come into it and the steward will kindly supply you with mineral water and black coffee. However, if what you have really is Stendhal syndrome, these specifics will not do the trick. Neither will shock therapy or any other magic potion. Indeed, in the fullness of time, it will come to be recognized that psychiatrists and art critics, far from being able to cure this disease, are among its more profligate transmitters. Stendhal syndrome is an historical disease, caused by living at the end of the second millennium. Though its crises are spectacular — one young man, standing in the Bargello before Donatello's David, started to undress in imitation of the statue's fetching pose — interventions at such moments will prevent neither its recurrence in certain subjects nor, more important, its already alarming capacity to take people unawares.

What is to be done? Let us leave the busy electrotechnicians to other work. This condition can be addressed effectively by using the familiar methods of feeling, thinking, reading, talking, and writing. Some applications of these old approaches to such predicaments are very well known. Aristotle, for example, advises that when we suffer from an excess of the feelings of pity and fear, the best cure is a tragedy, which allows us to experience these emotions and so void them. The famous talking cure of Sigmund Freud allows us to relive terrible moments in a new situation which is not terrible, and so rid ourselves of their worst effects. Neither of these reliable applications will work on the Stendhal syndrome, because it contains a new element, which may be called *ahistory*, the absence of history. That is, it certainly has feelings to purge, which we may call unspecified grief and unspecified rage. These feelings are both the causes and effects of immigration and revolution. But you cannot get at these feelings simply by remembering or talking.

For the roots of this syndrome are not to be found in your personal history. Consider: you are the heir of immigration or revolution, or both, but you may be as I was, and scarcely know how. These historical events are very large objects in your personal condition, yet they have sunk without leaving many traces you can find. Especially in America. But they push you and pull you whether you recognize them or not. They are why you get on the airplane. A whole nation walked out of the middle ages, slept in the ocean, and awakened in New York in the twentieth century. These persons, when I asked them during the years I was growing up, never could explain very well what had taken place while they were dreaming across the Atlantic. I held that against them, with the usual hard hand of an exiguous child. But later I came to see that there was nothing surprising in their incapacity: they couldn't tell me what they themselves didn't know. My grandparents stepped, you might say, directly out of King Arthur's stable and into the tinkery of the Connecticut Yankee. They had no more idea of all that had been required to make this possible than would you if you had spent your entire youth tending goats and chickens. My parents needed their energies for making sense of a world their own parents scarcely began to understand, so that the genealogy of their predicament was a luxury they had neither the leisure nor the means to think of pursuing. In my generation, time and money were provided, but it turned out that the genealogy was not on sale. The great migration was a revolution in which almost nothing had actually happened.

Thus it is that if you follow Freud's road backwards you will come to vast blank space. The migration, even as it is remembered, included very few events that could give you any clear idea of what was in fact going on. There is a limit to how much you can make of the cramped farmhouses, the horrible sea, the humiliation of Ellis Island, the hard times and good fortune of America. And most of what can be made has already been made. Often. It has a shape so firm that politicians have been leaning on it now for decades, and it does not give way beneath them. It is a wonderful story, rich in feelings, but it explains very little. It doesn't begin to account for the stunning passions I saw all around me as a boy. It doesn't tell you anything about the shimmering silences that occasionally appeared like sudden angels right in the middle of laughing, musical, stereotypical Sunday dinners. It doesn't, in short, and it never did, answer most of the questions I was forever putting to my patient elders. Paris, however, did. It showed me, in its blunt articulate way, how to find the path that led from where I began to the place from which they had begun.

That was the necessary path. It was a peculiar walk. It meant following a continental history backwards as if it were my own recollections. What happens to the victim in the Stendhal syndrome is that he suddenly is caught by something to which he belongs without knowing it. And the ordinary tourist transaction is reversed. Instead of his capturing a souvenir, a souvenir captures him. He becomes mute. He no longer knows his name because he has become this painting, this monument. It owns him as it owned his ancestors, because he has never lived through the story of how they freed themselves from it. All this happened to me in Paris; and afterwards in Brooklyn and in Rome I was working out, and writing out, what it had meant. I am older, I was better prepared for it, than some of its victims, so I did not go under. But I felt it. It tugged at me. It was an enormous struggle, where the personal pronouns began to dissolve, and only by the straightforward method of reading all history as if it were my private troubles rising to the surface of the dialogue did I succeed in escaping.

There are easier ways to do this, I suppose. Only after I had finished writing this book did my cousin Judy tell me the story of our grandmother and the brick wall. This was the mother of my father and of Judy's father. All of us lived in a six-family house in Sunnyside, Queens, in the early nineteen-forties. Across the garden from this house was a slightly smaller house owned by another clan, the Letoes.

— You see that brick wall, she said to Judy.

— Yes, grandma.

— You look at the brick, you look at the brick, then you become the brick, and you look back at you.

Since I was only a boy and could thus never be qualified as a witch, my grandmother's conversation with me was mostly limited to telling me how clever, how handsome, how wonderful, how noisy, how obnoxious, and again how wonderful I was or would be in time. She never taught me this practice of going out of the body and into a wall or a stone and looking back at myself. Nonetheless, in the fullness of time, I seem to have had to learn it anyway.

It may be, then (you are thinking), that the Stendhal syndrome is not a disease at all. It may be that this is a very old trick of the soul, practised for countless years by people who used to know perfectly well what they were doing. Perhaps it is something forgotten that needs to be remembered. It may be. I certainly would not want you to try to fit everything that follows into that straitjacket, attach it to those electrodes. Think of it, as I said, as a travel book. He went there. He was caught in his mind. Bit by bit, he managed to think it through, to travel through it. In a way, he escaped and lived to tell the tale.

He had four grandparents. His father's mother. His father's stepfather. They lived in Sunnyside. His mother's mother. His mother's father. These lived in Astoria, another part of Queens. They called it *l'Astoria*, which was unconsciously a complicated pun that meant *history* and also meant *ahistory*. Since they made nothing of it, he was going to have to do so. Astoria, l'Astoria, was a persistent trace. He kept finding it all over Paris.

But begin at the beginning.

The scene of writing is, of all things, a dark and stormy night. The professor has been out visiting an old high-school classmate of his who lives in the neighborhood of UNESCO. Walking down the hill from the Métro station, our scribe has passed a brightly lit shop that sells Italian sweaters. The shop is called La Storia. All through dinner, this unlikely name has kept recurring to him. Now he has come home, through freezing rain, to his little room in what is left of the Jewish quarter of Paris. It is very late, but like so many travelers, he does not want to sleep. He sits down at the table to write.

I

The Invalids

I have to my account forty-five years, quite enough, as it turns out, to look backwards and see not one or two but a dozen worlds, the closest to my sense of the damp being the one furthest away in time, most deeply buried under the avalanche of wet newspapers that ordinary conversation signifies with the name of *history*. *La storia* is for me not the newspapers but what still is lying there under them, the gleaming cobblestone in the rain stubbornly persisting exactly where some to me nameless Parodi-cigar-smoking man with red hands bent over for the six-hundredth time that day to set it into the mortar. *L'Astoria* was the name of a place as well as *la storia*, the name of the condition I am beginning to slip under your foot as if it too were a granite cobble able to reflect, at least in the driving April rain, the faces that still make me weep while I am sleeping and still come to mind if in Paris, on the way to hear Jacques Derrida at the École Normale Supérieure, I slip inconsistently into the cathedral of Notre Dame and give the tin box three francs so that I can light with a good conscience one of those slender tapers under the mosaic of Notre Dame de Guadeloupe or the statue of Sainte Jeanne d'Arc. Those faces of my mother, my grand-mother, my grandfather, all gone, my uncle Mike, gone, and of all of us not gone but none-theless by now so differently faced, so layered with passages and impossibilities, scribbled over with our choices and deeds and the gradual revising of the genetic transcript that, though we answer to the name in the tele-phone book, we are, even as we live forward, already, insofar as what we were is what we were together, gone: those faces of what and who and how we were there once upon a time in l'Astoria.

There were two kinds of cobbles in the streets in l'Astoria. One kind, the newer kind, were black asphalt, almost as flat as plain asphalt, but still a pleasant maze of lines and crosses. The other were real stones, much rounded either by age or by the custom of their cutters. And all of it was old already, already abandoned two other times before us. The mil-lionaires, they said, came here in the 1820s and built these palazzi and chateaux and Greek re-vival mansions with ghostly porticoes, and all or almost all of them in wood, sign not of poverty but of provisionality and frivolity be-cause this, at the bend where the East River begins to give onto the Long Island Sound of which it is after all just an estuary, was for those bankers and merchants the place of rec-reation and summer resort — soon enough to be abandoned for Newport and Southhampton, but not until they'd made and deployed for two generations a little hillside paradise of wide verandahs and trumpery crenellated towers, points of interest, points of pride, views of the East and Harlem Rivers and of the Sound roiling ecstatically at Hellgate. Who followed them when they left? The Irish, the Germans, filling up the big houses with more people and less leisure than ever they had been imagined to accommodate.

Everyone in it by 1944, when I was three years old, was Italian. So it seemed to me. We didn't live there but in a place a few miles to the south called Sunnyside, where the people were Irish, Lithuanian, Jewish, German, and Italian: America. On Sundays we went to l'Astoria to my mother's parents and sometimes during the week for dinner or coffee. We lived in a tiny Italy, a six-family house owned by my father's parents, who kept a factory in the basement where they worked seven days a week. Outside this palazzo, the sidewalk smelled of the refinery in Greenpoint a mile away, the people smelled of jelly donuts and crumb cake and pigs' feet and Virginia ham and boiled cabbage. L'Astoria, by contrast, was already what you would call *la storia* then, the past, completely Italian, completely composed and coherent: wines, onions, eggs, flour, oregano, figs.

A boy will make young what is already antique, will fill the sunset with powerful intimations of excellent pleasures. Young, I fell in love with old age. The trees lined the cobbled streets in a twisted exuberance of centenary growth, pouring onto the nubbled pavement in the fall red and yellow cataracts of thick leaves, leaves wet in corners of the slate sidewalks so that you slipped on them walking. Every inch of terrain expressed a crooked will, the slates that settled there at crazy angles to the grade, the granite walls along the enormous lawns and gardens so suddenly given into the hands of the humble immigrants, the roots of elms excavating the curb stones, the hills where the oceans of seeds buried themselves among the broken walks and ran in gutters down to rot in puddles the water rode along on its way to soak the lowland baseball field and leach at last into the river freedom of rats and barges and, in those days, LSTs and battleships.

If I begin this way with the streets and the trees and the houses, it's because some of these, at least, are still left, still sustain from some angle in some gray October moment the illusion, and give off the perfume, they gave. There are no horses anymore. There are no ice wagons. There are no trucks full of crates of grapes rattling up the drive to my grandfather's cellar entrance.

We were sitting on the cellar steps when the truck arrived, already eating grapes from the arbor at the other side of the house. My cousin was beautiful as wine, herself a pink and black glistening as she sat there considering the beehive in the woodpile five or six meters away at the western edge of the vast property. Grapes from California, brilliant indigo and orange labels, and we sat there for hours eating them drunker and drunker as Grandpa Di Rocco, coughing, carried and dragged and heaped the boxes in front of the press. The barrel he kept his wine in was taller than he, and twenty times his girth, but he was entirely the color of wine, my grandfather, he was wine in his every broken capillary, his long thin nostrils an instrument for finding wine, his skinny legs in long white socks a fierce concentration lugging gallon jugs upstairs, his stringy sinews wound like the cables of the Triborough Bridge for pulling, twisting the handles of the press, his grunts devoted fully, only, to exacting from the California purple every spurt of juice, and all his secret grace a dance for moving wine from press to barrel to jug to bottle to table, and made around him where we breathed it clouds of wine, rains of wine, snows of pulp, a nameless silence soaked with wine, laughter of birds, secret wisdoms known on other days to caterpillars, butterflies, chestnut trees, revealed this once a year when the cellar opened to us swallowing grapes the size of plums the mystery of what he was the rest of time, silent, laughing, angry, skinny, smoking, gentle, silent, red. Entirely red. Once he killed a man, I heard.

So this is not an elegy, it is an investigation, inquiry of beauty slipping, tumbling down the gentle sidewalk slope, catastrophe of flowers, complicit now with history, marks of what was done and what we aim to do tomorrow. Everything revealed itself to us sitting on those thick rough granite blocks, giggling, eating grapes, but uselessly revealed, as if one saw one day as plain as a walnut the fatal bump under the skin, all clear, all present, but no more use in the event than a newspaper to a stray dog. We saw it as blueberries see the rain. Completely, and completely helpless. I am sitting in Paris alone writing now, was never able to write this at home. There, one must always *do* something. Here, all I fail to do if I write this is to go look at another church, another monument, another warehouse of beautiful things, another train full of beautiful women, and beauty is the one thing I have never had in my life too little of, I have drifted and swum in it like my grandfather in his bottom of red wine.

Beauty has two ages. The cousins in a trance of fruit sugar see the first age of beauty, the vision of coherence and fittingness in the old man's ferocity and flowering decline, the living warm milk in the rolled and folded ravioli under the damp towels in the kitchen, the impossible magnificence in every muscle, the glitter of ecstasy along the rims of little coffee cups. The others see the second age, the agony of hanging the glass to the lips another time and regrets of what was lost or murdered, labor, lies, loss, loss, fear, a jealous death of appetite, and loss again, a boredom embroidered carefully across the stayed hand, the long-postponed departure. The second of these is invisible except against the first — and the first, that is the one we forget existed as much as we can, what bewilders you in the winter sky of orgasm, the membranes of doorways that might lead you out of there and into a music you remember as the thump of larger creatures dancing — past that wedding of beer and sausage, back to some window garden like a sunlit printed bedsheet in an English advertisement, glass the very gel of the luminous sky against the fragrant skin — what you only think of under the pressure of the irresistible flood of pleasure or else, if sometime meditating as the antiquary of your ordinary sorrows, under the aureole that makes the second age of beauty, giving work and sleepless fear their echo of purpose, their sleazy vibrato of tourism and white pianos, so that you may, with or without assistance of gin, masturbation, conga music on the radio, Sunday supplements, or airplanes painted Kelly green, contrive the reasons you continue, all awaiting you among your children speechless as they see the thing itself themselves the first, the second time, incapable of telling you what you can't at any rate bear hearing, let alone make passes at making sense of it, because, although you know it is there, you only know it as the pain of what you do remember even as you can't remember it, a great golden eye thus erecting itself forever between your pleasure and the child's vibration in the age you see but cannot recognize for what it is, only, at your best, walk gently past in honor of what you know it was and always must, always secretly, be.

These are the two ages — la storia and l'Astoria. That's all. My cousin and I among the grapes tasted what the grapes have always taught: complete delight, liberty of bodies to which sexual concourse is the natural but for us forbidden even unmentionable consequence. That is la storia. That is passion and renunciation as in holy pictures. Nothing personal about it. Only the force of the event and the force of the absolute division, later to become a change of tastes and of conversation. The rest is l'Astoria, the archeology of removals and rearrangements — Astor leaves for Newport, Di Rocco leaves for l'Astoria.

Merely that and that, he said, smiling that quiet smile of imitation superiority, his only product when trying to pretend that clarity might be the solution, might, at least while one was achieving it, replace the narrow walls of the low-ceilinged corridor, damp and impermeable, he sees as history.

— A depressing vision, she says. She is

making pancakes. Summer, 1982. The hills of Putnam County. Go for a walk after breakfast. Cheer up. My mother's last good summer, years after l'Astoria. So it would appear there *are* other ages, ages of real estate speculation in the country, winters on the Gulf of Mexico, gardenias in January. So it would appear. I never could, he never could, argue successfully with my mother, his mother. She was in fact all history, all force of removal, sitting knitting as the television blandly tumbled carnage like shirts in a washing machine, planning new wings on the house as the loose platelets worked their way up the arteries to her lower Pons.

The car turns in off the road, up the cobbled drive, bearing left around the circle, under the Dutch elms (all dead now), the gladiolus in the heart of the circle around the flagpole, and stops before the pile of concrete steps. The father, his father, my father, speaks of the carburetor like a priest considering the hymen of the mother of God. The mother, his mother, my mother, directs the children to go upstairs. The Fanaras are playing pinochle. His father joins them.

— Joe, come upstairs.

— One hand, Vera.

She takes the girl and the boy into the glass vestibule, an aquarium of mildew and milk bottles in metal crates. She leads up the stairs. Forty years later she is dying, trying to spell with her eyelids, 'My chest hurts.' This rapid retrospect, this hard similarity of pushing ahead despite her husband, his father, my father, playing pinochle and discussing the broken carburetor over the broken heart, this steady misalignment, this breaking twinge of climbing stairs wherever they present themselves is l'Astoria, the form history takes forever the minute it ends, and it is the nature of history that it has already ended before you even know it is there.

Not that it never returns. Every day offers the chance, what some people call the lottery and others daily mass, there will be a moment of history. You wait for it, look for it, turning your head like a horse with a bee sting most times it appears, and almost never see it unless something, some person, some instant of torrent in the rarest weather, some catastrophe of joy, might suddenly seize you in its grasp, or hers, and hold you still long enough that a history happens as it did that day sitting among the fruitflies and the gothic butterflies and gorging grapes.

But you will run from it. It will run beyond you if you don't, but you will, one of those occasional moments, have written in you with a burning stick some heraldry of pleasure, some purple of connected desire, some wire you'll be hanging on forever. Then begins again l'Astoria. L'Astoria is the paradise of sociologists, rooting about everywhere in the attics.

Down the street they come carrying tape recorders, cameras, metric scales, barometers, indices of folktale motifs, typologies of eyebrows, exchange tables for all the moneys of Europe, bottles of vitamins, laxatives, the encyclopedia of toes, dissertations on the average heights of children. They are not harmless. Nor are they irrelevant in l'Astoria. L'Astoria is history as she is available to the ministry of agriculture and the secretariats of information, whose capacious enterprises cannot proceed without her. She is the iron paling on the Tuileries and the number of eucalyptus trees per acre in Pinellas County.

You understand already, no doubt, what I can't quite keep clear when I'm writing, how la storia and l'Astoria are also the same thing, at least when he speaks of the one as happening in the other, only my name for his childhood interpenetration of the fig dish or for his hand on the polenta board, his dream of what it was when everything, even to the cast-iron nymphs in the Victorian fireplaces there, gave off a thick aroma, what a dog knows as articulately as you know the prospect of lower Manhattan at twilight, and only can speak of it now inside the frame with the brass plate, ASTORIA.

On the other side of the big house from the entrance to the wine cellar were the little formal garden with its rain-worn marble benches, the huge grape arbor made of pipes and buzzing with heavy bugs, the thick red tree, the file of fig trees every winter wrapped in blankets and tar paper and baling wire, the broad walk between all this and the stone piers the house was resting on, the picnic tables, the six-car garage, the mouldering stables. Behind the house, a farm tumbled down the hill all peppers, lettuce, escarole, beans, tomatoes. The house had a double verandah all around, fifteen feet wide, concrete and stone on the first floor where the Fanaras held their title, wood and tar paper upstairs where my mother and her sister had married out of, and their younger brother, those days, had parties and slept till two, so that he sat down to Sunday dinner with the eleven of us, still rubbing his eyes while chewing celery. All of this on top of a hill that commanded to the North views of Hellgate and the Triborough Bridge at the foot of the little street that descended outside the front gate a hundred meters to the water, and to the West, the skyline of the Upper East Side, still smelling of spring chickens to me when I see it as I did first as a boy, it seems, at sundown with the lights like punctured holes in the papier-maché buildings of a crêche in our church in Sunnyside, and the sun lowering itself behind it like a well-positioned lightbulb sending an art deco neon glow along the horizon and sharpening the points of the flat towers against the radiant sapphire of the improbable night above.

So what is that? L'Astoria, corrupted by la

storia in its most intimate guise, my absurd pride in my thoroughly provisional command of this lordly eminence. My grandparents paid the Fanaras $40 a month for their suite of huge rooms, their verandah, their views, their share of the farm in the back, the wine cellar, the freedom of the estate. Thus begins the fantasy of ambitious youth, that carves his chevron in the snow and breaks the tiger lilies to its pattern, completely insistent that l'Astoria unfolds in every direction the narrative of his criminal delight, the innocence of his trance crawling up its steep walls like the roses on the trellis at the back of the house, thousands of them come June, his one conviction the absolute correctness of a passion *as* a passion, sin or plain stupidity being no more questions to him than parliamentary politics to a conger eel, his passion driving only — as they see — towards survival of the species or — as he would always say in those days — 'up the hill', the hopeless twist of function we know as its only conceivable pattern here, careering through the streets with its accordion on its arm and its heart made of marzipan held up between thumb and forefinger offering itself to the vibration of a woman who might any moment reappear in any form, your wife on the telephone, and the force of la storia is the only one you know at any rate, so that l'Astoria, even if you call it Roma, Paris, is the lines of houses it throws up the way tectonic plates emit the Alps, churning corkscrew staircases of the up-and-down in a carapace of what keeps out the rain. This moment where the one becomes the other, the trance lays out the tiles of the roof, awaits you at every step, a possibility to step across into what he remembers and foretells. Only order, you say? Only disorder? Neither as yet. Only terrain of the gathered rediscovery.

— There is the house with two glass porches, he says.

— I always wanted to live in such a house, she says.

— Will you buy me a Hershey bar at the corner?

— That little stand on the corner of Trowbridge Street, my father used to stand there talking with his paisans for hours. We have to go visit Uncle Rob. Maybe they'll give you something there.

— They never do.

— You see this street?

— Twelfth Street.

— We call it Trowbridge Street, that's before they changed the name. And here on Twenty-seventh Avenue is where my cousin Bill lived.

— Are we going there?

— You want to see Zi' Anton'?

— They always give me *pizzelle*.

His mother's cousin Bill swam across Hellgate at age thirteen, not long before he went to jail, exploits which gave him permanent lustre in her conversation, *la storia* which needed no detective. And Bill's sister Lina Di Rocco had married *her* cousin Rocco Di Virgilio, age sixteen. And their uncle Roberto Di Rocco, and my mother's, was my namesake, or to be precise, shared with me a namesake, Beato Roberto, patron of Salle, the little town in provincia di Chieti where they came from, where half the men are called Roberto. Uncle Rob in l'Astoria was a ward boss. My grandfather, his brother, had a job in the civil service — sweeping streets, with an excellent pension and plenty of time to drink wine — though he could scarcely set down his name in Italian, say nothing of passing a written exam in English. Intricate weave of things or flatness of stale bread, two names for feelings in the face of the absolute writing of la storia. I never knew this until I went to Salle in 1977: the old women, my mother's aunt and her friends, are in love with Beato Roberto.

He lies there, the sort of mannequin that used to appear in the windows of the people who rent tuxedos, at the end of a long aisle with coffered ceilings, the only bit of luxury in the bare church built by Mussolini after the *terremoto* destroyed the old town in 1928, Beato Roberto in a floodlit glass box under the altar and dressed in a cassock and a surplice only a little finer than the one I used to wear as an altar boy in Sunnyside, and the old ladies stand in front of him exclaiming, *'Quant'è bello!*

43

Quant'è bravo!', as if he were a glorious young stallion just out of school. He was my model though I never saw him. *Bello, bravo*, I conquered all the mothers and grandmothers and *comari* and aunts and neighbors, not a question of intent, but merely and exquisitely the play written by the audience.

And la storia. My mother always admired reckless Bill in his troubles as a boy and his wild career in the South Pacific during the war, and, at the same turn of her impassioned glance, could rarely value except *as* value my father's genius, his infinite ingenuity and secret desire to be admired as an artist and a dandy. My cousin married a doctor who went to my college and, as I did, played the piano. Always bored, she hung empty picture frames on the wall of their splendid house in Short Hills until they were divorced. How do you make this out? La storia is the law of incest, of circumcision, of turns and fractures and reasonable facsimiles in love. My mother's mother was married, twenty-one, to a man thirty-five she didn't know, just back from America, on the basis of her father's respect for his father, and *his* admiration of her beauty and balance. In Salle a woman is only marriageable if she can dance a tarantella with a jug of water on her head, no hands touching it. Which is exactly how she lived her marriage, a story she always told me in the form of a tragedy. 'My father said, "Do you want to marry him?" and I said,

"What do *you* think?" and so I married him.'
The woman does not have to admire the jug,
only to carry it. La storia, as you turn it over
in memory in the cafe, is the wrong drink, the
wrong road, the dirty window, the political
economy of cold coffee, and the magnificent
counterpoint of mandolins advertising rubber
tires. My cousin's doctor wanted to be taken
for a philosopher.

L'Astoria survives in the trees and little
streets the real estate novelists will make exquisite and impossibly costly. I have aunts and
uncles there and cousins, *paisani* forming
folkdance societies to preserve the dialect and
the music. The priest comes by Alitalia from
Salle carrying the saint's jawbone in a sterling-
silver arm with a finger pointed to heaven and
a little round window in the palm of the hand
through which you may peer at the relic while
kissing it, and they print this in the local paper
and put him on the Italian television program
on Sunday afternoon.

I cannot leave Long Island. I was born in
a hospital in Brooklyn in the rain. I live in
Brooklyn. Sunnyside and l'Astoria are in
Queens, all parts of Long Island, whose
beaches are my summer resorts. Once I lived
in Ithaca ten months, Bronx a year, Manhattan
a year and a half, weeks in London, weeks in
Rome, weeks in Paris, where I am writing this
swiftly because it is a narrative of exile. Sort
of.

So l'Astoria for me, for all that I have separated it out from the other, has become la
storia, the situation of some powerful cloud of
dream romances, incest, jealousy, murder, paradise. I see its large houses at the scale of Versailles, a giant drama of habitation. I see its
streets full of old men and women heroically
passing down to the bakery like nobles in a
procession. Every tree, every rippled pane of
glass has not one but two identities. For me
English, for them Italian. Thus it is that Italian
remains for me the language of the gods, the
masters of l'Astoria, which is, as a town, the
physical form of la storia, the shape in English
recollection of an Italian reality. This place of
migration, of loss, of exile, of wreck is also for
me the dawn of an Italy entirely visionary, a
prospect of pleasure and assurance to which I
remain entirely attached as if something
glorious were waiting for me inside the painting if only I could find myself somehow there.
And I have done so. I have been painting it
around me for years now, thinking to offer it
as a patrimony to my children, who, of course,
may not want it at all. What we take as children
from our parents so thoroughly differs from
what they think they have to give that l'Astoria,
which is what they made of la storia in their
lives, the drawing in two languages, becomes
again for us as children la storia, the babble of
non-communicating emotions, from which we
are obliged to take our own paintings of —

what? What our children can make of their endowments notoriously eludes our intention.

Le Comte de Paris, Pretender to the throne of France, I read yesterday, has separated legally from la Comtesse, a woman by whom he had eleven children, of whom three of the boys, at least, have led disastrous lives in their headlong effort to escape the father's elevated notion of the historical parts they were to play. What happened to him? Did he first taste joy in the precincts of the Tuileries and devote his life ever after to drawing all this back to his hand? In France, one always can dream of the return of the party, left, right, right right. Someone told me his dentist, an excellent dentist, said to him one day, by way of explaining some other remark, 'But, of course, I am a Royalist.' So, as the painting of L'Astoria grows around me, as I call into, drag into, being the bilingual Jasons and four-winged Phoenixes of a world both American and Italian, I see my son sometimes wondering about his place in this, and I think of the Comte de Paris and *his* sons. What choices do we have, though, after all, the Comte and I? My son and I?

Surely I have more choices than the Comte imagines himself to have had. Surely my imaginings of Paris — memories from films I saw twenty years ago, memories that turn out to be precise in every detail — imply both a fatality and a mastery in my composition of the prospect. For this is, in my case as in that of the Comte, entirely a matter of politics when one considers it at the level of choice, and politics requires a just assessment both of fatalities and masteries. *Fate*: I have inherited a double world of words, a world in which one mastered English as if it were a musical instrument, against the background of an Italian which was no more nor less than the world itself, the theatre which projected onto its ample stage little me and my magic violin. Was it not natural that, coming to manhood, I should think to assume the responsibility of the theatre? Was it not like food and weather and sex that I should find the language of Italy, that built the theatre, the voice calling my body, driving its movements, hinting its rewards? *Mastery*: was it not for this, I say to myself as I look up from my window at the roofs of Paris, that I was born — that I should come here to the capital of Europe, where these thin tall chimneys stand up to the gray sky like totems of Europe's weariness, where the timbers of the ceiling in this room have rattled to the sound of bombs, where every house is old enough that you know murder has been done in it, where the wooden steps of the turning stairs have heard the boots of the Gestapo, where, even as I look out my window, I see each day the little sign on the house to the right opposite, *Mort en déportation, 1943*, where the very city was rebuilt by Baron von Haussman in the 1860s as a rattrap, so there could be no barricades, where the cathedrals have certain floors especially designed to support the furtive movements of tanks, where political struggle is the secret plot of life, enclosing in its grim parentheses how many nights of good food and good love, the furious gaze of *La Marseillaise* bearing down on Paris forever from her grotesque eminence on the Arc de Triomphe, that guardhouse, that I should come here to this empire of stares, and write this book? Was it not for this?

Perhaps not. Fate, which lifts us up, also carves us in tortured marble like that Medusa of war who keeps plainly under her eyes the pleasure gardens of the Champs-Elysées, the Place de la Concorde, the Tuileries, the Louvre, a monument of disaster and fear that, after all, doesn't *have* to be there. It might not have been built. Some day, it may come to appear so obscene that they'll take it down. The Comte de Paris might have decided, in such a spirit, to become a disciple of Jacques Lacan, as Princesse Bonaparte had been of Freud. His sons might have devoted themselves, if they did not want to revive their ancient perquisites, to the creation of Europe, that dream of a new life for this old set of barriers. Might have, didn't. Some do, no doubt. I don't know the careers of the *other* eight offspring of the Pretender. As for me, I have open before me a very wide range of possibilities. I can be an American *tout court*. Live in America, give my children American educations, and so on. Or I can play my double concerto, half in English, half in Italian.

That sounds very thin, but nothing in writing so freezes the pen as the history of the future, and one must address the subtleties of projection into what is ahead even to write of what is passing in the current at the moment of writing. The future is not a set of details but a set of options, directions, goals, objectives.

There is not one France but very very many. A country, which we speak of so simply, in one syllable, really doesn't have any existence at all except in language. Nature does not reveal nations to themselves. Nations are made through language and through war. One does not touch a nation. One lives in it, as in a language, completely subject to its effects as to the laws and to the value of the money. The money is the main physical presence the nation, *as* nation, takes in one's daily life, the constant reminder of the collection of pacts and privileges, dreams and territories that make a nation. Reminder, too, of *la storia*, the anguishes of those who cross as well as of those who defend the boundaries and definitions which make l'Astoria, or France. The city of Paris speaks through its monuments and its Métro stations concerning the real intersection between these two histories, where every great arrangement is the replacement of another arrangement, itself slipped into place while putting the widow of the dead king into the boat for England. But of course Paris is the memorial of all such events, their necropolis and gallery of trophies, all summarized in the Nike of Samothrace headless at the prow of a double staircase as you climb into the Louvre and are set adrift in an ocean of recollections which the collections aim to make your own, floating you upon the fragments of endless wrecks — in the midst of all, you come upon the raft of the Medusa, as much a self-referential gesture of the Louvre as the painting — also in the Grande Galerie, that massive, endless, revival of a Roman bath — which imagines the Grande Galerie as a ruin, with people wandering in it much as they are when you turn from the painting and look down the very prospect it represents. You are caught here in the circles of l'Astoria, in the sense that it was invented by J.J. Astor: here you are inside the dungeon of reference and referent built into an ocean of money and will and violence, its impossible wealth of refinements and acquisitions towering over you, rising up before you, falling into the cellar and writhing in ecstasy in the apparition of Michelangelo's slaves. And here I touch the place where Paris spoke to me exactly in this doubled voice: the voice of the captive Italians, their sweetness and grace, their generosity of gesture and thoughtless abundance of thought, captured and smiling pointlessly under this northern sky, this frost of intention, this all-devouring *taste*, this churning maw that gives to Paris, after all, its homogeneity, a city where one eats. So there is a single gesture, even as there are millions slipping into it and it is not remaining still.

We were in the hospital. At the foot of the beds of my mother's cousins, there was a tray of loaves of bread.

— Why are these here getting stale?

— These are our babies. That happens. Sometimes a loaf of bread is born.

— Why don't they take them away?

— You would think they'd slip a baby in when you were still out. You'd never know.

I go to the *caisse* and buy a ticket for a baby for her. I come back.

— But you must tell it before it grows up who its real parents are. I look at my grandmother, who is getting up to leave.

Helping her on with her coat, I say, 'I hate how you are getting old.'

— You must not let those women take you in like that, she replies. Is she angry because I have referred to the family secret or is she telling me something else?

I am waiting for the policeman to bring me marijuana which I will try to persuade my wife to smoke. She does not trust ecstasy, but, since she is a Celt, like the French, she resorts to the Italians to find the way back to it. Italians carry the collective memory of having lived in the ruins of their own collections forever, eat-

ing and being eaten, and of having passed beyond these geometries of death into the final
monumentality, a perfect unconsciousness you
see in slaves repeating itself here not in
masters but in abandoned heirs.

This is the real poignancy of historia, when
it peels back the cover and shows you, not passion, but the openings of passion, the skin that
ripples over the muscles and mounds, the
huge forward thrust of the hip of the Venus of
Melos, the delicate topography of nipples,
glowing in a shaft of sunlight, recalling you to
possibilities and lusters, but what of this conjoins itself to some actual touch of one to one,
some dizzy haze in the western sky on a summer afternoon, is not specified, the precise
measure of your throb of response to the
statue's blunt allure composing itself as the articulated table of debilities you correctly read
inscribed in cypher as the lines of mortar joining limestone blocks that mount on either side:
l'Astoria, the coffered ceilings of desire, what
forces you and drives the stag, the dogs, the
hunters' trumpets on their horses in the
tapestry, another autumn of chateaux, and ladies drawing needles patiently, methodically
remounting lake and leaf as just so many
strokes of green, of yellow, blue and brown.

I had expected this in Rome, not Paris, and
perhaps will find there some other gaping
crevasse in the endless fault line that has
opened in front of me here. But Paris, I have

seen, draws its unmistakeable murmur from its dramaturgy of a double play. Its *mise en scène*, entirely l'Astoria, attracts interest by its placement, as of pieces on a board, of desire against its residue. One follows, in the guidebook that reads like a lawyer's digest of decisions in surrogates' courts, the battle which recurs, always as an afterthought or consequence, when, amidst the patterned gardens of l'Astoria, the eye awakens and the hand approaches with its thumb and index like a perfect O the perfect tip of the sibling breast, and some new conjunction of floral satisfaction carves itself extravagances not to be denied. Dynasty slides under dynasty like Beethoven replacing Haydn on the pedestal. Or like an avalanche the arms and bayonets, the mad mob, the songs and drunken unity of Liberté — to cut, to slice, to make the pleasances of queens the avenues of Sunday leisure. Every move implies abandoning, defying, forgetting, encapsulating residues of other moves, so passion never rests and never lasts in Paris, moves itself below ground, concocts a pyramid, and rots. Is this Parisian life? According to the guidebooks and the passages of pilgrims, for whom the city has arranged itself along the pattern of processions.

For this, the city spills and overflows, the very things one buys with the money one is able to garner where the river flows conveniently being, as they only are, the ordinary food and drink, clothing, shelter, persistently transformed, like relics dipped in holy water, by their participation *here*, their glimmer of this spectacle — this epic nostalgia, this haze of triumphs and absolute eradication.

You see it, or I show it to you, as if one looked up from a sidewalk in l'Astoria and found it looming beyond the border where the man pushes the roller over the grass in front of the tulips: Paris, sprouted in Queens among the milkweeds and sunflowers. Paris: an American delicacy, imported in cans and canisters, rolls of pressed Paris, sliced Paris, six dollars the hectogram, Paris delivered fresh by jet daily; one hundred pages of old Paris; Paris by Night; Melodies of Montmartre; Paris hats; two free weeks for two in the sewers of Paris. You can't see it without seeing this. Paris to you is what l'Astoria is to me: what you can buy but could never inhabit once you wanted to, because it was never there as even a phantom, was never more than, even when you were happily strolling in the Luxembourg gardens with an ice cream in your hand, an effect of the brain working full tilt to translate all of it, its music or its silence, while you might murmur comfortably in the language, back below to what you knew and to what you return even as you race blindly away, which you would not call l'Astoria or perhaps anything else either, it being not what you call it but what you call it *with*, but it is what I call l'Astoria, the sliding of the vowel under the apostrophe (prosthesis), la storia as it becomes what keeps writing itself under what you write or hear, a dialect inaudible, invisible, and if heard then only as auroras around something inescapably lucid and vividly wrong, but nothing more palpable than the sign that even under the nymphs at the Opéra, you weren't there. I mean two things. I mean what the philosopher means: *there* is the name of the place where you aren't, of the condition of your never being able to be in it, what never quite becomes *here*, no matter how patiently you pitch your tent in its midst, eating its pastries and mastering the forty shades of pastel beige in its jargon. That's the universal *there*. But another *there* has a more precisely crystallized vertebral articulation in the glazing of your eloquence. In Paris you, as in l'Astoria I, contrive to hear an ancestry you speak and never utter: your American language, how clean and flat, conceals the sausage and pistachio more subtly than the *brioche* they bake them into — all these gestures like a polished slate exhibiting the death of a fish with sharp teeth or a chewing bird whose chatter you imagine only too readily, but you can't hear it, as you can in Paris hear the Latin in your English, extracted, dressed, tied with a bow, up and walking about from jewel box to jewel box, a total resurrection, your own inconceivable past exuberantly present. Where you aren't. Even as you decode the organ music, reading the stained glass panels like a guidebook, the haze of the place lingers, a frame inside the picture, every part of it marbled with indistinction, every new prospect dewy with reiteration. None of it *there*. None of it *theirs*. You move among them with the clumsy stealth of a stereotype, clattering into the café like a horse, all of it pressing tight against you, and you, as if you were an immigrant, framing your order carefully in your best French, where you never will be a native.

You aren't *there*. But no one can be for himself *there*. Another favorite of the philosophers. Somewhere between this *there*-ness of the *there*, otherness of the other, at the bottom of the kaleidoscope where the eye peeks in, somewhere between this exclusion of the inspector outside the glass at this end and the glamor of the recomposing rose window at the point of light, at some point between these, comfortably in Zion among the laws of refraction, fall the boundaries that, altogether taken as one finds them, weave the texture of l'Astoria, a tapestry or photograph that must be, upon minute consideration, a dialogue of small distinctions. For there we had the notion of living on the rough underside of a floral print, where the fabric speaks only of how it holds itself together and presents its camellias and gardenias to the slanting light. Ordinary philosophy must call this an effect of language, which it is, but what is language?

In my two classes in Paris, the student lists

began with the names *Aglossi and Alingue*, without-a-tongue and from-a-tongue. Wonderful names for what it is to find oneself repeatedly among people whose language not only is not the one you speak but one that, even after you learn it, repeatedly and crucially makes mention of things that you, not having lived among its speakers since forever, have never seen or known. In the Italian school in New York, they could not think how to explain to my American son the meaning of *vendemmia*, vintage. L'Astoria wove its fabric of those who could not speak the English or speaking it deploy its referents as instruments. So it wove in literal cloth, cutting, sewing, fitting; the Fanaras used the half of the second floor opposite my grandparents not as an apartment but as a shop. All the doors in that house, being old and mostly needless, swung open without turning the knobs, and in we ran. The smell of dry goods has its own spectrum. A store full of wrapped shirts can make you gasp. The Fanaras' shop smelled of heavy polished cottons with backings as ribbed as sailcloth, thick foodlike substantial heavy bolts of vegetable pattern from which they cut and sewed, almost like sculpture, slipcovers like monuments, drapes that required good stout bars of spiral pine to hold them up. The air this made was at the same time dry and thick with pleasure, an almost digitated fullness of the round women, smooth-faced, smiling, handling the rich stuffs, or of their cousin Angelina, white hair in a great Gibson bun like a triumphal pasta, every strand in implausible parallel, in the chair at the window infiltrating a frame with a needle drawing purple threads into some floral crescent, or all of them talking over the wide parenthetical ruminations of the power machines making double stitches in the rugged piping, a driving opera of absolute occupation, the only part of which might leave the room and join the general conversation elsewhere in the visible city across the river being the mute extent of measured wing chairs, camelbacks, throws, an overwhelming stillness, tonguelessness that soaked up every sound, a sweet dryness muffling any possible song, any possible protest or explanation, a universe of gleaming brown paper into which I darted like a blackbird practising his devil's trill. This doesn't answer the question what is language, not directly anyway, but the answer is hard to give in *words* because they have a way of appearing ethereal, spiritual, neutral, and benign.

Words are perhaps border conditions between speakers and objects. So some philosophers seem to think. I think the old expressions *hot air* and *bag of wind* get us closer. Words are aromas. Perfumes, in many cases, speak so bluntly they reach us as if they or we were gods, transfigured, transparent, translucent, transcendent transmitters and receivers, no static or obstacle between us. In the air of the Fanaras' shop, the fabrics rolled and spread and heaped on the long pattern tables spoke unmistakably of an oceanic aglossia, pluckers of cotton, balers, heavers, weavers, teamsters, factors, stevedores, printers, polishers, and the enclosure of all this room's conversation in this room, a chattering, pleasant, even roaring silence I had the power to break. I had the task, that is, the role, the praise, the mission: all of that.

They always stopped as I stood there, asked me a question, exclaimed over the answer. I could breathe English as they breathed cotton and Italian. I could, he could, be counted on to inhabit a halo of lime water diffusing its scent of disappearing mastery lightly in a sprinkle of innocent wisdom and startling information that left some faint watermark on everything. La storia, their own passion for children; la storia, their own passion for speech; la storia, his own surprise at the suddenness of fame; la storia, his words, his reading of the ribs of the drive wheels in the Victorian machines; la storia, l'Astoria: the passion not only constructing a memory in the form of a ritual — all of this in my retrospect as rich in gesture and pattern as a portrait of Napoléon by David — not only making this, but made by a prior, chronicle of separations. Passion lifts its head up from the sea of diplomatic dreams and dreams a diplomatic dream.

Like Paris. *Diploma*: a piece of paper folded twice, single sheet given an inside, an outside, a left and right inside, a front and back outside, a secret writing always folded in, a double face of waxen seals and ribbons always growing around it. Paris is the theater of diplomacy in this sense. It never lets you omit the other face. The big buildings are big because all the other ones are not allowed to be, so that the whole city lives inside a set of Chinese boxes, cramps enclosing cramps, doors inside doors, that the Madeleine may rise up before you like a pedant's nightmare of the Parthenon or that the lofty eye of the Tour Eiffel may follow you persistent as the moon between the branches. The scarves are brightly colored because the buildings and the sky are gray. The life is completely regulated so that it may explode every twenty or thirty years in some carnival of distilled development. Revolution everywhere inscribes itself as cemeteries, ministries, academic sculpture, wild excitement perpetuating solidly a planetary flatness, anarchy as cosy ease. The buildings are Italianate so that they may be more absolutely Germanic, all the extrapolated logic of garlandry, all the pedimented windows, the trophies and the cofferings only to declare the tensions of the angles, the straight lines, the intersections, the buttresses as technology, the gargoyles and humped roofs as witnesses of endless rain and snow — a southern garnish on a city which seems in consequence more absolutely northern than London. Paris is poetic, the name of poetry as a city, because it is entirely in prose, a city like a shelf of novels, every little street debouching like an eccentric character into the fluid of a boulevard or *grande famille* concluding in an ending at Les Invalides, the Opéra, indeterminacies being thus firmly in the embrace of happy closures, tragic arches, finishings, stops you spin around in taxis if you like until you're ready for sleep. This scene of countercurrents, paradoxes, and face-to-face contradictory sentiment — all summed up in the Janus hat of Napoléon Bonaparte, rebel and emperor, anarchist and lawgiver, hero and monster, lover and user of women, Frenchman and Corsican, Caesar and Hannibal — is the much-advertised mobility of Paris, its function as theatre and graph paper of other dramas, other divisions, its glory as a universal hotel.

Astoria. Waldorf Astoria. Astoria as a style of opulence excluding virtue, rigor excluding discomfort — that is the style of the Pont Alexandre III and all it leads to, including the original Astor, Louis XIV, whose notion of comfort, one knows, is hardly comfortable but is, nonetheless, an ubiquitous *suggestion* of repose upon Olympian cloudbanks, whose opulence extended to the portrait of his own head as a gold piece, whose rigor was precisely the discipline of an innkeeper, whose whole object in life is to attract the bugeyed farmer from the provinces.

Or at least whose *strategy* is thus to draw them in, where they may beggar themselves with magnificence and contribute to this glory. Paris gives lessons in strategy. On the quais, the spectatorial cosiness overwhelms the tourist in an indiscriminate mound of options. You might sit almost anywhere and watch. But the spectacle defeats you nonetheless, its convenience the convenience of engineers and generals, cavalry commanders, impresarios. The ordinary stroller rests a cheerful smile of expectation from some artificial eminence upon a composition of trees and lawns and flowers and bronzes. But strolling is an ordeal. The eye and the foot measure differently, and what pleases the one defeats the other. Arriving at the focal point, one thinks less of glory than of the weariness to come going home. This, I suppose, is what they mean when they say Paris is Cartesian. The systematic elegance, the chimera of complete design, arouses emulation and discredits modest wisdoms. Against the paradise of shoppers and the Elysian fields of food, the little pockets of croissants and sandwiches, the boutiques of embroidered sweaters, every step a new Easter Egg, stands the blackened Louvre too high to think of vaulting, too long to walk around. No building I have ever seen conveys precisely its consummate force. A calculated ugliness — they rejected Bernini's elegant plan as not rigorous enough for Paris — and a calculated mass of splendor in the galleries, dizzying ceilings, dizzying accumulations of wealth along the walls — Aladdin's cave for dictators, who visit on a rotating platform to learn the style of shameless opulence, to keep before them signs of what they cannot have succeeded yet in buying, howsoever thoroughly they have impoverished the provinces, and to dream of Hitler: the greatest success is to steal Paris, bringing it home in crates, at least provisionally, until you might put the whole city, as it often appears to have put itself, in a box with a silken ribbon for presentation. And strategy is, after all, this: the ease of vision and the fatigue of soldiers, directly related by inverse ratio, calibrated grades, so that troops emerging from the Étoile come rapidly down and crowds struggle up from below. A sliding pond of order.

And easy, as a resort, to keep in mind when you have left. In Paris, I thought of Long Island. Back now in Brooklyn, I think of Paris. Bombs go off in the shopping malls on the Champs Élysées. People are killed. There is no better battlefield, no more perfect stage of resistance than this theatre of the Grande Armée lined with royal boxes, gift boxes, chocolate boxes, coffee boxes, the South and the East encapsulated like books or movies in tins along the shelves of an emperor's library, and every now and then one of them explodes. So the emperor thinks. Back home in Lebanon or Tunisia or Chad, they are packing the boxes with dynamite, plastique, whatever they can devise, and this, in the end, will make their point for the moment, though the balance of forces and the gravity of the grade in that astonishing street will not have been changed.

A city of philosophers has produced, has been produced by, or lives upon, a city of strategy. You will elide that sentence at your peril because all its options are true, and the degree to which they appear to contradict one another simply suggests how difficult a study arises before you when you leave your bunch of Parma violets absentmindedly upon the tiny circle of black plastic in the café and begin to descend the granite steps along the Seine, considering how the place, or any place, contrives to appear so vulnerable, so open as the naked woman you see everywhere extending her arms to the wet haze, while it is, as you know it is, a sunken cathedral, a sunken pyramid, Napoléon's tomb crashed through the floor of the Dome, a bunker, and a battlement, all of what's visible only the necessary index or gunnery map of what can't be seen, and you dig through Paris, footstore as if you had been wandering up and down the unforgiving halls and steps of the Louvre for a week in search of a painting no one had told you had been lent for the year to Buenos Aires, looking for the actual plan, the ruin-built-in-advance, the absolute scar of its intended and indented persistence, the stubborn intelligence of what resists, the hard stone of what they have in mind, not so much finding it wherever you descend, however filthy you get in the bowels of inspection, not so much *that*, not so much any chart with Christmas tree lights they give you in the Métro to tickle your intelligence, not anything you see so much as what, climbing out of it, aching in the joints, suddenly easy prey to every knife, every infection, you just as suddenly, though you have not going down ever seen it, remember.

So they built, you reflect, subtler than you saw. They were shameless. They draped everything in a fraudulent antiquity. You knew it. The *Guide vert* told you it was only eighty years old though it looked eight hundred. You read the lintels of the Opéra — Rossini Beethoven Mozart Spontini. Spontini. You smiled and went to buy a lizard wallet in the Japanese tax free shop across the street. You read the signs and dismantled the objects. You saw the whole bazaar under the rawest weather with the holiday plumage of metaphysics drooping in the remorseless drizzle. You were not fooled. But you were cut. Not caught, you avoided that. But cut. Ribbed, tattooed, visibly striated with the sudden density of what you walked between, a waffle, pocked with Paris as deeply as if you were Belgian. It drew you and drew upon you as it moved. Why?

No one is surprised to hear l'Astoria is why. You are, I am, he is the struggle of displacement walking. He has grown completely apt at finding and losing, completely alert to how people will want to persist. L'Astoria is there, but for him not even as a ruin, simply the mouldy marriage between what lingers and what has taken its place. As a boy he was up to his knees in someone else's recollections, staggering through a swamp of useless gorgeousness under the illusion he was dancing, he was investing the flaking paint on the pillars with a chronicle of lovers and stately crimson skirts, long ringlets troubled with ribbons and rubies, armies of yellow-breasted birds on an arch every Easter as if invoked by the gypsy lady in her corrugated tin shack down the hill in the hollow under the field of peppers, a liturgy of tiger lilies and tomatoes dictated to the great Lord Montezuma by the God of the Sun one afternoon when night delayed itself so that the feasting and drinking and talking might seem never to have an end — he was, that is, inside la storia, which is not merely fantasy, as you supposed, but the actual viscid greenness in the estuarial flick of the tidal tongue under the bridge when the morning of late March drills into it all the cold brilliance that gives New York its air of being not a city but a citizen itself, belonging to a larger body,

a location in the solar system, a metropolis discussed among sharks and whales as a source
of the ocean; there he was, as you might be
one sunny afternoon for an instant looking up
from your newspaper at the dust as a radiance;
there he came down the banisters sweeter than
a pinky on a harp; heir he was, though unaware, to a certain nervous soprano lifting
under the baritone bellies of the men in their
chairs at the window, a design of theft and
murder hatched every morning and cooked for
lunch out of a deeper spring even than
courage, out of a blind mind that has no way
to think or act about defeat, but always replies,
as all of it gathered and boiled down to an
exquisite flavor, to the incremental pull of
Need.

People there are who pretend it isn't working every minute, that spaces of simple delight
exist, envelopes of simple — or, as they call it,
pure — contemplation: art as a pleasure; history as thought; thought as freedom; freedom
as play; play as random chance, unmeditated,
unconstrained, so utterly contingent upon the
motions of chance as not to be contingent, really, upon anything else. Such persons are not
Marxists. But then, neither am I, except in the
no doubt utterly *American* sense that everywhere I look, I see l'Astoria, I see what he in
his minor freedom could not quite make out
among the jugglery of gravity and light, that no
one drinks a cup of coffee or offers a child a

slice of roasted meat with a little glass of cooked blood at its side except because someone left l'Italia, someone rolls up the drive in a 1932 Chevy wearing inverted commas in the purple sheen of the black paint, each departure owing everything to the great god Need and his consort Desire, each departure a rupture in the seamless silk of la storia and each arrival a stitching of l'Astoria, the very condition in me, or him, of what they ripped and tore in order to make my uninterrupted, edgeless afternoon in the company of Brother Sun and Father Montezuma. So this knowledge grows an appetite, every rise into the clouds lands me again in l'America, l'Astoria, an open grid through which the sun sets precisely, and there I find, not myself, though you will say I'm looking in a mirror, but what my grandfather found in Queens — not, to be sure, *as* he found it, but as he taught me to teach myself to be in the end what he would have been from the beginning had he been able even to imagine it, though he couldn't, could only indicate a set of directions that, not precise for what they aimed at, were equally misaligned with what I was able to make of them as I heard them — this double misconstruction not cancelling itself out at all but erecting instead a cat's cradle trusswork of contradictions resting and rising in a hyperbolic arc under the actual tower I managed to construct, which moves rattling and rumbling like one of

Leonardo's engines of destruction through the lunar valleys of *Star Wars* as I appear to you to be strolling through the Rue Saint Honoré while actually I am only asking it the question my grandfather, if he had done what I learned from him has taught me to suppose I'd have been better off if he had actually succeeded in doing, would have asked of it: how do they persist?

For they do, in Paris, seem to persist, not as some of us in l'Astoria, simply by failing to move on, but rather on *purpose*, as a form of success one only succeeds in America by forgetting, all persistence here being the effect of enclosure within expansion and most success being not even expansion across or certainly down, but only out, up, over, beyond. The great capitals of Europe do not abut the ocean or even the Mediterranean Sea. Rome, Paris, London are all upriver. New York, San Francisco, Chicago, Boston, have the dramatic force of seawalls. An ancient theme, this one, how every place in America speaks of another place, here perhaps merely opening its wing to draw in Paris, the only city, after all, in the West which confronts you in its sacred places with the names written large in stone of foreign cities: MOSCOU IENA AUSTERLITZ ROME RIVOLI PYRAMIDES ULM. I grew up thinking of Napoléon as an Italian immigrant, short, quick, determined, who made good.

These are terms no one can accede to, perhaps, without a lot of replacement of mine with other narratives, more consecrated, more true, and you will say to me, the reason you see Paris as you see it is because you came there in bad weather and because for you Paris is merely a mirror. I will plead guilty on both counts. For me Paris is an American World's Fair, seen under the weather of Greenland. Napoléon Bonaparte, one of the fathers, after all, of the Risorgimento, was therefore also one of the fathers of its bastard offspring, the vast migration of the Southern Italians which landed my grandparents in l'Astoria and, by a commodious vicus of recirculation, me in Paris. You will say that I do not owe Napoléon what, perhaps, was due him from Champollion who achieved eternal glory by deciphering the Rosetta Stone Napoléon's army found. I have less, at any rate, to owe than Champollion, but, though I freely admit how long the strands of filiation are, how circumscribed by chance and thoroughly diverted by the agency of others, I will nonetheless stake my claim, which is, remember, not merely mine but that of an ancient people great in numbers and in virtue, drawn or flung across a sea, an ocean, a continent, to plant in California and in Uruguay the sprig of rosemary, the vine descended from the seeds and branches ferried from Troy or wherever by Aeneas or whomever three thousand years or whatever ago, their claim, our claim, to see in Paris what Aeneas saw in

Carthage, a place we didn't want but wanted us and had its piece of us, and I will reject your implication, your perfectly agreeable suspicion, that in thus laying my finger on Napoléon's untouchable tomb I am engaging in a politician's invocation of the Origin, Authority, and drawing down into my breath the breath of god or gods, because Napoléon, as I saw him at every turn in that city, played a tragedy not of origin but of repetition, crossing the Alps because Hannibal and Charlemagne had crossed the Alps, Vercingetorix descending upon Italy in the avatar of an Italian, Rome revenging itself upon Rome, in his sinews and his portable presence chamber an indissoluble clump of friable rubble, whom it would be understatement to dismantle as a shape of lateness, whom one only experiences fully as a piece of candy concocted so obsessively that one has enjoyed it for hours, days, years, suckled on it as long as all of Hecuba's children in a row, getting down through its hundreds of layers infinitely thin and intricately delicious before the little taste, as fleeting as an afterthought, reminding you the meal is already ended while you search your teeth with your tongue, the sudden shaft of bitter almond, over before you stop looking down to catch your balance. Not an origin. Not even a conclusion. But certainly an overture, certainly a great crescendo followed by another great crescendo landing in the silence of yet

another great crescendo. Neither Rossini nor
Beethoven alone, but both of them together in
the soundtrack of a movie that goes on like
the anonymous great river.

I stood in Paris as every American stands
sooner or later, Dorothy in Oz interrogating
the dishevelled Wizard. This was what my
grandfather had been hearing, I thought. My
father's stepfather, whose ear I have been constructing all these years, not to catch it, but to
hear with it, sitting at his drillpress in the cellar
factory sixteen hours a day — a matter, I imagined, for pity, afterwards for pride, and after
that just whatever it was that without having
the immediate fur of curiosity still moved me
through all the upper hells or lower heavens
of speculation into the labyrinthine suite of
concentrated colors and high polishes that became my ordinary place of work — listening
at the same time to the fourteen hums and
buzzes of the machine, alert for any trouble or
sign of resistance needing oil from a popping
can or grease from a thumbflick, and to the
overt radio hanging by a wire from the ceiling,
its inner city of glass buildings glowing as the
cedars of Lebanon would if they were lit from
the core by a flame of desire, and its hardy
little cone of black paper roaring at him all day
long the arias of Bellini and Donizetti, the
strong smoke of shouted and wept melodrama,
the announcers like the surf at Rockaway in
October, which poured into him, the whole

noisy jumble of it, without seeming what it was in one sense, a part of the darkness and struggle that laid its grimy fingers on every calendar of saints' days, every forgotten green glass vase on a shelf, the old breakfront full of drill bits and wrenches, and tumbleweeds of random orange wires, the radio seeming instead somehow the unwilling vessel of something my grandfather was sucking at with his ear, a sound he could not bear to miss, like a seagull far inland cocking his head to strike some echo of the ocean, because he was hearing it all the time, I finally understood without knowing what it could mean to me if I tried to give or allow it meaning, was, in his little cellar factory with the ivy growing in at the windows and the brilliant glare of Calvary cemetery lighting up the whole of Sunnyside outside, receiving at all hours the thin unmistakeable anchovy voice of Europe, a brittle tenor howling down a tunnel, to my deafness or literality nothing more than a high color frantically stroked across the illimitable cosmos of harmonious static that enveloped it with distances of blacknesses whose nominations require mathematicians rather than poets, but to him precisions of assurance, doves alighting on his hand as he gazed about him at a circular horizon of rolling water. Precisions, yes, to him. To me they were syrups, liquors, dark bottles full of lizards dissolving in poison, distillations of flowers I had never smelled in blossom or touched in their sexual softness, weeds I had never chewed in a field, as I came to know or imagine him to have drawn in breezes full of Africa and a mother who smelled of a wood fire in an oven like a brick burial mound, a continent lost in the Ocean he could hear whose echoes I might catch in Caserta or Napoli, and all this privacy of wheat flowers or sprouting artichokes complicit, recombined as in a soup you eat two bowls of before the texture of it parts and begins to unravel its flavors, in the hoarse ironic voices of Parisians, their elaborate insistence that they are Gauls merely underlining with its total lack of instantiability the actual case it states, that they are, they have aspired to be, they have become, and they have failed to sustain, the very throat of Europe, its synthetic music, its comprehensible rituals of cutting and chopping and steaming and boiling a stalk of celery in the company of the testicles of a horse or the eyeballs of a pig, its open matrix of its own meanings, its visitable tomb, its caves of illiterates, its solution, in short, in perfumed water of the dried and folded paper flower on my grandfather's ear. So might he, or what I mean when I write *he*, have opened as a possible chamber of audition for me — what I mean being in no sense *he* as he is even to my sisters or my father at this moment, nor even to my own placid reverence for the passing icon of so appreciably personal an exhalation as that regal pronoun, but some sort of processed and processing algorithm, *he* as a set of data and statements about data, and instructions about data and about statements about data, all of these various levels of order notoriously existing in some musical *modus ponens*, such that as a texture it all looks much the same and only playing it through will allow you to begin to make distinctions among motives and themes and the larger patterns and that you will play it through again and again, four times a day for forty years, never arriving at some settled order of distribution among these varied levels of attention, music even appearing to draw you most certainly with the triply assured instability of its patterns, and that being a mere suggestion or synecdoche of what happens in the interminable program of nomination, where *he* is not only some large set of recollections trailing their soaking jacket across the linoleum of the landing but also up and down the stairs a number of times not assigned a numeral in the memory, and branching or stumbling into every room, every broken *poltrona*, in the house, cellar to roof, coalbin, birdbath, everywhere plus Connecticut, to say nothing of how he smells on each of the parts of each of these occasions: what he wears and what its collections independently include, how he sounds or doesn't sound, and so on through the fifteen or sixteen *main* organs of sense which one might think loosely of, then as the data, statements about the data having need for a so much larger valise of categories that one describes the plan of the library before beginning to suggest its inclusion of every possible kind of story or conversation but knows at least then how inexhaustible a conversation might be available even if you had died and gone to one of the more sedate Methodist heavens supposed by astronomers of a certain persuasion to be located in the air directly over central Ohio, which is not what you did at all, however, all your geology of frozen slabs of meat and all your biographies of Felix Mendelssohn having entered the score as themselves while at the same time having moved as a fluid into winter shapes, nighttime magic, and moved, subtly but remorselessly moved by instructions, themselves having become instructions instructing, and all of it changing together, teaching itself its own calculation of change as instruction, conundrum discarding conclusion, as the railroad train shortens the pillars of churches and lengthens the roofs and the eye of a reader reconstructs a finger as the letter *I* and the death of the object gives pearly smog a magnificence of forgotten sunsets, which monumental instability or vagrant foundation is the special charm as an index of *he* — had I paused there to think of him and what he might have wanted to do. Why waste words? I didn't. In the senses I have been lecturing on just now, I *was* he. He was, I was, he said, guiding you into the train as the whistle, sounding as you leave the station, figures miles away in his niece's dream, whom you've never met, as your own name pronounced by a buffalo wearing a paper hat and chewing a briar pipe. His pipe.

Quick-witted as you are, you suspect me of meaning to announce by this logic that I am, or might as well be for all the difference it makes, Napoléon Bonaparte wincing at the unexpected brilliance of the sunset of early spring here in the smoking car as it rounds the bend and heads for Patchogue, *he* being by my account some absolutely shifting designation whose finger writes a finger which rewrites the finger that wrote it on a magic pad that offers its freshest invention as its most carefully represented memory. But you have already perceived that this is a vulgar simplification and a trap for the unwary pride of the too-clever, too-suspicious, too-tendentious reader, someone you resemble only in the eyes of those who either dislike you or like you too well for their own freedom of movement. The real case is that each of us, you and me alike, is *almost* Napoléon.

What is Napoléon Bonaparte? If Paris is a novel, and if a novel is built around its suggestion of a secret which it promises to reveal and either does reveal or pretends to reveal while in fact diverting one's attention elsewhere (as Roland Barthes suggests in his amazing novel about castration *S/Z*, a work pretending to be an essay in criticism written with the same honest abandon that moves me to imagine that what I am composing here is a novel), and if the secret of a novel really does resolve itself with a certain uncomplaining readiness into a question of identity or classification, then the question asked by Paris is this one: what is Napoléon Bonaparte? This, at any rate, was the question I heard, listening in a pattern whose model, let us say simply, is my grandfather to the radio / me to Paris. This is the pattern that, at a completely different order of magnitude, reconstitutes the molecular *he* of the data, the *he* as a hemisemidemiquaver whose identity is inconceivable outside the inverted mordant of statements and the *presto ma non troppo* of instructions inside which it occurs, the *he* transmutable and apparently transferable beyond origin or filiation, the delusional *he* of the Bedlam Napoléons and Lake Geneva Jesus Christs that readily breaks its fall in a clump of leaves and dry twigs or stubs its toe on a broken cobble in l'Astoria, here (that is) recurring as the so-called motive, what you know and know again at first sight or upon closest consideration as the famous gesture in four notes, the perfectly lucid stand upon the triple dominant and the tumble to the minor third, a juggler's orange you might find anywhere at any speed and never once take it for a grape or a stuffed tripe. He is, you know, both the little black ball and the mordant, the impersonal empty staves and the key signature, or (rising through the crystal spheres of neurology) the motive, the melody, the repetitions, the canon, the progression, the title, the signature (even), the recording, the announcer, my grandfather whistling the tune of 'Questa o quella' in time to his fingers feeding the machine the little oily nuts that the drill would thread, and me, not listening to it, but listening to hear the sound of something being listened to. That's a different sound. The difference is that other listener, my by-now ubiquitous *he*, as you might think, but not really ubiquitous at all. *He* is the sign of my guess that he might have been there, should have, no, but wished it in such force that it propelled me there to stand listening to what the world offered but always as what he'd have advised me, did advise me, to hear, a sound he knew as well as I knew the sound of him, which was not the same. This complication of wills, his and mine indecipherably distinct so that one looks to separate them knowing all the while the desire to do so is merely a version of a desire to see them as identical, is the secret music of l'Astoria, which is what I hear in the question: What is Napoléon Bonaparte?

Not a delay. Not this apparent paratactic or retreat into the next alley and the next courtyard and the window above and the window within. Though you might think so. One of my instructions is this: Do not trust strangers.

Another instruction is to travel, and alone, when necessary. From this, it follows that I find people who are known somehow to me and that I rely upon my own eyes and nose. And following these instructions is how I came to this point, because my friend told me to walk up a certain street in search of something that turned out not to be there, but since I was walking and since we had had wine at lunch so I needed to walk anyway, I kept going, thinking it would bring me somewhere. That is, when the friend's instruction leaves off, the street's begins. The street would lead me. I asked a soldier what is this. This is the École Militaire from the back. What is that? That is Les Invalides. I don't know why I always avoided Paris before this. I feel ridiculous at my age not knowing anything so obvious, so poking itself into the skyline as this. Nor am I able to rid myself of the sense that it is all something in my memory. This is a complication, no doubt, of my having studied French at school, having been reading French writers all my life, having seen dozens, hundreds of movies set in Paris, so that everything has a certain veneer of familiarity and yet all of it is new to me, its distances resist as distances do the mind's attachment to the map, interposing their sheer piles of actual gravel and bleak windows. And when you arrive there is no trumpet but the question of how to cross a particularly busy street, and there is no sign saying

Napoléon's Tomb or even Les Invalides but only the blunt seat of the dome and as you get across the street the actual invalids, despite the guidebook's assertion that the name of the place is hardly justified anymore, very much in evidence and even in your way as they labor slowly across the well-drained grade, their progress on this artifice of flatness and presentation made to seem by the largeness and angularity and shadeless brilliance of reflected sunlight so much the more deliberate and painful, the large wheels of the chairs and the hunch of the old victims as they lean to their propulsion all adding to the illusion that one has stepped into some tank at the zoo where an ancient and curious race of snails is being observed with care, against its possible extinction. The authors of guidebooks perhaps do not themselves walk so quickly past this spectacle of prehistoric deliberation and visible anguish, not themselves unsusceptible to its place in the panoply of transformation of la storia into l'Astoria, the broken limbs and ossifying sinews and stiffness of purposive progress filling the empty moat with uselessness and working on the apprehension of the hiking tourist like a staircase, steeper by far than the ceremonially shallow rises of marble up which Richelieu and a regulation retinue might pass without pause or sense of effort, a palpable break by contrast from the unconscious energy of exploration and discovery or even just the ordinary pump of ordinary business, verging suddenly into this dance of heroes as they transform themselves, even there on the path and even as you pause to let them struggle by, to stone. But the authors of guidebooks, cheerful and sober bureaucrats of travel, disregard these casualties, refrain from suggesting that you might not so readily be able to slip indoors to what they excellently catalogue awaiting your elucidation, your acquisition as a trophy or justification of the trouble, the time, the expense, the danger, the discomfort, the confusion, the dreams, the lonely sense of not quite being able to make sense of even the things that are most thoughtlessly familiar — the light switches, the coins, the girls in the shops as they murmur helpful suggestions that nonetheless keep reminding you of lessons in grammar books, the indefatigable cheeses, the murky soups full of vegetables you can not quite taste or name that are grown in places you have neither seen nor read the names of, though you do eat and from no ordinary hunger but from the mouth seeking reassurance it will find here only in the crude temperature or texture of a thing and not at all in any of the distinctions and colorations it will have been trained to expect and can be expected later on to know how to praise or employ as a criterion lending itself with a remarkable suppleness to all sorts of comparisons among complexities, contradictions miraculously sustained between

dialogues of appearance and of aftertaste, con-
trasts among identicals, explications of left-
overs more than adequately full of authority
and accurate prolepsis to make the name of a
professional fortune-teller, one having come to
Paris, as always, to acquire not merely perfumes or maroquinerie or silk ties at Sulka's
or a handsewn set of Babar and Celeste stuffed
and elegantly dressed at Au Nain Bleu, but for
another arrow of authority, another scrolled
parchment written over with names of streets
and shops and favorite waiters and little-known
paintings in the Louvre and an opinion about
Beaubourg's toy-blue ventilation ducts, to all
of which those assiduous scriveners offer up
their effective arrangements of information, so
that circumnavigating the Place de la Concorde, you may be able to point with assurance
to the allegory in marble representing the city
of Brest and tell the girl whom you have just
offered the hot chestnut from the little white
paper bag in your hand that it was precisely
here they set up the guillotine which was to
separate from the body of Louis XVI the
anointed and embattled head, repressing in
their dutiful adherence to your appetite's imperative every impulse to tell you what they
have been led to suppose that you will have
no use for when you have returned to Long
Island, such as their own personal relations to
one or more of the young persons battering
guitars in the Métro or their undeniable knowl-

edge, these authorities of tourism, that the name of Les Invalides is no empty recollection or totemic persistence of an otherwise forgotten function, what might more plausibly be suggested if not sustained concerning the relations between name and usage at La Sainte Chapelle, but arises from a policy not of mere glory but of necessity troubled by glory, of glory *as* necessity — glory, as it seems here among the scallop shells deposited by the receding moon, imposed upon France always a little unexpectedly, glory arising into the sky to be mistaken for a cosmic body when it had been recognized from the start as the curled and gilded lips of a muscular evacuation spattering the boulevards and cemetery walls in moments meticulously recorded in the dialect of l'Astoria — the *grammar* of iron spikes and naked girls cast in bronze — but each turn of the narrow street showing you as the most ignorable shadow of la storia, that ready argument at the ticket office, that grim beauty with the low voice asking you repeatedly if you have made up your mind in the bakery, all of this rumbling sullenness parading as a sort of style in its heraldry of Burberry scarves because this is Paris, they know, with or without the hand of some constantly reflecting haberdasher, Paris where all the fault lines are always on view even in the form of the most sedate compositions of grass and marble, to say nothing of the terpsichore that springs into articulate movement each morning when the shop girl touches her ears with a drop of Deneuve while the veteran of Saigon straps the braces to his legs, so accustomed to this winter of groans and stabs he can't imagine other seasons of the body any longer but faces this weather with a permanently settled squint and flatness of the mouth, drawing his dry solace from the customary coffee and croissant and beginning in his bathrobe his slow progress across the operatic backdrop of Les Invalides, a pitiless beach the Sun King could imagine as a provision of exquisite reward and comfort, having some bitter thought for you as you might have been expected to pass through in the body of your grandfather's grandfather's grandfather in order while selling silk or buying felt to acquire some accurate notion of French clarity, then more famous perhaps than now, consisting of its capacity for making what hurts even to look upon, to stand patiently behind as it drags past you with or without some hopeless salutation, into an ornament of glory, the soldier become the medal, the body of the building become his body, so that his actual collection of betraying joints and decaying tissues appears to him every bit as useless, as quickly to be disposed of, as it does to you or to your cicerone, who directs your eye to Hardouin-Mansart's dome and begins to recite its excellences with as extreme an energy of details as he can muster, reserving for these human beings only the polite patience to sustain his own title to membership in the company of sensitive observers — people, monsieur, such as yourself, people whose instinct of acquisition allows itself that scope always commendably visible in the masters of any destiny, howsoever modest, without losing its nervous periphery, its alertness to the demands of the humbly inconsequent, who require no more than a nod or a handful of centimes, offering in return a reassurance of one's own sensorial balance — and avoiding the fall into memory and fear, into recognition that stops one in his tracks, as it were, as I was, waiting on the pebbled walk for a fat old corporal in a wheelchair to negotiate the narrow gate, not even thinking to offer assistance, partly as he seemed not to look for it and out of the consequent fear of meeting a refusal I might possibly not understand, there being nothing quite so unsettling as insults in other languages which may not after all even *be* insults, and partly out of my own attachment to the guidebook, my haste to get inside and see what was to be seen of Napoléon Bonaparte and of the answer to the question what is Napoléon, partly out of all these ordinary social self-containments, but mostly out of a knowledge that, once you put your hand to the handles of a wheelchair, you will not be able to take them away.

You will see, I have seen, the same army of caterpillars and snails, looking out the windows of Goldwater Hospital on Roosevelt Island, looking out to l'Astoria on the East and Manhattan on the West. Welfare Island, it used to be called, a little more candidly, and before that, Blackwell's Island, when they would ship tuberculosis patients there to undergo a cure for years or die without even telling their families. It occupies the center of the East River and might have become an Île de la Cité, a place of churches and palaces and restaurants, and may yet in another five centuries, but now it is an island that even the Queensborough Bridge, which used to send an elevator down to it, no longer wishes to know, passing overhead like an infinite column of trucks in a painted dream of war, and you can only reach it by a cable car from Manhattan, as if it were a mountain, or, if you want to stay close to the ground, by a small bridge from l'Astoria — the way, often, my father drove me there in the nineteen-fifties on Sunday mornings when I was working as a Sodality boy from the Jesuit school, and would go there to meet my friends and the girls from the Dominican Academy, to push the wheelchairs to Mass. The Hospital is long, having five pairs of wings, five five-story V's in parallel strung out along the ground and first and second floors by straight empty vanishing-point corridors lined with tiles and windows, into which we would run and skip, astonished by our adolescent immunity, our sacramental radiance, touching jaundice and polio and leukemia and the all-inclusive stink of urine and despair without feeling, afterwards, the need to wash it off with anything more weighty than the river air and the passing butterfly touch of the fingers the girls might bestow, giggling, and carried this sense of good fortune, of impermeability bought at the price of these habits we developed in doing corporal works of mercy as our form of mating, twenty-two years, my Filipino friend in Paris among the most innocent of us all in this gleeful sobriety, until the summer of nineteen eighty-three when I went there again, this time because my mother had suffered a stroke so totally devastating that, though I was still hoping for some better fortune, it had begun to look that no place else would take her, and went in with my sisters, dismayed and startled by their horror of it because I was still supposing it owed me some absolute guarantee of happy developments which in fact were not going to be forthcoming except in the most subtle ways imaginable, most of these owing to my deeply inscribed sense that all would be well even in the midst of the most excruciating deceptions and agonies, not deserting me through six months she lay in the hospital in Danbury able to move nothing except her eyelids and, as the extent of her rehabilitation, her left thumb, her lips, her wrist on good days, her tongue, her head from side to side sometimes, her facial muscles as time went on, enough to convey the illimitable terror of the prospect, clear-headed enough to write messages by blinking out the spelling, even to make jokes —

CADMIUM IS THE METAL USED IN FACES.
WHAT FACES?
EDIFACES.

— or if the doctor had been cheerfully describing some Rube Goldberg arrangement of computers, bells, pulleys, wheels, and whistles she might be brought to use after a year or two and we asked her what she thought of it —

IGLOOS ARE FOR ESKIMOS

— and every such item a cause for rejoicing on long distance telephone, my cousin in Connecticut having premonitory dreams of different developments as the months went by in my car racing back and forth between Danbury and Brooklyn four and six times a week, or my mother's cousin in Los Angeles calling up because she had had a vision at a healing service, all of us gathering in the hospital to christen my daughter who had been born five weeks before this disaster, my mother driving down from Putnam County at eighty miles an hour to be there and help, doing this as she did everything, so quickly you were still reading the newspaper and thinking about getting started when she had already done it, now lying still in the bright cheerful room as the priest went through the motions and my son kept imagining that either it wasn't really his grandmother in the bed with her face sagging on the side or else she was suddenly going to get up and be better, a belief I myself never got rid of even after all these emergencies, sudden pulmonary edema, sudden pneumonias, sudden unnameable infections, oceans of mucus drawn through a tube in her throat from her lungs with a machine, because New Year's Eve we had a party there, even gave her a sip of Asti Spumante and even, using devices and patience, played cards with her and she won and we went home full of bitter-tasting optimisms and all of us sick from the strain and sorrow, and finally that month gave in and brought her to Goldwater where they said, give us six months and you can take her home, and after a month, on March 4, we celebrated her birthday because it was a Sunday though her birthday was the sixth, and the morning of the fifth she had a heart attack from which she amazingly recovered most of what had been left of her, except that lying in a coma and fragile for days with no muscle therapy, she began to stiffen up and suffer awful pain but kept getting better till the night of April 1, I came by subway and bus because my carburetor needed some adjustment and my father came to drive me home, her complaining of her chest, which we told the doctors, but she had another attack the next morning and another, them reviving her seven times between April 2 and April 4, my forty-third birthday, when she woke up and even, rolling her eyes like Jesus, always a trace of blood on her lips, smiled at me as I wept and returning from dinner alone in a driving rain found the monitor shapeless and they revived her three times in an hour but she had had and had given enough and died, me knowing all through that hour there was an incredible blackness and loneliness in the endless straight corridors of the hospital that had never been there before, so that I called her brother and sister-in-law in l'Astoria, very near, you can almost see the spit of land their house sits at the start of, and they arrived in time to be with me when the doctors came down the wing to where we were told to wait and told us. March 6, 1986, I was in Paris. It was her seventieth birthday. I had had some notion I would fly to Italy that day and kiss the ground she was born on. But when the day arrived, I was too weary with the weather, had too much still to do in Paris, said to myself, I will go back to Notre Dame and light a candle, I will do something to mark the moment, and went however, as I had promised, to UNESCO to have lunch with my friend, which we ate after all at his apartment because his son was sick at home, and went afterwards in search of a place I didn't find but

92

found instead Les Invalides, never once thinking of my mother, all these parallels and intersections having come to me afterwards, but
only thinking, as I went, that I was following
a path I ought to follow, observing my reactions, such as they were, of impatience with
the veterans, as if these reactions were merely
a part of the architecture I had come to see,
or part, according to another program, of a
scroll of what's already written I had come to
examine: this whole experience as I tell it
being one instance of how the past presents
itself persistent in l'Astoria as the most com-
monly understood text of the future, the act
of travel as the adventure of reading what has
long since been prepared, including in its preparation your sense that all of it has been prepared for *you*, so that it is but an easy and an
abrupt glide from your recognition of what you
had been so lovingly and long ago formed to
hail as yours, to your, which is to say at least
my, easy sense that the chronicle of the tomb
of Napoléon includes among its possibilities
before and its actual events, now that I was to
visit it on my mother's seventieth birthday, my
visit to the cemetery of Europe where she had
been born in the mountains of Abruzzi during
the World War, unseen by her father in America till she was three years old, and that this
tomb would become for me *her* memorial, my
instinctive answer to the question what is
Napoléon Bonaparte being, my mother.

How do you love your mother? You do not love her in the contemplation of her beauty, her swift fingers and her grace at conversation, admiring these excellences of course even as you tot up the things that, over the years, their sustenance might have cost you or drawn from you as a sign of your own always amazing *virtù*, as you know, because loving her in the contemplation of these things is only too likely to lose itself in their own goodness and estimability, but you love your mother differently from all these perfections she has surrounded you with and left ready to hand like so many ripe pears and plums silently set down for you on the table (as in the poem) when you come home from school even though she is out for the moment, love her with something very terrible to name, some desire to stand at her door and hold up a mace or a club against all possible entrants, tell someone else, not me, that you don't, or never knew, even a moment, that you did, which was, under everything else, under the spirals of fear and delight and resentment and tenderness, what I had discovered, a plain black animal inside that would not let her die and would fight her death for her when she could not, no reasoning able to reach him, so that he only howled at his failure when she died, only later quiet enough to hear the 'all's for the best' and the rest of it, him loving his mother as an involuntary act, as a form of breathing and turning under water in

his sleep as he dreamed of it, a great pool
through which he ran, fully dressed, in water
up to his waist, only a great hanging on for
dear life and a roar of pain when, at length,
he had to lay down his armor by the side of
her bed and confess to her helpless there in a
body so ruined it was horror to think of her
waking up again into it that he had not been
able to talk or think or run or tug or charm
or frighten, or in any way change the course
of, the fates or whatever they were into some
new gesture, into some lifting of the iron hand
that had been laid on her and had pushed the
life so far inside it had no room to act any
more and was looking to escape, to fly in its
invisibility into that illegible suspicion of a
touch beyond death, that calm recovery of
what cannot be solved or even discussed, and
when she died, her body still warm and suddenly without pain, he whispered in her ear,
you told her you loved her or, what you can't
remember, made the hiss itself the form of
your gratitude to her for giving you life, pouring out of you as if you had no need of it any
more, all of this because in holding on until
his birthday, as his sister had predicted she
would, saying 'I will envy you the honor,' the
dying mother unable to use ordinary sentences
and given now to speaking entirely in Cy-
clopean rebus, said to him now you are entirely born, though he'd have preferred remaining in the water up to his waist, so that his

aria of pain arose, as he understood, in the air of l'Astoria coming in at the springtime window through the roaring rain, his mother's ambiguous and embattled brother at his elbow, into a great fountain of roses and hyacinths, filling the room with cardinals and wrens, taking into himself and giving out whatever it was, entirely beyond the reach of conversation, she released to him at that moment, whatever it is your mother is carrying for you and you don't want it because though it is yours someday you'd rather not arrive there, but when you do the power is like nothing so much as, when you'd expected a bottomless void, the feel under your foot of dry land and an easy grade. In other words, you love your mother in silence, it is altogether ligaments and fluids and undetectable frequencies, mirrors and tides, spring rain and spring air, all of it when dragged into a story or an explanation hopelessly riddled with paradox and oxymoron, as if you looked through a mile of veined marble to find a perfect rectangle or a line of the Bible, naturally occurring, in Gothic type — not to say, however, that you never find anything, and indeed, the truth of this impossibility of truth being just the opposite, that you always find it or at least are always open, as I was, to find something so much like it that you know it when you see it, and without words or announcements, its addition to your understanding speaking directly to other parts of your body or brain than the ones devoted to receiving, processing, translating, switching, and producing expressions with the mouth and hand.

This is what I met in the Dome, altogether a surprise I could only experience as one might a change of weather, with not much thought for myself, having begun to enter, been told to get a ticket, naturally not there but at a *guichet* around the corner, annoyed by this typical inconvenience and slightly exaggerated price (20 francs), came back to see the famous tomb of Napoléon with only in my mind the notion it would be some vast imposing thing one looked up at like the Arc de Triomphe and walked into this more or less perfect Baroque church to see the floor had been removed from the entire center, a great round railing of marble around it and below, submarine, a huge catafalque of polished red porphyry with gleaming scrolls carved rising along the top, sitting like a sunken heart in the pavement surrounded by a mosaic of laurel and a sunburst mosaic of gold enclosing the names IENA AUSTERLITZ RIVOLI and so on, saying nowhere Napoléon, no *N*, and all around the circle tall statues of women, Victories, with wreaths in their hands and eyes cast down, while, looking up, a grandiloquent church, all domes and coffering, Louis XIV presenting his arms to Jesus in the sky, a desecrated sanctuary made over into this operatic tomb, what you might call camp and would be hard put to call serious, but I knew when I laid eyes on it that because it was so lucid, so tacky, so entirely an act of vandalism in the exquisite church, so gross a violation of all the canons of geometry and grisaille that render the taste of Paris invulnerable to the sneers of other protocols of self-possession, because, descending, one enters around the enclosure a circle of bas-reliefs of Napoléon like a Roman Emperor half naked and half divine, lit by lamps not out of place in the lobby of a Hollywood palace of the 1920s, because, exactly because it announces his reforms and memorializes his stature as the captain of dreams with his headlong expressiveness and brutal sentimentality, abjectly in disregard of that Roman purity aiming at spectacular immobility which one sees indelibly in even the vaguest reminiscences of the great Arc, because it speaks in a thousand ways despite the gilt catalogues listing achievements and battlefield triumphs, with the undisguised sincerity of defeat, of a fall from more than royal heights to a bottom below the floor of tragedy itself, I knew that I had stumbled into what Paris had been holding for me, that this inferno of bad faith and bad taste had more to tell me than the familiar excellences of the Musée Picasso or of the music at Saint Gervais, that this echoing inconsequence of ruined altars so precisely answered my sense of what the city was telling me that I had no choice but to attend, and so, sleepy with wine, foot-sore, and appalled by my own fascination, I began at last to discover in myself, under the character of irascible and disappointed tourist, the incommensurable energies of a pilgrim, arrived at last at what I had been seeking all along in this city full of imperial attitudes: Italy, in the worst sense of the word, Italy the symptom, Italy the residue, my Italy, what I would strain to find even if it were not there, but there it was.

There so many hands appeared like soothing mothers stroking and polishing the unlikely scrolls of the wine-red stone. There, its architect a Visconti, the tomb gave the game up without an effort at dissimulation, Buonaparte who made himself Bonaparte, la storia straining past l'Astoria, returned here to the operatic recollection of points of departure. He was us, Italian to the exact degree he had escaped being Italian, Italy because he had succeeded in escaping Italy, his great originality nothing other than the completeness of his recapitulation of the whole story, the outsider in Italy become an outsider from Italy become a general and a republican become first consul become emperor become his own successor become an exile become an exaggeration in red stone, he was everyone from Romulus and Servius Tullius down through and including Julius Caesar, Machiavelli, Cesare Borgia, Mussolini, and my grandfather, that much of him was as clear as if the pool of tears around his tomb had been filled with the orchestra of La Scala playing *Aida*, clearer, as we were, out of Italy than he could ever have been inside it.

Gate of Heaven Cemetery is in a town called Valhalla. This is either precise or redundant, as you will, but standing there in the April sunlight looking at the brass plate with my mother's first birthday on it next to my forty-third, March 6, 1916 — April 4, 1984, all I could think was there had been too much to do, she had had to come too far in one lifetime, from those ungenerous steep rocks in the highlands under La Maiella, where it snows half the year and the priest is still the most important person in the town, to this final rest in upper Westchester, languages changed, cities changed, food changed, again and again, one whole civilization replacing another and again another another, all well within an ordinary person's span of years, and that ferocity of Italian poverty sustaining her and us through victories and removals like an army of angels, all of it rolled up and distilled in her quick hands, her quick glance, it was this of her and of us I saw that afternoon, like a prepared demonstration, at Les Invalides, Napoléon who used up all history in the attempt to make a new gesture, whose real contribution was the rate of his consumption, could display and exhaust the lessons of a thousand years in a single season, who aimed to found a dynasty but turned rosy himself in the general sunset he drew down over a longer afternoon of Europe than had been calculated before, his contribution to the decoding of Egypt having been one step in the process by which he had made the entire chronicle of Roman Europe into something recent, contemporary, secondary, belated, hopeless, finished before it had properly begun so that even if it continued after him, as it did in his nephew's career and in Hitler's and Mussolini's and may yet again in someone else's, it would no longer be visible except under the glaze he had given it, his re-processing of all that had ever happened since Achilles left for Troy, spinning it all out in a perfected form they would soon enough be using as the pattern of railway stations, and leaving behind him after all this stupendous course of sudden transformations and debilitations — among, you would say, his more notable deposits — this pathetic extravaganza underlining, as no historian could ever manage without laying himself open to charges of lurid simplification, that all of it had been some horror of melodrama unsuspected by the Greeks or Romans and never, indeed, imagined before this. And it was, I think, to this comprehensive brevity that I responded as I did, for what in Napoléon had taken place as the outcome of a meeting in him of character and events altogether special to him and to them, had become a century later the ordinary experience of any ordinary person alive to what was happening in the course of all those uprootings, all those crossings of the ocean, all those messages, and the suddenness of the changes of scene and of rules, what had been the unique cataclysm, so unique it was mistaken for glory, now become the typical life to be endured and decoded a million, a hundred million, times over. We were, like Napoléon, every one of us a capsule of all that had ever been remembered of our race, startlingly enclosed by our distance from where and how it had all happened, no longer receivers or transmitters but ourselves become transmissions, messages, lives of a new sort, more alive than before because everything we carried was so completely no longer alive to all the dark doorways and valuations of animals that even those who had known them could not remember well enough to explain, even supposing they had imagined some need to do so. I was standing in the Gate of Heaven thinking it wasn't any time at all, but now it seems that it was more time than anyone could have expected to know, but it was arranged differently, it wasn't all laid out in a line, it was rolled up and stood on end, and, like Napoléon's time, the amplitudes of achievement it contained may have been very great but the amplitudes of recollection it had wrapped up in it were even greater, so that in both cases you could never find a point of balance because so much was moving so rapidly along diametrically opposed axes, and the lack I felt was not of time but of rest.

You'd have never thought of this, I never did anyway, all those years in l'Astoria, going there at least once every week my entire boyhood till I was eighteen. When rich Americans built in the 1820s and 1830s, they did so with an eye that Jefferson had educated, so that, whatever the style of the houses, the general aim looked for a Palladian ease and dignity and sense of settled spaciousness. The halls were enormous. The music of voices and footfalls had air to make itself heard, giving to this settlement under the eyes of Manhattan Island a civility of quiet and exaltation of human noises I never have met with again except in some out of-the-way corners of Venice. When I go there now, I still can see some signs of this, but there are the inevitable condominiums, a vast brick apartment house advertising excellent views sitting, for the moment, where the Fanaras' house spread itself across the crest of the hill for a hundred and forty years. It is clearer if I think of it as I pieced it together in my mind growing up, Our Lady of Mount Carmel where my parents were married and I was christened sitting at the lower, eastern end of it, where we turned the car in the direction of Sunnyside to the south, and the pizzeria off Astoria Square with the green lattice-work outdoors where you could pick roses before they brought the food, the hill street with the cousins on it, all seeming in my mind the order of the stars and the moon, not only because a boy wishes to make sense, but also because it is reasonable in him to wish this, because it is explained to him that way by his elders, who also want everything to stand in position, even as they, and he, are busily planning those excellences of gesture and trade that will leave standing only enough of what was there at the outset to make it plain that everything has changed. A great return will occur, of course, but the heroes of this resurrection will restore what they find to a clarity of detail and an inspectability of texture that is the clearest sign, you see it in the obscene perfections of Notre Dame, that the place has been embalmed. A certain brand of posterity will always be willing to accept the ease of textbooks as a substitute for the terror of love. The silence will not serve those who admit, even as they polish the censer at the altars of the dead, that memory makes an ineradicable tracery whose persistence gives the howling lie to these suave reasonabilities of decor, that the only hope of a moment of real life, of passing thoughtless through a door and finding an instant that will impose its own order forever as another trophy of loss, grows with the lilac and the tiger and, like them, makes of every garden prospect the broken paradise of funerals.

When I went to the florist's, my sisters had been there before me and had ordered baskets of spring flowers, light, contrapuntal, elegant or at least impeccable they seemed to me, but I bought one of those big bleeding hearts of red roses and carnations on a stand, the very thing we had trained ourselves rigorously to refrain from, because our whole education had been a way of putting a distance between ourselves and this continuous explosion of ormolu and mirrors, Louis XV sofas and French Provincial bedrooms, white Cadillacs with downy rugs and plastic headrests to protect the velour upholstery, thick brick houses with ornamental parlors full of Capodimonte flowers that were covered with clear plastic, starched embroidered doilies, white-on-white shirts and shiny white ties, huge sad-eyed Jesuses bleeding to death over the marriage bed, polychrome accordions with electronic rhythm attachments, pink tuxedos, second kitchens in the basement where people actually lived and only used the Kitchen-Aids and Hollywood counters upstairs as pedestals for glazed porcelain statues of Saint Rocco with his dog and milkmaids with Marie Antoinette simpers idiotically atilt over their creamy bosoms spilling out in the direction of the glittering electric can opener that had never been plugged into the wall. We were students of our own specific fate, which had marked a course around all of this Bourbon floridity, landing us in post-revolutionary Astoria where the magnates had built their diversions according to a taste we

could recognize as quietly monumental, a series of austere symmetries that encouraged in
us a steady avoidance of the extravagant Sicil-
ians and dramatic Neapolitans who, being the
most warlike of immigrant Italians, were the
first to grow rich. We — were we too feckless,
too clerical, too mathematical? — flinched at
the very sight of their mammoth concrete-
mixers painted red and gold and metallic green
that shimmered like snakeskin, the huge
chromeplated mascots on the radiators, the
garlands painted in pinstripes on the hoods
and doors surrounding the names of their
wives and daughters 'Rose Ann', 'Marie Rose',
'Lisa Marie', 'Antoinette'. We were not rococo.
Indeed, we predated the Renaissance. Our
towns in Italy still convey the handmade heroic
scarcity of the Middle Ages, where every piece
of furniture, every tablecloth and wooden
wardrobe has a history, represents a triumph,
displays itself as a treasure. All through our
years of growing up, we held to these simplici-
ties, seeing in them and in the bright calm of
those high-ceilinged plain rooms of l'Astoria
the same possibility of possessing, eventually,
some distinction that did not require us to become violently wealthy, and this passionate
little snobbery of ours had no stronger apostle
than I was, seeking out everywhere in New
York Federal restraints and Greek Revival
bull's-eye windows, at least one whole lifetime
spent compiling an Augustan vocabulary and a

closetful of gray suits, an expedition into being American and Italian at the same time without conforming to the style of brutal opulence that was being canonized for us by a generation of bricklayers and truck drivers, as we saw them, whom Hollywood and *The New York Times* would later teach us to think of as gangsters. But somewhere in the midst of all this, it began to dawn on me that we had miscalculated the progress of manners, that the children of these vulgar millionaires were, since they were rich, already outdoing us at our own game, that elegance, like everything else, is much easier to buy than it is to grow in a garden, and that I had merely myself replaced one form of pointless appropriation with another, not to say that now the overstuffed manner of the Southern Italian had become mine any more than to deny that the austere Americanisms I had been cultivating had yet appeared, either as ivy or as icons, along the walls of those I had been flattering myself were incapable of appreciating them, but rather to admit that suddenly I found myself facing the difficulty that with neither of these performances could I hope to disguise from the mirror the naked displacement that had become now the fullness of manner for me, a dilemma that rendered poignant the memory of all those lessons we had administered to our mother in the dictates of restraint, imagining ourselves to be instructing her in this silent semiotic much as she had

107

taught *her* mother years before how to speak in English, and touched a well-known pedal tone in the by-now-perpetual hum of regret swelling up to paralyzing guilt in me, this time for the part I had played in our general march towards everything that belonged to American life, as if in following this familiar imperative I had myself become, rather grandly, the responsible mover, so that I began to wish for a way to play a mandolin at family dinners, restoring what we had either given up or simply never chosen at all, partly as a way of lifting my own burden of culpability and partly as a reminder, constant and nagging, to the rest of them, and particularly to her, of their own enthusiasm for abandoning the comforts of ignorance and the consolations, as they irresistibly had come to seem, of shamelessly bad taste, the good taste, really, of being shameless.

It is to this I have learned, now that I have learned what it feels like to be safely ensconced on the other side, to aspire, and for this I have cultivated a nostalgia that does not lead me astray. In the long run, only that which visibly exceeds the limits of taste has any chance of becoming visible at all. So it was for me in Paris, where the perfected fabric of this tourist paradise unveiled its treasures under a gray sky of remorseless predictability one experiences only in overdesigned environs like that of an interstate highway or of Disneyland, but not at Les Invalides where the gross wrongness of the whole spectacle made me understand in an instant, viscerally, that Napoléon Bonaparte had touched a nerve that has not ceased to vibrate. My first thought was, naturally enough, that this was only true for the French. Certainly, the Musée de l'Armée into which I now passed, gives the impression very forcibly that Napoléon is still with them in Paris, for his every relic is preserved and displayed with a thoroughness of verisimilitude in decor and taxidermy that in the United States is generally reserved for panoramas of mastodons eating buttercups among clouds of pterodactyls. One may count the veins in the legs of Napoléon's stuffed horse. One may examine his dispatch cases, his camp-bed and also the beds he used when he was dying in Longwood House on Saint Helena, his grey cloak, his battered hat, humble indumenta like the rags of Saint Francis in their glass case at Assisi, bringing you to the point of touching this unresolved contradiction. It was these clothes, thoroughly simple and devastating in effect even hanging empty, that finally awakened me to the force of my own reaction, a vibration not to the man Napoléon, about whom I knew too little, but to the faults and fissures he bestrode, called to attention, announced, was constituted by — breaks and false doublings returning, like my bleeding heart standing its vigil in the Egyptian gloom of Morisco's funeral parlor, into the places they occupied with an air of belonging that convinced everyone and no one at the same time, a demonstration of ownership complete enough to leave even the casual viewer with an oddly unshakeable sense of empty hands. For Napoléon, even into his grave, is the great demonstration of what you get when abandoning everything in honor of a single fidelity.

You might call it his mother. The painter David showed Letizia Buonaparte, her satisfaction presenting itself as thoroughly legible, as she presided from a box over her son Napoléon's coronation in Notre Dame. The painting, like all of David's Napoléons, is truer than one recognizes — for, in fact, Letizia was not in the church. She stayed away from this event, disapproving her son's elevation of Josephine to Empress. Napoléon's relation to her has in it a little of Coriolanus and Volumnia. And more. Much more. Still, despite all the themes any competent analysis would elevate — the death of the father while little Nabulio was still at school in France, the boy's immediate assumption of family responsibility even over his perfectly competent older brother Giuseppe — Napoléon's resonance certainly subsumes, but it does not simply echo, that of King Oedipus and Prince Hamlet and Lord Jesus.

You might call it, more grandly, his family. Surely no *capo mafioso* has shown a more persistent capacity to trust and reward liars and

110

cowards above friends and heroes only because of the Swiss credit of blood ties. But the very splendor that displayed itself developing this theme — the endless variety of kingships and principates and grand electorates and grand duchies that flowered all over Europe as the visible witness to Napoléon's impotence not gloriously to reward those whom the lessons of experience had long since consigned for him to a limbo of vile stupidity and vain imaginings — this very glory, this already tragic carelessness that scattered its magnificence helplessly, more like a blossoming dogwood in a storm of rain than in any way resembling a 'man of destiny' or a demigod of willpower, gave the sign that Napoléon's attention was not very fully engaged by these little splendors, that these crowns were never more than viceregal, these gifts never heavier than the strings that held them had been tested able to support and draw back home at an instant.

You might call it himself. This is perhaps the grandest of the possible Napoléons, certainly the one I heard most frequently spoken of growing up in the United States of North America. The captain of destiny. He would have done well in railroads or real estate or the stock market, this Napoléon, but of all American things to do, he would probably have founded a religion, a religion one can imagine as the uncreated lost chance towards which the Church of Latter Day Saints and the Church of

111

Christ, Scientist, can still be seen clumsily striving. This Napoléon is the god of meditation, taking council with his own secret sources of might, from every crisis stepping back across a tessellated pavement in his mind and lifting up his eyes to the open dome of the Pantheon, where the clouds racing by are writing in a ragged hand legible only to him the ineffable wisdom that their arcane calculation ceaselessly scribbles towards the interest of his growth in riches and power and beauty and joy. But to call this studious rapture by the name of *self-reliance* is to accede to an Emersonian sleight-of-hand that conceals, during the instant of the snapshot, every item in the ensemble that might detract from the effect of the keylight transfiguring the forehead, with the result that you consider only a problem made ridiculously simple, ignoring, as it were, the ground he's standing on, who paved it, when, for how much, why, when and how it changed hands, the price for the horse that brought him there, what he's about to eat, finding yourself set down full of air and energy, on a Platonic picnic blanket, a vacuum you are abundantly able to fill with seeming-innocent platitudes that leave you, when you are done, hungry but include no hint as to how you, any more than the Emperor Napoléon, are to go about procuring a meal. The 'himself' so beloved of American theologians like Whitman and Mary Baker Eddy resembles a village in a

112

valley. Anyone can take it. The Marxists have marched through looting and pillaging. The Freudians have flooded it by damming the brook. Napoléon's 'himself' is, if anything, much better defended than this, indeed is part of something quite different from what these Gnostics have imagined.

Marx said that Napoléon represented the small-holders, the peasants who now at last owning land also populated those armies he blew across Europe year after year like heaps of leaves. With Marx's analyses one always feels the ground underfoot, and this reassuring solidity gives them their recurring worth even when, as in the present instance, one feels the volume and weight of things disappearing under the force of the observation. For surely Marx was right about Napoléon even if, after considering why, one must take a step to the right. Precisely the simplest and most direct notions of glory and power, of revenge and satisfaction, notions one recognizes in Napoléon's costume and attitudes, policies and manners — precisely these are the things which, though they undid him in the end, endowed him with his appeal for those millions of families who sent him, year by year, in lieu of ruinous taxes, their sons either to be put the sword or to bring home from Milan or Vienna the wherewithal to keep the treasury of France moderately solvent. Accurate description of Napoléon's functions for a whole class of people does not quite, however, answer the question I posed, of his fidelity. Perhaps fidelity is the wrong word, you are thinking, but I am speaking of one's sense in him of an adherence that underlay all his shifts and turnings, lies and betrayals even of the passionate arrivistes who spawned and supported him. This fidelity has a shape of its own, which gives to Napoléon's life the narrative splendor it has always possessed, even for his enemies.

One is tempted to see the faith of the hero in a revenge play, little Nabulio the Corsican hatching in the École Militaire at Brienne and later in Paris a balancing of the scales between himself and the Rohans and Bourbons whose inferior, whose charity case, he was made to recognize in his own instance, day by day. But the Vindicator in Napoléon is only a passing mask, his debt to and protection of the regicides who were all going to have to flee France under the Restoration (twenty-three years after an event that had as much appalled Buonaparte in what it revealed of the king's pusillanimity as it had opened to him yet another avenue of opportunity). And one is familiar with the tradition, very close to my own chronic uneasiness, of Napoléon as a *parvenu*, a *nouveau riche* willing to do anything to get ahead, never satisfied with any victory, ceaselessly inventing new outrages of self-display, self-glorification, unable, even when his own best interests so obviously demanded it, to rest content within the most expansive border, with the most appropriate wife, the most abundant good fortune. All of these explanations cover the truth, but none of them covers quite enough of it to answer to the sense that in this individual, something held firm, despite everything that might be supposed or has been said concerning the chameleon fingers of his bridle hand, and beyond the power he sustains for anyone's desire to see a model demonstration of possibilities from the start designed, if not destined, to shudder continually in the vanishing point that began to appear like a universal chimera outside the gates of every shtetl, every narrow alley perched aslant a cliff, every watering hole and post-change in Europe. What was that something?

Napoléon learned as a boy he was the wrong person in the wrong place, would always be seen to be such, and that he had the ability to make of this perpetual disqualification a flowing river under the foundations supporting his opponents, and he could do this, for the most part, when and as he chose. This much is clear, and it makes the first uniqueness in his complexity — that, always misplaced, always embattled, he nonetheless did not succumb to the sense of persecution one immediately encounters confronting such apparent brothers of his as Robespierre and Hitler. His fidelity did not attach itself to some weakness of judgment, despite the notorious string of bad choices and miscalculations that finally brought him to grief, but it stood instead foursquare upon the impossibility for him of his ever doing anything justifiable. In this respect, the little Corsican who was never to learn properly to pronounce such shibboleths as the fluted *u* in the language of the kings who had bought his ancestral island and had become, more or less as a natural result of this purchase, the patrons of the boy's military career, found himself — not the only one of his kind exactly, but still years ahead of the event already taking lessons — taking profound lessons deep in his muscle and spine, writing bottomless lessons into Euclidean demonstrations at which he early excelled, carving angry lessons into trees and stamping determined lessons into the dust with his marching feet when he was not scratching them across it with a pointed stick, lessons that mingled inextricably and gave to him while he took them as one the double truths of what might be calculated and what might not, so that there grew, it would appear, at the same rate and to the understandings of science and of illegitimacy, just that two-handed knowledge which events would call for at the critical moments of his rising career, the capacity with a single gesture to move and to remove forces with musical fittingness and to lay claim to authority in this act, because authority required to be claimed, to be stolen, to be inhabited, in the interim every other French sense of heritage and habitation, of filiation and command having come round and rolled neatly into the slot where Nabulio had been whirling in orbit already for all the years of boyhood and of youth, with the startling effect posterior analysis has neither been able to diminish or even to deny the power of growth, Napoléon continuing to figure in ordinary conversation as the name of streets and museums everywhere in Latin Europe, because he continues to stand with his ridiculous scowl and impossible glamor squarely astride an abyss of what no one can open to question without appearing not to know that from the start he grasped it and held it aloft as the banner of the completely dubious, the completely desirable, the chalice brimming over with stony water that no one will ever even want to pretend to change to wine.

His faith is to nothing he did but only to our desire to see him do it. He is not an actor so much as the phantasm of an audience writhing in the final throes of desire. His copious *curriculum vitae* splinters and branches like the history of a cell, dividing everywhere you look into yet another duplication of all that had been squirming under your eye the prior instant, the Italian and Frenchman being neither of them present except in its qualification and negation of the other, the studious general with his annotated copy of

Caesar's *Commentaries* rising in your estima-
tion at the same speed that the looter of
churches and thief of treasuries sinks, every
possible motive dividing itself neatly into its
own perfection and its own possibilities, set
free in either case from the elaborate codes of
what might and might not be done in Paris or
in battle, and allowed in its liberty to arrive at
the splendor of completion an audience always
recognizes and seeks, for which reason arenas
of combat always have exquisitely articulated
boundaries and protocols that, in this case, had
every one of them been suspended by that Revolution whose failure Napoléon is usually supposed to mark unmistakeably — a wishful
thought, that one, which overlooks, let us say,
three basic changes the Revolution had made:
first of all, there is the freedom the Revolution
had endowed him with in the matter of choosing which restraints would do him least harm
to accept while most thoroughly hobbling his
old-world adversaries; second and most to the
point I have been making, there is the by-then
decade-long habit of creating new spectacles of
domination, instantly out of cardboard, in strict
accordance with the perceived notion of what
the audience was most likely to applaud,
government for the first time by the methods
of popular science or market research; and
third, most conclusive, was the endless string
of bad debts that was the propeller behind
most of the Revolution's conquests and the

118

thing in Napoléon to which we, or at any rate I, most instinctively, according to the reflexive laws of second nature, respond — his capacity to spend more than he could borrow, his willingness to conquer the world twice if necessary in order to protect the power of his constituents to lurch unaffected from one bankruptcy to another, a characteristic that would place him somewhere between a parent and a god were it not for the equal force evident in all he did that underlines at every turn the insincerity — nay, the futility — of the gesture of provision, leaving us with the persistently returning reflection that he paid bad debts with bad credits, that his complete inauthenticity was the only genuine thing about him, and this vacancy, while it reduces to the noisy trash of a children's party all the great rumblings of war, also as it dwindles erects before us the palpitating heart of stone which is our truest portrait of ourselves, a triumph of sentiment that feels nothing even as it weeps because all of its rage had stood at a thousand yards in square formation and all of its weakness blown itself across a valley in volley after volley of exploding shot, a placement of pity and terror into the icy fingers of murdered monkeys where they resist any attempt to give them diagrammatic identities and are no more merely alienation or 'acting out' than they are, in any sense beyond the purely filiational, some expression of the 'general will' that Saint-

Just or even Robespierre could have recognized, but are instead our own prospective memorial, a marble of movement predicting migrations not just beyond the Kingship of Christ into the Kingship of Satan or the Kingship of Nothing, but beyond even nothing into a bleak paradise of fury without object and payment without debt, sonship without fatherhood, citizenship without nationhood, number without quantity, intersection without destination, removal without motion, death without life, so that as he separates himself with a logician's ease from any settled meaning of each thing he does, enveloping it every time in its own extremist contradictory, Napoléon Bonaparte stands up for what we are condemned to continue, the charade of value where all guarantees have been annulled in the hope that, at some chance turn of the path, some idiot inventive bestiality will suddenly appear not just dreadful but dreadful *because* there is some other thing visible in its baleful radiance that is clearly, is demonstrably, a place from which once more we might begin, a hope that division is also combination, a forlorn sinking into feelings because the voice of pain at least remains, against the general muffle, conceivably audible, and he holds out to us with a ponderer's security his one perfect invention, his invisible but impermeable mask, enclosing like a skin an epoch of mathematical torture, a stinking gutter of blood, a confused exhaustion lifting itself to the strains of Rouget de Lisle's glandular anthem and walking, for all the world like a nervous bureaucrat pacing in front of a desk, across every swamp and prairie, every range of snowbound mountains in the ancient continent with no clearer object than to erect this mansion of catastrophe you recognize at the first glance as your own eternal collapse.

So this is Paris, I thought, wandering among the battle flags and hussar's uniforms. It was only afterwards that it began to dawn on me how honest, how ruthlessly blunt, a city this is, and only after that I began to understand how this crude edginess of the city of light was not, as I had kept supposing, some puppeteer's shadow thrown across the screen by an unhappy middle-aged paterfamilias deprived for the moment of his consoling wife and effervescent children, was not an illusion in the bad weather, but was instead the actual message in the all-too-famous charm of this capital built with such harmonious insistence along the banks of an open sewer where the tourist boats glide and send up their improbable brilliance, illuminating these monuments of dominating will and reminding you at every bend in the river that these pleasures belong in a complex way to this alone, where to all their intrinsic excellences is added the Argus-eyed reminder what it costs to join the middle classes in their revels, so that the tourist in

Paris stands sensibly upon ground soaked with the blood of duchesses and buys cashews from North Africans — is able, in short to visit not just the pleasure gardens of divertissement but the pleasure gardens of Terror. I had a dream of Sanson, the master of the guillotine. It was the summer of 1794, at the end of the Terror, after the fall of Saint-Just and Robespierre.

— Justify yourself, they said to Sanson.

— Let the knife justify me, he replied, removing his clothes and lying down naked so that the knife would cleave him into two tines of a fork from forehead to groin and he would fall in two equal halves to the sides.

Let fall the knife, he said. Down it came, and he fell in two on either side the guillotine, and then his two sides joined and stood together, justified. The guillotine, nonetheless, does not appear to have been a sacrament.

II

The Terror

All along the Rue Saint Honoré, looking for gifts for my wife and children among those concentrated cubes of snakeskin and those lacquered objects of explicit utility, walking again and again through the route of the tumbrels to the place of execution, past the house of the carpenter Duplay where Robespierre had lived in ostentatious, or at least ostensible, moderation, unaware of all of this but aware of something in this street very different from the rest of Paris, aware of the place's name as a melody I hailed at first sight for being somehow attached to my information though I was unwilling in the act to pause long enough to find the pathway that might help me to call all of it up to the screen of conscious review, uncurious (more curiously) even to dip my hand into the deep vent of my raincoat and consult the Michelin *vademecum* because in that moment, though afterwards at home I read and reread many accounts of the doings of the Convention, all the actors who played this interminable allegory of class warfare, if that's what it was, appeared to me under the leveling haze of a doubtful clarity long familiar, even definitive, like the names of the *grands boulevards*, without having been allowed for more than an instant to revisit the focus of attention they must have occupied, indeed burnished with their own glamor, during the hot summer many years subsequent when the houses were knocked down and the new pavement laid in a straight progress like the lightning forearm of God Almighty poking through a cloud of orange dust and a hailstorm of tobacco spit. Not recalling anything more than the vague numen attached to the name of this surviving alley and its association with movie stars and parfumerie, but relieved for once to find a street that did not present the by-then-all-too-familiar rhyming sequence of *boulangerie, patisserie, charcuterie* that reminds you sadly all over Paris how love is fleeting but food is forever, I implausibly haunted that narrow place, avoiding the department stores as altogether the dingy inferior of what New York City or even its suburbs had led me to think of as minimally glossy and spacious and cheap, concentrating instead, as one always seems to do with unfamiliar money in hand, upon a set of shops whose Madison Avenue branches, if they have them, would scarcely divert my attention from the usual winsome project of looking at the decorative women and surviving the homicidal bus drivers, having decided once for all and years ago that the boutiques were offering nothing I wanted that a little industry couldn't find downtown for half the price and without the withering radiation of the salesperson's eyes sizing you up and offering, in a shop full of diamond bracelets and wristwatches more precise than the orbit of the moon, to show you a fifteen-dollar mechanical pencil, but here, protected by strangeness and ignorance and unable to feel very reliably the cost of the money, drawn free of all those carefully inculcated restraints and spiderwebs of hesitation, peered greedily into the windows of Gucci and Hermès and Dupont and even plucked up the adrenalin violin loud enough to stroll carelessly in and discuss, in an exaggeration of incompetent French, with some impeccable creature who I hoped could not possibly begin to assess whether or not I might not, back home, present to my neighbors some substantial array of white-jacketed assistants and views from the bay window, the desirability of a two-hundred dollar pinafore for my two-year-old daughter. We named her Victoria, out of an agreement we have never much discussed but I have privately supposed founded itself upon our mutual recognition that we had indeed a triumph to celebrate — indeed, more than one — over the fearsome doctors who told us a caesarian would be needed, though my wife's determination and courage proved that wrong, over a host of our own doubts of the same possibility, but even prior to this, over our own monsters of anger and fear, separate and shared. A legitimate victory. I did not, nonetheless, buy the pinafore, though I spent money enough on a selection of exquisite things, having decided that this particular bargain, being neither good nor necessary and the item in question revealing itself upon examination to have been made, despite its imposing price tag, in a sweatshop in Taiwan, would, with its refusal, open the door, as in fact it did, to a subtler range of options. Never, travelling, have I given so much impassioned attention to this collecting of trophies as here, in this battleground of shopkeepers. Transatlantic reconsideration has led me to suppose these little acts of election possessed an importance for which I know many modes of evaluation but none that specifies just what it was that drove me back and forth in front of the Église Saint Roch so very many times in search of a pocketbook, a model car, a sweater in twenty colors of wool, as if, so the tourist must suppose, the very effort of hauling a thing out of Paris and across the ocean were certain to make its mark, not only on my mantelpiece in Midwood where the miniature Renault landau in green and cream and black and silver rests unobtrusively among the household divinities, but there in the street just under the scars in the masonry left by Napoléon's whiff of grapeshot. For, despite your lack of enthusiasm, you have seen in every flash of appetite the repeated demonstration that Paris *is* a writer's city, a city written in the diverse script of carpentry and plaster, vermiculated quoins and painted stars in the ceiling, to which you have wanted to lift your piercing needle full of would-be South American poisons, leaving on the wall your own deadly and intensely interesting stain, with, it must be admitted, always a sad or at least flatfooted recognition that the fables of your poets and readers of poets had failed to convince you that there was anything exceptionally different to be found in a careful examination of your signature upon a pedestal when seen against its signature upon *you* — *you*, like *he*, resisting all unification, condensation, and enclosure, more *it* than *you* or *he* because what one carries along has no person, more *they* than *it* because everything is always in motion, more *which?* than *they* because the place is old and the names of the streets are always changing — *you* dissolving backwards into as many pieces as there are words at your disposal, a riddle even you will not solve. So, to consider the souvenir in the severest of modes, it might be said that who buys it is obviously bought *by* it, carries its tattoo proudly onstage back home, but perhaps less clearly to be seen is the buyer's desire thus to carve a sexual frame in the oak tree, break off a chip of Saint Roch less for the pleasure of mounting it in a frame or of wearing it on her neck than for the satisfaction of being able henceforward to contemplate some return, possibly in company, which should feature in its itinerary a dramatic inspection of the scar

129

left behind once upon another descent from the sky.

There might be, then, a case to make for the art in being a tourist — the practice, that is, of painting a red squiggle down the middle of the Boulevard Raspail at two in the morning when no one is looking. Or it might be the other thing, so secret even in broad daylight, the thing without a name, because you can't call it vomiting and you can't call it just bleeding and you can't call it just suddenly, when the fellow with the great closed parentheses scarred into his cheeks steps into the Métro and says he's going to kill anyone who refuses him money to eat with, the mere faint clink of the coin submitting to the threat, and you can't it call it any other name than the one they give it in Paris that you found yourself strangely aware of, the Terror. How, reasoning always backwards, I said to myself afterwards, they must have loved Bonaparte because of the Terror, which he did not so much bring to a conclusion as regularize to a degree more than adequate for ready exportation, as the historians in their savage concert mightily conclude, but be not confused, it is a simple thing you can buy, and you will see no more there than, curling its tiny fingers into one of these cherubic pink fists, a little reservation of some other pleasure yet to display its palm before the ecstatic pilgrims in procession, far too pointless to require its special thesis, excessive in its moderation, avoiding even the tinniness that suspicion always seeks when the telephone rings and triumphs are requested with the episodic regularity of rents growing further and further out of reach, settling instead upon the full unremarkability of a potato peeler or a fork or a table knife, though it is nothing even so vestigially terrible as one of these. That is the Terror, nothing more or less, as the newspapers and television have been teaching us, than the breach in the wall, the gaping wound in the fuselage, the exploding souvenir folded into a pile of shirts and wrapped in birthday-present red and blue and gold. Surprise! in the bottle of headache pills, the ill-sent question in the symposium. And by what name are you going to call this ordinary thing?

Is it a grammarian's subject, a movement, as is said, from the first person to the third person? Supposing it were the case that such an elision of responsibility were, if not the thing itself, the enabling condition or *sine qua pax et ordo* of the Terror, it might be worth a tourist's travelers' check to watch, hoping in the slow motion of repetition to catch the magician's fingers in the plunge of transfer, the energy of these words, faster than a speeding bullet and silent as the dining car in the Trans-Europe Express — which is to admit that the pronouns go not softly at all in their slide, but noisily in a thickly registered burble of comfort and dispatch towards the supposed target of your arrow, always itself another city or, in our terms, another flight of birds between a thousand steeples and chimney pots and down into secret blackberry troves or farms of crickets busily rattling their legs under an invisible umbrella of 'Bruxelles' or 'Paris'. And were we to make this investigation, it would surely display the usual properties of language as a prison, a pauper, and an idiot's two-stroke engine, delighting your persistent appetite for something to blame it all upon, growing thus into yet another triumphal arch or repository of Terror and an excuse for further investigations whose conclusions are as predictable as the climaxes of Agatha Christie, where, though you don't know which it is, you know there is a deadly culprit lurking among the far more radiantly shameful lilacs, and you won't be cheated of the price you have paid to have that person absolutely named, bound, and mailed in a steel box to Reading Gaol. Then, assuming your quick-drying polyester as if it might hang as heavily as an embossed and embroidered golden cope transmitted ecumenically from the few Jewish survivors of the Marais to the convert who is now the Cardinal Lustiger at Notre Dame, a sort of gift and reminder to the son in New York from the father in the rest home at West Palm Beach, something so heavy as to wall out the thought, to flatten and roll into a crimson drugget, the possibility of the impulse to move ever so slightly too quickly along and in the twitch miss the thaumaturgic thumb at its work on the rounded ruby, you might begin some careful looking about at the innards, carvings, windows of these transforming monuments.

I. I write *I* continuously in these pages because this is after all a work of fiction and *I* is the most popular of all romantic heroes, selling more books over the centuries than Don Quixote and Don Corleone rolled into one. Shall we call *I* and *me* 'necessary fictions' or 'pointers' or 'shifters' and have done with them — that is, go on employing them as creatures of fancy whose limited powers of amusement now stand revealed? Also available at moderate cost is the guided tour of the speaking subject, where the strawman illusion of individual self-to-selfness is neatly sliced into a square of four equilateral triangles, ghost of mother, ghost of father, ghost of self, and self of ghost. This is the famous Lacanian theology, complex enough to satisfy anyone wanting to write a medieval telephone book of phantasms and energies who own houses and have pedigrees on file. What else does *I* have to say for itself? *I* is not so clear, doesn't seem ready to play Hegelian Monopoly, has been looking admiringly down upon the washbasin of Napoléon's tomb which *I* sees as filled this time not with the band from La Scala but with heaps of books among which children with thick slings over their shoulders carry aluminum radios larger than themselves, the air riddling with dozens of different rock and rock'n'roll and cabaret renditions of what sounds as if it might all be the same song, and *I*, turning away and climbing the steps, passes into the cobbled courtyard of the Invalides, imagining horses easy on the stones, begins to read the decorations on the windows, goes back inside, inspects the postcards and guidebooks, can't find a telephone. Has *I* got lost in the blur? Has *I* revealed itself to itself as a baroque construction, a Romantic illusion? *I* thinks otherwise, I think. *I* is an other who is also what Lacan once said it couldn't be, what he said couldn't be imagined, the Other of the Other. Lacan said no, we can't return *I* to itself. But the case isn't so simple, not now. *I* is the place of passion and also the place into which it has disappeared, leaving that interesting foxing absorbed into the expensive patina gleaming along the invisible ridges of silver that bind the autobiography — the place of la storia and l'Astoria and the sign of nostalgia, the power making all that remains possible of the first in the looming erection, draped in pigeon shit, of the second.

Nostalgia wants to go, find, recover, invent, buy, sell, rent, lease, paint, plant, dig, decorate, display, leave, and return. *home*. And under that flag, armies blossoming in May, the tourist begins to march outwards, securely circular now as every road has become, every cannonball another bead in the rosary, every Rimbaud

134

another Columbus approaching from the East, every innovation another repetition. *I* conjoins all nostalgia, deploys all global stratagems, sees in every knifeblade the puzzle piece of an equator, and though suspicion might wish to do away with its claims, and dismantle the altars to ego hanging like eagles above a hundred million hearths, it is neither suspicion nor the philosophers nor the poets who are its voices that can do this deed, for the visible *I* stands over Paris in the form of a great *Je* in imperial steelwork and likewise in that great plains of water, New York Harbor, where the urine of workers has drawn indelible strokes down her copper cheeks, like an inconvenient stubble of beard sprouting platinum wires: this divinity owes its birth to something wilder, wider, and more insidious than armies, even than Terror, which of course is its child; something nameless it names, some millenarian desire to begin again, has driven us back to this worship of the mobility of the ocular muscles, for indeed upon so fragile a scaffolding rests the illusion of liberty, but Liberty itself contrariwise stands solid upon the ground of death and dishonor and shows, hundreds of years in advance of the event, the allure of apocalypse.

— Or so says who? say you.

— Says *I*? I say.

— Says a certain stinking revisionist, you say.

— What says him? say I.

— *I* says, you say, the whole of the Revolution, from Rousseau to Robespierre to Babeuf to Marx to Lenin to Castro in fact devolves, goes backwards.

— You don't say, say I.

— You say so, you asshole, you insist.

— *I* says, I say, something of that sort, but thusly: construct the *cogito ergo sum* and you have made a radical move not against doubt but against security which merely accepts the structure of vision, its empire its freedom, as one among the phantasms. Construct the original equality and liberty, then, on this model of visual life. Then are kings in soup. Descartes and Rousseau.

— An old, *you* says, story, say you.

— Ah, *I* says, say I, yes.

— So, says *you*, I says (you say), you say, the Cartesian turn turns toward apocalypse?

— Or South America.

— As l'Astoria?

— Thank you, as l'Astoria.

— As, you might have said, says *you*, la storia stumbling upon its own moment before itself?

— Excellent reconsideration of the possibility of Apocalypse, l'America in every sense of the word: closing of the circle, reopening of the quadrangle.

— So, now you are talking, now you are talking, if I am reading you right.

— What are you reading?

— What you write, you write. The waiter brings in the coffee.

I looks up and lights a cigarette.

You searches in his pockets, none left.

I offers him a Marlboro vert.

— Here, *you* says, is the café, this very place, le Sarah Bernhardt, where my wife used to meet her lover.

The streets are full of rain. *You* has parked his car illegally, but it is late at night. No one will bother *you* except memory.

— She thought I was stupid, *you* says.

— *I* says, You aren't stupid.

— *You* is not stupid. *I* is not stupid.

Here have first and second become third persons, confused but not stupid, bored but brokenhearted.

— Are they / we / you monkeys after all?

— Say yes, you, and you say nothing material.

The question of Terror, let us try this a little more straightforwardly, is the question of fear and anger displaced. My friend divorces Sarah Bernhardt. The Palestinian blows up the shop where there may be Americans or at least French people who buy from Americans who support Israelis who kill Palestinians who live in the house that Jack built. Something like that. Everyone knows the dominoes from the newspapers. But many things happen in the parallel tracks while the counters are neatly knocking each other over in turn. One admits

137

from the start that oceans of air and lakes of water pass through a human being mostly unaccounted in their capacious flow except in moments of unusual pleasure or fear whose character may in an instant induce angelic receptivities, some circumstance of life disposing the whole apparatus to glow with the aroma of gardenias or to detect across water the intimate breathing of household cookery or to see the stars as if all of them were rapidly spinning about the earth because of an arhythmic stillness hanging over the wet lawn where you stand with your bare feet, and, though elevators fall dazzling with lights through pools of carp in marble lobbies twenty stories deep and you have submitted a long monograph analyzing the relationship between this foam on the crest and the mammoth swell of commodification which has thrown it into the air and will redeploy its subsidence, you have failed to provide, there has failed to be provided, they have not attempted, we do not possess, I cannot begin to offer, the streetmap of the undertow.

I was dancing at the dance with a dark beautiful Puerto Rican girl who knew how to dance, which means in the hands, the slight turn or extra pressure that speaks to the hand of the partner, and both know what to do, adapt to changes in the music without stumbling, making love last longer.

A crowd she belonged to came in, and the

boys were looking at us dance and saying threatening things we could see but not hear.

She walked over to them.

— He's no more white, she said pointing to me, than he is black.

This must have satisfied them, for now the dream changed. I was at a party for my mother's cousin Bill. He has lung cancer. In the party we must have cried. I only remember looking at him, his barrel chest and muscular neck, this cousin my mother loved so well.

Our Terror came from this, that we were no more white than we were black, we said.

— *Da Roma in giù*, they say in the North, *comincia l'Africa.*

From Rome down begins Africa. We were the beginning of Africa, our blood is mixed of Oscans and Umbrians the Romans subdued 2500 years ago, as well as of Hannibal's soldiers and who knows what Carthaginian slaves, to say nothing, said we, of Macedonians, Egyptians, Libyans, Jews, Turks, Goths, Ostrogoths, Visigoths, Arabs, Spaniards, Moroccans, Cretans, Catalonians, Basques, Celts, Greeks, Franks, Corsicans.

— So, he says, *I* sees where you is going to.

— Where, say I, be that?

— That be up slavery lane, say he.

Well of course, right you is. What makes all this distancing of *I* and of *you* if not the buying of us and the selling of us? This too is the Terror, not as an historian's Gotterdämerung in the Jacobin Club, full of speeches admirably argued and citably phrased, framed before painting, but as the breath and drink of everyday misery and the sticking pain of unrelievable want. I grew up hearing these stories:

— A lady poisoned her sister for a cameo.

— Two cousins fought over their mother's deathbed for a hat.

— One day my mother's cousin stole her father-in-law's pocket watch after he died.

— My grandmother's mother loved her chickens. One day she left my grandmother, then six years old, to watch the baby. She rocked the baby to sleep, but one chicken kept waking the baby up. Chickens are stupid and willful and will not always listen when you tell them to shut up. She shook the chicken. It made more noise, the baby started crying. She shook its head. It squawked louder. The baby screamed. She wrung the chicken's neck and killed it. *Ah, che maledetto!* She threw the chicken over the cliff at the side of the house, two hundred feet into the ravine where the river carried it away. The baby slept. Her mother came home. Where is my favorite chicken? I don't know, the little girl replied, shrugging her innocent shoulders. Her mother decided that the neighbor, a witch who had put the evil eye on her baby son who had died of fever, had stolen the chicken out of envy. She went and accused her. The neighbor, naturally, denied it and, naturally, counter-attacked. They never spoke again. A year later, my grandmother, thinking the chicken so long dead it would be safe now to unburden her conscience, explained the whole truth to her mother who listened to the entire story and then beat the little girl for an hour with a wooden spoon, screaming and cursing and chasing her up and down the picturesque streets of the medieval hill town with its simple Romanesque church so charming to tourists.

— My father's mother said to my mother, 'You do a hundred good things, I no can remember. But you do one bad thing, I no can forget.'

— My father's father worked six days a week twelve hours a day in the G.E. factory in Schenectady. The seventh day he played cards and got drunk.

— We have a *paisan* in Florida who retired in 1969. There was a sale on fluorescent light-bulbs. He has not yet used a third of the ones he bought. He also owns four thousand rolls of toilet paper.

As I write these things, I keep feeling I'm doing something very wrong, putting down in black and white these ordinary stories of ordinary life lived, after all, in broad daylight. There is a Terror in this too. I frighten them by telling these stories. They frighten me by saying, as I write, in my secret ear, 'Why tell these things to strangers? Traitor!'

It's a radio full of melodramas that hangs by a wire from the ceiling wherever I write.

Not in Paris, though. This is why Paris touched me as it did. There the *omertà* was at last broken. That is its everlasting glory. The Revolution was a war not against the aristocrats or for the bourgeois or with the proles so much as it was a war against silence, the discovery of a universal third person that neither Descartes nor Rousseau, though they were its progenitors in some way more visible than the way you are descended from Mark Antony or the King O'Neill, could have expected or would have countenanced. Saint-Just was more than anyone the voice of the Terror. He invented the formula by which it became possible to execute the King, declaring him not the Father of the Nation or God's Legate but, revising these notions from the bottom up, an Enemy Alien. Once said, a phrase so precisely answering everyone's sense that the husband of Marie-Antoinette had more in common with his Habsburg in-laws than he could with Mirabeau or Roland or Vergniaud or any of the well-meaning bourgeois or even aristocrats who, both in his secret pay and out of it, would have saved his neck, became an irrefutable truth, an invisible palsy everyone could see, as if it were aspens in a March wind when the doomed fat gentleman stood so calmly sweating in the dock. Saint-Just with his earring and his steady good looks and his silver-buttoned rhetorical glaze, the passionate chill of Robespierre's powdered wig, invented the accusative shuttle or guillotine of heteroglossia that afterwards operated at such an astonishing rate of acceleration, wherein the Revolution named itself as a purity of adherence so like to an academic book of shibboleths that the great similarity between its ordeal and the possible intricacies of a great linguistic consonance became, in the course of months, a dazzling appearance of ontological reality based upon nothing and crowning itself during Robespierre's infamous celebration of a gerund he was able to call Supreme, above all others, consecrating a phenomenon philologists would find troubling for more than a century before Saussure finally laid it down as a postulate that between a meaning-maker and the meaning it makes there is no connection either necessary or even possible, so that language cannot be politics without doing murder, and if you try to turn it around, making politics into language, you come up against the same problem that actions do in fact go forward in ways beyond the reach of words at the same time that words, themselves actions, do produce actions which are connected neither to the meaning-maker nor to the meaning made but to a thousand other sets of exigencies and instrumentalities equally exigent and instrumental with language, thus language-like or even languages among non-communicating languages, with the startling result in this case that once the phenomenon of unlanguageability had become a crucial point in the language of politics it was only a matter of time before even the greatest virtuosi of the podium were going to begin, for their very transparency of manner, to appear incomprehensible and, drifting near it, finally fall into the hole of the foreign word, or thing or King to be killed and so become unutterable, for as is well known, the liquid eloquence of the lucid Saint-Just stopped suddenly the moment he was arrested and, from having been the voice of the Revolution, he became until his execution the next day the very silence of untranslatability that, it now was plainly to be seen, had itself been giving voice all along, had been the first person as the third person, all *his* authority an attribution and his own voice only an environment into which the word of the Revolution might or might not go, not a voice at all but a glass of warm water or a bosky dell, a silence the Revolution might break or leave to its own device, a freedom obtained at the price of preliminary disjunction in the interests of a third person which only could father other thirds, bastards of bastards, propriety-less and, for their deepest claim, free to give what it gave, say what it said, *be* said, in fact, by it, as if its Saying like its Being were, or had to be, enough. There has been told in this vortex a spiral narrative of philosophy and pornography so often, under the Old Regime, changing places as one blinked in their direction that they came to occupy the same position, so that the most serious reflection always had the character of a libel, and a libel, one came to see during the Terror, could parade itself as the unveiled torso of Principle. One has reason to hope that the needs producing this confusion have now long since disappeared for some persons, that two centuries of splenetic sentimentality and philosophic scurrility have cleared a high, well-drained flowering liberality of polished oak in a temperate climate, a San Francisco of the moral imagination, where this intersection appears truly strange and pointless, not out of a well-fed American blankness, nor through the spun-sugar tunnel of Ralph Waldo Emerson's eyeball, nor yet because chemistry has been supposed to render these matters obsolete, but rather because of something I only have known through the twin deceivers of lack and of envy, what waltzes past Sunnyside along Queens Boulevard in a communist's Jaguar, what looks down the Congregationalist aisle in Scarsdale hopefully to welcome the Salvadorean refugees, and that for the persons who think hard among the azalea banks a genuinely calm look is possible. Not for me.

— Who are *me*? asks *you*.

Me. I. Two definitions so far. First, the usual legal hero. Second, the name of the desire to go home. To which now, a third: *I*, *me*, is the name also of the breaker of silence, the accuser, the traitor, the teller of secrets, the libeler, the philosophic smutwright scribbling in the diner at daybreak.

That is to say, given that *I* is a lawyer's invention and given that *I*, once invented, is the site of many crisscrossing emotions and beliefs, and given that there is a favored coherence to this fiction, an adhesive and absorbing syrup full of a sweetness it attains in narrative when it becomes the bond linking starting-place and ending-place, celebrating home tacitly under a cartload of sensitive drunks, reformed call girls, charmless rogues, determined ideologues, maiden aunts with Shakespearean vocabularies, detectives with cocaine in their wallets, and all the rest of the wooden Indians of the best-seller list, and given, in sum, that *I* is mostly a piece of religious furniture, a pitted marble angel or dented ciborium, left to the merciful fondling of the auctioneer, there still remains an *I* to consider, not yet ready to be sliced in neat strips like beef jerky or taken down like a yellow brontosaurus fanatically compiled of Lego blocks, not to be reduced but to be constructed, yet to be built for the wreckers, still proliferating itself like shanties on the high ground outside the silver mine.

Not that this *I* is unprecedented. This *I* belonging nowhere in particular has a force you specify when you say that it has nothing to leave and nothing to welcome. It exists by virtue of place, of motion, of context, defined clearly enough by that, all that, to which it belongs but is not; that is, it reflects precedence and causes it, lives inside it, is an effect of perpetual liturgy upon which it forms its observations, against which it aims its angry denunciations, its philosophy growing entirely, out of, being the source of, its sense of arrangement, de/arrangement, re/arrangement, not of the world in general, but of the world in ceremony, in its representation of itself to itself. This is the *I* that's talking to myself at this moment of writing, altogether heedless of ordinary mumbling while cutting grass and hosing down the T-Bird, an *I* in this case not always available to talk this way, completely dumb if at all possible if happily eating breakfast at Howard Johnson's or answering theoretical questions on the blue telephone in the office, but, too frequently experiencing that subtle discomfort which produces a vivid sadness, this *I* gasps for air or tries at least to get comfortable with the wrong set of cushions and then finds itself noisily putting out its manifestos, libels, broadsheets of scatological biography of the wealthy and well-favored, and, in the present case, treatises on reminiscence.

That is, when you read *I* in this book, you are encountering a character you best think of not just as something possessing a name — even the name of the personal indicator — but having, instead, a clearly defined point of blindness. This modish entity is so exactly and in so many respects like a point of view that you may be helped before you are puzzled by thinking of the two as identical in their capacity to work as sorting programs that order a pile of scattered material, in their compositional power to arrange even the wildest juxtapositions under the steadying weight of a rhetorical necessity that the sentence, although made as it is indifferently out of jade elephants and strawberry popcorn, carries like the girl in spangled underpants or, in another sort of procession, the old porter the bleeding plaster heart. The familiar technological miracle grammar can perform, when informed by a clear sense of what might or might not be needed to secure a good fit, provides us with the steady reassurance that goes by the name *point-of-view* or even, grandly, *character*, or yet more grandly, *subjectivity*. In the present case, however, all that can be claimed has no title to anything beyond a persistent hole in the field of vision, a steadily missing point, not always in the same place and not even always able to be detected but ready, anytime, to put in an appearance not by showing up but by moving into play the fury I used to call loneliness but now recognize as helplessness in the face of incapacity — one part of the organism attacking another for having failed to supply the new Mercedes, the timely breakfast, the desperately needed rest.

Neither l'Astoria nor Paris appears to know of these divisions, for architecture expresses mostly what is there, especially in Paris where a certain evidentiary fullness is the leading theme of the shops bursting like bookmakers' pockets and of the bellied roofs rising everywhere like bubbles in glue. Buildings subdue and subsume windows into rows, signs of structural argument, symmetries of architectonic force, adjustment to site, ease of ingress and egress, splendor of crested chimneys, offering little to guide one's sense of how life is actually lived in these places, their very complexity a residue of cross purposes and a mask of articulation obscuring here what is more visible in the countryside, the notorious muteness of rocks and sticks. Working backwards, you always know that every *hôtel particulier*, every bend in an alley has its set of lost reasons and its unrecorded log book of jobbery, adultery, and simple revery, but you need a library, you need an age in the archives to recover even the faintest traces of what any of it was like. The tiniest part of it in that case serves as the stark admonishment how it would be a fool's errand to get up and cross the room for yet another dusty box of crumbling letters. Why widen the diameter along which one sees the horizons of dark death and fruitless enterprise?

The Great Terror strung its beads precisely along the line I have been disentangling for the length of a few centimeters here, it wanted to be l'Astoria before la storia, without it, or including it. It wanted everything clear and palpable for good. The Terror was politics as sculpture, its dreamers saw themselves as marble Catoes and Cincinnati singing an opera like Tritons on a twelve-decker fountain. Not that they knew nothing of inconsequence and contradiction, not that they had forgotten the rotted cheese of the Old Regime, but sadly that they had thought of nothing else but that. For all the bravery of calendars and togas, standing scratching its arse under a placard painted with republican laurel wreaths, they saw only *that*, their new beginning unable to think itself even for a second except as something they did to *that*, to an invisible net of protectors and protected, no one able to take off his clothes and swim in the river without continuing to be culpably someone else's uncle, someone else's nephew, everyone becoming the third person all the time, his sins in bronze, not because the first person had ceased to matter or to exist, but because it had flourished so grandly that when Brissot said *I* in the Convention, he was referring to a great multitude of spies and spymasters and when Robespierre spat back at him *I* he was invoking an army and painting around it the stumps of a thousand burnt bridges, so the room, large as it was, began to grow unimaginably crowded, the air getting thicker and harder to draw as the months went by in their new names, *Pluviose, Floreal, Prair-*

ial, Thermidor, like a ballet of fat old draymen in pink chiffon tutus, and all one could think was how no one's being a god meant that you couldn't quite tell any more where a person's doubles stopped duplicating in the invisible mirrors, an intolerable compounding of the throng that the guillotine, to everyone's surprise, failed to assuage, it turning out that people could not acquire genealogies by killing them but could only, in the end, contain the confusion by admitting aloud that even greater than anger was fear, a point they made at last when they brought down the Committee of Public Safety, keeping it vague by exporting their use of murder as a sorting device through a whole generation of wars which established, for good and all, that the execution of a King did very little except underline how difficult it was going to be, having separated head from body, to get rid of the corpse or stop thinking with its brain, a nation of loyal and disloyal subjects no more able to think in concert than a crowd of assassins to conduct a New England town meeting, and the oldness of the Old World rolled along, not because no one knew any better but because no one knew, or knows, enough.

So we landed in New York City without a pot to piss in and far from going, as the saying predicts, from shirtsleeves to shirtsleeves in three generations, we went instead in less than one generation from nothing to *padrone in palazzo*. When my dentist came to Sunnyside in 1959, he opened an office in a new apartment house, his mother sitting all day in the waiting room knitting, aiming to give to the occasional wanderer with a swollen cheek the illusion of heavy business, but nothing happened until one day, my grandfather, my father's stepfather that is, having a toothache and refusing to set foot in a dentist's office, a man with a hernia so bad his balls were at his knees twenty-five years in a truss he made himself rather than give himself for one minute over to the dangerous mercies of a doctor, and my father and his brothers all unable to move him or their old dentists, someone, my mother I suppose, suggested asking this young fellow who was just starting out, so that he made the house call to do the extraction, gaining with a shove and a pull of the pliers a hundred lifelong patients, all of whom had friends, and still tells the story of this square-headed bull-chested man sitting mostly useless in this room surrounded by men and women in their fifties and sixties, people of substance, anticipating his wishes, hopping to his commands, the most powerful man, he says, he ever saw, except possibly his own father. I love to tell this story through the caps my dentist has put in my mouth while telling it every few years to me. My grandfather, beginning as an excrescence and a homeless hero, stole another man's wife and sons, and he became great by the same

152

process that has made him greater, year by year, as my dentist recites the episode one more time and the details line up more closely with the theme of power. 'A man like that makes life easy for everyone,' he says. Just what my grandfather used to say about Mussolini, whom he bettered by getting away with everything and living to die in, finally, a hospital bed, aged ninety-three, the mound made by incremental repetition still today accumulating moss and glory together with his Cleopatra on a concrete shelf behind a polished green granite plate in a mausoleum laid out like a shopping mall in Saint John's Cemetery in Queens, where they await those curious antiquaries who, bating the resurrection of the dead, will attempt to construct from the names of all the contractors and doctors and landlords that gleam in the silent corridors under the polychrome light of the rounded windows some sense of the heroic sweetness of the Italian migration of the twentieth century. All we knew, it appeared, was what was remembered, a random catalogue of attitudes and proverbs that grew new force and power as one clasped to them more tightly in the face of the strange things one was learning in New York, things one needed to master for survival, but things it was impossible to assign a certain value or assimilate to an overall composition or lean upon as a steady point of reference against the prospect of an American future glittering all

the more brightly as the years filled our pockets and widened the beams of our doorways
but glittering with a brightness belonging, as it
blossomed more richly in the rainbow opales-
cence of American apples, to an Italy we had
never possessed to begin with and could only
imagine here as the combined product of obsessive recollection and compulsive digging,
planting, hammering, sawing, sweeping, painting, cooking, sewing, talking, and writing. So,
like the Jacobins becoming the protagonists of
a million nightmares even as they were weaving daisy chains for the statue of Marianne, we
were making ourselves American by the unap-
petizing process of becoming more Italian than
we could ever have aimed to be in Italy, where
to be Italian is neither remarkable nor men-
tionable except in deference to strangers, while
here in America the more we became a part of
the landscape the more we were visible against
it as objects of a high color and an assignable
price. This phenomenon had its own inelegant
duplicity, for the very things that placed us in
the general architectural chiaroscuro as decorative stumps whose pinkness or crimson was
symptomatic and, under the severe discipline
of the black-and-white camera, invisible to the
very degree that the Ionic columns of the police station and the immigration court were rendered as vivid as they had been under the de-
signer's stylus, also married us for generations
to the perishable heraldry of plaster flamingoes

and platters of yellow peppers into which, given the dynamic of ancestral desires, we were forced to compress an amplitude of potent longing that always reached the screen as laughable or pathological until, suddenly, with a Technicolor budget and a Frenchman's mobile camera, Francis Coppola showed how to make this parade of food and polished black fenders into a visible semiotic of dominion every bit as resonant as the gilt in a Corinthian capital or the blank windows of the Los Angeles City Hall. And opened the way to a long series of panoramas of Orchard Street, Hester Street, Mulberry Bend, Essex Market, Tenth Avenue, streets where the people, buying, selling, marrying, running, cooking, against a mountain range of whipping sheets and longjohns, figured as buildings, their very nakedness of resource, their debarrassment of any decency of shopfronts or dignity of Shetland ponies, petrifying poverty in the heroic glamor of naked origins, like Napoléon who, when he was about to marry Marie-Louise, daughter of the Austrian Emperor, refused the intricate genealogy the Viennese bureaucrats had prepared for him, saying to the Habsburg inheritor, 'I prefer to be the Rudolf of my line.' There was a biologic fatality about Napoléon's career, condemning his tribe to hail him as the very opposite of what he wished to become and forcing him, as he went, to answer the salvoes with each time some new exuberance of discipline and labor depositing his signature, in the end, upon the historian's page as the Rudolf of the impossibility of lines except the ones that stretch backwards, Rudolf of the by-now-universal accommodation to dynasties that are born, flourish, and die in a single life-span, the bulk of the estate left to the winsome chambermaid, the sons having not status but careers, the daughters thus unable to acquire husbands who are in real possession and so themselves required to have careers, the glamor of originality impossible to lay to rest in a tabernacle, and a polished effectiveness competing at every fruit stand on the highway with the universal aspic of high good cheer one has learned to recognize as the dialect of powerful persons, my grandfather's style like those of Napoléon and Mussolini having disappeared into the television set while the clasp of recollection that made them what they were has only gone underground in order to live a more comfortable life.

I dreamt of a series of little shelves that hung each by a nail in a hole in a triangular stamped tin backing. Each shelf was about an inch and a half wide, was painted with red lacquer, had a low railing across the front and held a pair of tiny clay figures of a husband and wife. On one shelf they were in a sailboat, on another they were in conversation, and so on. Over every shelf there was a pencil drawing showing the scene the figures were enacting.

There were over a hundred shelves. On a tab under each was painted in red strokes against a white background the signature of the artist who, it became clear, was the husband in this couple. The drawings bore dates, one per year beginning in 1840. Towards the end of the series the couple sat in rocking chairs or were in bed. In 1941, the husband died. In 1942, the wife, who was shown in the drawing being led to heaven out of her body by her husband who, though already dead himself, had made the figure and the drawing. I was born in 1941, my wife in 1942, and I took this dream as a gloss on what you have been reading here, as a clear way of thinking what is born with us when we are born, which is to say the memories of our parents' grandparents, whom we never see, even if they happen to be alive, except as the invisible amniotic breeze in the bedroom, full of aromas and admonitions, but anonymous, impersonal, ventriloquial, unanswerable because it has no habitation and only the wrong names, like Grandma Marguerite, my cousin Marjorie's great-grandmother and her namesake, who slept in the hall bedroom and moved so quietly through her business that you hardly knew she was there till she broke her hip and died, ninety-six years old, while her daughter ruled the whole clan with a quick mind and a settled Sicilian sense of order that showed nowhere in her perfect English, but you might want to read this dream as telling something about the relationship between body (clay), signature (the Chinese-looking initials), narrative (the drawings), time (the dates), death, and the personal pronoun as it discovers itself in the relation of love between a man and a woman, which aims to transcend the separation of death as the husband does here, either painting a picture after death or preparing one beforehand, it scarcely mattering which, and finding itself as an effect of a process we mostly encounter in the waterfall of years, the twistings of the body, the composition of scenes, and the astonishing persistence, which needs some name better than *I* or *you* or *love* but would come back if it could to the broken body and take the tender wife by the tender hand. So you might call it a dream about life insurance, that machinery for blurring obliteration of the *I* in a ritual of payment, perhaps the clearest sign in bourgeois culture that freedom is not everything, for the gesture of life insurance does not merely, as the cynics point out, perpetuate possession — it rather underlines the rigors of mutual dependence in the harsh poetry of money, there where no other poetry gets a hearing. And once you have begun, you find with this dream, as with all others, that you not only cannot encounter it untainted by its interpretation but that its interpretation appears to be theoretically interminable, not restricting itself to a predictable registration at the conference of Frankfurt School Marxists, Lesbian Feminists, Jungian Tai-Chi masters, though enough of these are sure to arrive on the bus from the airport to keep the conversation full of abrupt shifts that it will plaster over with gossip and flirtation, but extending itself gracefully, agreeably, into the convincing garden of endless dialogue where only a little patience will be required to bring the figures, using the handy index of annualization, into imaginable earshot and focus enough to attach and insert *ad libitum*, drawing from the overloaded context like a priest in a pornographer's back room.

1840: birth of Rodolfo and Annunziata. Descriptions of weather, childbirth, babies in handhewn cradles worn and creaky from constant employment. Lists of siblings who did not survive. Digression on meager but stable economy of the region, where famines though frequent are almost never severe, allowing for survival of at least one child in four, on the average.

Marriage of Robert Schumann and Clara Wieck.

Publication of Proudhon, *Qu'est-ce que c'est la propriété?* Answer: *La propriété, c'est le vol.*

Publication of R. Browning, *Sordello*, A. Manzoni, *I Promessi Sposi* in Tuscan, P. Merimée, 'Colomba', G. Verga, *Cavalleria Rusticana*.

Birth of E. Zola, T. Hardy, P.I. Tchaikovsky,

J. A. Symonds, A. Rodin, C. Monet, death of Beau Brummell, Niccolò Paganini, Maréchal Macdonald, erection of Nelson's column in Trafalgar Square, marriage of Queen Victoria and Prince Albert of Saxe-Coburg-Gotha, deposition of Napoléon's ashes at Les Invalides.

It is a fact, part of this *récit* though perhaps not that one, that the number 1840 occurred in the dream without any reference to Napoléon, though certainly in my reading I had gone through many descriptions of the arrival, Macdonald's desire to greet the Emperor and his remark to his servant afterwards, 'Let's go home and die,' enough of such that when I opened the *Timetable of History* to see what had happened in 1840, what I felt when I saw this little stitch taken up was not simple surprise or pleasure but both of these wrapped up in a filial glow of reassurance and gratitude, as if I had been given a bicycle for my birthday, or been treated to my favorite supper on a Friday night visit to my mother's kitchen, securely nestling myself into the gratuitous relationship between the *I* that writes, the *I* that looks up in the middle of writing because the girl has come with lunch including a Kosher pickle (which I had requested) that comes in a plastic sac like intravenous nutrition and turns out to have been packed by a Dutch or Flemish company in a Wisconsin town called Waterloo — all these numerable *I*s and the other *I*, the one who writes dreams that include the crucial date for sewing together the cut parts of the narrative. The generosity or good housekeeping or perhaps secretarial efficiency of the dream-writer forms the basis of one way to look at dreams, a prospective mode allowing dreams their full place in the process of making plans or of choosing among possibilities. So one might read this dream as an alternative plan for the present work; I thought that perhaps I should revise the plan I have been following, of a three-part essay on Les Invalides, the Terror (which you have not forgotten is what you are reading at this moment), and the Revolution, which will come up in while, and instead regard everything you have read so far as a preface, in the old-fashioned manner of the Victorians, to a narrative that might draw freely upon the sorts of texts indicated above, weaving together the liberalist resurrections of Browning and Manzoni with the protoanthropology of Merimée and Verga, beginning the narrative proper with a double evocation of metropolitan and peripheral antiquities that alternatively bound and weighed upon the lives of the babies whose convoluting clay we were to follow for a little over a century, through the collapse of world after world after world, punctuating itself with rumors of war and accounts of Universal Expositions to which Rodolfo and Annunziata might play sometimes witnesses and sometimes would serve as the excuse for the after-dinner account of a neighbor or the implausibly informative letter of a semiliterate cousin driven to authorship by the boredom of the trenches or the loneliness of a migrant in a boarding-house in Oneonta, New York, the whole edifice of little tin shelves rising like a flat pyramid upon the ashes of Napoléon Bonaparte as reflected in the disastrous career of Beau Brummell, the splendor of Trafalgar Square, and, eventually, Tchaikovsky's noisy reply to the sun of Austerlitz — still played, in wild disregard of its plain ideology, as a set piece in the United States on the Fourth of July — and Thomas Hardy's blank-verse epic *The Dynasts* to be cited now and again as evidence of a persistent preoccupation in Victorian England and America, a symptom showing that what Napoléon accomplished lay beyond the power of his own military victories or those of Wellington and stood instead as the force of what, repressed, would neither be forgotten nor slacken its hold upon the wheel, a power of unification by consumption of boundaries.

Is it a mistake to attempt to introduce these considerations to the narrative of my ancestors? Or to do it this way? I agree that it would be better to achieve this in the manner I am here abandoning either to someone else or, what amounts to the same thing, to myself at a later date. But I am driven my present way by precisely the engine that drove the Terror: a profileration of first persons so exponentially vigorous as to render impossible, until its curve approximate the asymptote, any pretence of stable masks, even to make suspect, as the Terror did after a very short duration, the desire for such a clarification — not that it might never have some worthy function but that it is likely to be premature, given the situation of a Revolution, for a very long time — even though neither the Revolution nor the Terror nor the present narrative moves at all except under the power of this desire that it must suspect and postpone at every turn, for home always beckons in the shape of what makes sense, feeds you on time the food you need and prefer, keeps out the rain, the servants begin at dawn, the lights work, the TV is not broken, the toilets are clean, the sheets are regularly changed, and make no mistake, even the Terror requires regular meals, its protagonists the ordinary range of domestic cosseting and predictability, to which we owe its place as the loudest sputter of an experimental horseless carriage that was forever breaking down and refusing to go another inch. There was no question of its stopping, however, either before or after 9 Thermidor, though its progress more often stood apparently still than it moved forward, for the Revolution was, and is, the justification of all those metaphors of avalanche and flood and runaway wagons that have been called into play to make plausible a series of events as startling to the familiar retrospect as they must have been when they first presented themselves as hearsay in taverns along the French border of Switzerland. It was impossible while these events were occurring to fix them for more than a moment in the image of a convulsion, an earthquake, an apotheosis, and it remains a sober paradox that though many of the men who made the Revolution were writers by trade, they have left us only a handful of songs and an attic full of pamphlets and speeches, it having proved as implausible to them as it does just now to me to compose a frameworthy narrative when the best you can do is bet your life on one of a hundred equally likely denouements of whatever is supposed currently to be the real plot while instead there is an effect growing that is changing the name of the novel, its principal characters, its locale, and its action, rendering all these desperately considered wagers mere irrelevancies.

This is why the French Revolution has become an historian's paradise, because though it began two centuries ago and though the libraries are stuffed with its effluvia, it has in fact scarcely begun to take place. The only thing truly clear about it thus far is its success as a consumer of barriers, boundaries of nations, definitions of divine powers, centers and peripheries in schemes of influence and maps of commerce, borders and passes of every kind and, among these for historians most of consequence, the supposedly impassable divide between the past and the future. We have by now, after nearly as long a period to consider Hegel and Lyell and Darwin and Marx, begun to accustom ourselves to the sort of time Max Beerbohm tried to represent in *The Mirror of the Past*, time that moves forward and backward continuously at the same rate of speed, never stopping in either direction, so that as revolutionary duration has whirled us through eons of industrial ascent it has moved us palpably closer to some perfectly visible recrudescence of what is most primitive, planetary, homeless, and naked, the carefully bred broccoli glittering in the dark, no longer fit to eat, while Milanesi in cafés speculate on the chances of survival in Greenland, Nepal, the Falkland Islands, Yucatan. But this of course is the grossest order of effects — preoccupying as always, it goes without saying, but nevertheless familiar and so spectacular one is likely to overlook the less glamorous among its friends and relations. The truth, as it turns out, cannot be said to exist or not to exist, but only, but persistently, to work as a name for the space between two things that need to have a connection if you are not going to disappear into a hole in the air as you walk past the restaurant, while at the same time you cannot discover a trace of just how it is that they are joined. And nothing does what it is supposed

165

to do. Who would have predicted that a collection of lawyers and prize students with impeccable prose styles would become the catchword bogeymen of ten generations?

It turns out, as usual, that my dentist makes better sense than he does caps, which are always splintering into my mouth when I bite a pencil during a meeting. A man like my grandfather does make things easy, but it has taken me all these years, and my mother's long death into the bargain, to see how it was so. For we always thought of our trips to l'Astoria as the dispensation of heaven and our everyday life in my grandfather's factory as the terrible grimness the optimistic ideologues of American social mobility would prefer to pass unvisited as they stroll down the avenue in a glass bowl of reporters eating pizza. But this, I now see, was the shadow of my mother's discontent that wove for us a truly astonishing narrative sweater of weddings and villages, a near distance one could visit and touch but unknowable to us in the absolute narrowness of its range of allusion, and it is in this steady snowfall of misconstruction, misapplication of wishing, and in the infinite residue of slipping sidewalks that I begin to locate the real vibration, for me, whoever I am by now, of the Terror.

My cousin Judy tells a story about our grandfather in Sunnyside that lifts a single edge of an old dark fabric for me. During the war, she was five or six, living on the top floor of

the three-story house and liked to play bom-
bardier into the garden where, as she had no
reason to know, our stepgrandfather would
sometimes stand to take a breather from his
labors in the cellar or else to watch for one of
the cats he used to catch and drown. One day
she almost killed him. It was a Monday, I suppose, because her mother did laundry re-
ligiously on the same day that Don McNeill and
Arthur Godfrey made laundry jokes on the
radio and, in our house, the man left the big
blue jugs of Javelle water on the white tile of
the vestibule. My aunt had put her iron to cool
on the windowsill, and my cousin dropped it
on the Germans (her mother was German) in
the garden, missing my grandfather by a hair.
He came running up the stairs and through
the door to give the pretty little girl a terrible
speech, an entirely unprecedented perform-
ance for him towards any of his grandchildren,
all of his own fear and frustration aimed by the
event and coming out, I easily imagine, in the
Neapolitan flow of blue vituperation that made
him such a pleasure to listen to when the subject was one of the neighbors or one of the
many bosses with whom he had parted ways
over the years before finally getting the point
and going into business for himself, and absolutely scared the wits out of the poor child
until, done at last and leaving, suddenly
turned, laughing, and said, 'Don't you wish

you *had* killed me? Then you wouldn't have had to listen to any of this.'

My mother told a different story about her own father. This was in l'Astoria, when they lived on Trowbridge Street, next to a little cemetery, not the big house on the hill, but a tiny house in a tiny street full of tiny gardens, front doors you stepped down to from the scanty sidewalks, a replica in l'Astoria that could have been designed by the Ellis Island Restoration Committee for an exhibition of how, even in America, the overwhelming stinginess of Italy took forever to lie down at last and relax, played in fact the architect in all the houses these immigrants built for themselves, squeezing basil out of squares of dirt with two-inch borders, erecting doorways that even they, undernourished and undergrown and sometimes misshapen as well, had to stoop to enter, bedrooms like closets, kitchen like bathrooms, six-foot cement-block walls studded with broken glass to protect areaways that bruised your shoulders if you walked through them too quickly, a poem of starvation that ended at Di-liberto's on the corner where you went every day to smell the cheese in its hard rind and look at the prosciutto the way King Edward had looked at Mrs. Keppel, as if a mile away did not begin a vast continent on which God was pouring sympathetic rain but instead a long dry gulch punctuated by *banditi*, *monsignori*, and *carabinieri*. My mother was five or

168

six. Her father whom she adored was shaving, and she was teasing him and he was laughing. He cut himself laughing. Stopped laughing. Went after her with the razor and chased her all around the block until finally she outran him.

Was this a simple difference of adulterer and husband? My stepgrandfather who could laugh and point out to his stepson's daughter that in some ways she'd be better off if she had killed him was, after all, a successful wife-stealer and a veteran target. When he ran off with my grandmother and her four sons, her husband tracked them down in a coldwater flat in Greenpoint where they had fled from Schenectady. The husband had a shotgun. The guilty couple didn't come home that night, and for a long time, every few months they would get a message that caused them to make sudden moves in the night until eventually the wronged man lost interest or found a wife (she had four daughters), I don't know what came first. Indeed, I never heard the whole story the same way twice. But the object that eluded him, the man I came later to know as my father's father who had, unaccountably, a different last name from ours, was given to settled opinions producing long discourses on Mussolini, Dante, Verdi, but none of this paranoid violence that appears to have driven my two real grandfathers, the one I never saw and the one who chased my mother round the block with a freshly sharpened open razor and blood streaming through the lather on his cheek.

Why did we, living in the midst of this difference, get it so wrong? Why did we suppose l'Astoria a paradise and our own life its opposite? Distance and relative rarity: we went on Sundays mostly to l'Astoria, it was our holiday place. That is part of an explanation. In the division, though, folded under it like the eggs and ricotta in the belly of the ravioli, lay a deeper separation. In Sunnyside, we were working out the hard bargain of an American future, where there may be much to be had but where nothing will be got for nothing. My grandfather there had arrived finally at a certain substantial possession by the very difficult path of following his own inclinations. These had not merely given him another man's wife and four sturdy, brilliant, impossible sons, but had also made him a very troublesome career of important jobs his talents won him and then lost him because, whatever he learned, he did not learn diplomacy.

In his household there was also what he had once been, that magician of immigrant stories, the boarder. My grandfather as a boarder had made love to the wife. His own boarder, however, was more carefully chosen. He was a Yankee, a genuine old Connecticut tinker with dormant gonads, a mind like a well-oiled electric drill, a heart full of cracked pebbles, a mouth full of Poor Richard, and a desk full of uncashed dividend checks from General Motors whose stock he had bought at fifty cents a share during the Depression when he was earning $175 a week and spending about five of them on board, room, and pleasures, wearing clothes fished out of the garbage can and leaving for work an hour early every morning, so he could save the nickel trolley fare, to arrive at the factory he directed where everyone in our family worked, where the Yankee made double fortunes for the owners partly by his diabolical sympathy with steam presses and grinding wheels, partly by the whimsical thrift that led him to take the doors off the toilet stalls so that no one would be tempted to linger there, and largely by the straightforward policy of never sitting down, never stopping, and never letting anyone feel satisfied with anything. This man, who finally decided it was time to stop working and get married when he had six million dollars in the trunk (a million of it in gold certificates the government had stopped issuing in 1933) in 1954, age seventy-nine, played the role in my father's family of financial ideal and ubiquitous adviser. They all got rich, none as rich as he, but rich by the standards of their barefoot beginnings. All four of those brothers, still alive, ages seventy-six to eighty, are living as well as their various views of human possibility will allow, because there is no shortage of money. In l'Astoria, on the other hand, where my mother's family lived without any Yankee tinker to guide them, there was no money but a great deal of pleasure. This sweetness, a familiar Italian concoction of women's work and men's extravagance, presented itself to all of its participants as an endlessly blossoming rose of coherent splendor, the prize of thousands of years of practice, a way of life whose parts are completely interchangeable and thus can always produce, against the background of a large, dependable harmony like polychrome sunset, surprising but not disturbing combinations, for it is always a matter of interest and never of distress that there are radishes in the salad or this time anchovies rolled up around the salami or soup with croutons instead of ravioli or polenta when you were expecting gnocchi or a trip down to Our Lady of Mount Carmel to watch a third cousin get married instead of a late afternoon cracking walnuts and playing briscola. Igloos are for Eskimos, as my mother said, and l'Astoria was for Sallesi. Salle, my mother's family's little town, two hours drive from Rome, is one of those places, Italy is filled with them, that have gardened the universe so obsessively for so long that they can, like Dante, suppose God is a flower. Or else his mother is a flower. And his father is a pigeon. In l'Astoria where the skyline of Manhattan seemed as dumb and as terrible as do the unthinkable heights of La Maiella that display snow to Salle in July on the Feast of Beato Roberto, we were able to move completely at ease in an ancient universe of dandelions and escarole, tomatoes and grapes, eggs, chickens, goats, my father, my mother, my cousin Michael, Gesugiuseppemaria, every family including at the terrible head of the table a probable Joseph, a great stag so powerful that the flickering shade of the great copper beech did not play across the greens and braciola on the blue gingham tablecloth on a summer Monday without seeming to be the size and veritable glory of his immemorial horns. If you want to understand the sweetness and the delicate anxiety of this feasting, you must study the paintings of Tiepolo, where the faces of the incredibly beautiful characters are as compact of varnish and *bella figura* as every drifting tail of drapery, and the only verisimilitude is this: that the painter gives them exactly as they themselves mean to look.

Conversation in l'Astoria was, as I see it now, almost entirely a textile of avoidances, every single scrap of perfected ritual designed to assuage fears and doubts that almost never had any chance to surface directly. This probably was not nearly so stultifying to the participants as it was to me, because they at least knew most of the secrets, imagined crimes and real ones, but these were doubly closed to our finding out, because we did not know, and never learned, how to speak Italian. So that the old habit, carried across the ocean, of observing all the decencies of dinner and wine

173

and coffee and pastry in the interest, among others, of keeping the face of the family as presentable as possible, assimilated to itself in this new and strange situation a new and strange absoluteness it could never have possessed when the children at least could understand the things they heard eavesdropping. We did not have that privilege. My mother, as I approached the age of thirty gingerly holding the hand of my friendly psychotherapist, one day told me a handful of secret stories which I vowed not to repeat and so can't tell them even now, I suppose. It was useful to me to learn them, nonetheless, because the compact of silence under which they had been withheld was an old institution never meant to be so utterly sheer a wall as the difference in language had made it, had never meant to have, as it did have, I afterwards saw, so many uncommunicating branches, or to become, my mother plainly saw in my confusion, the knot of a system of nickel-steel interlocks, each leaving out some other thing, not any of them so resonant as the monstrous central truths but each endangering the other with the monumental effect that in the end we sat on the porch behind a reticulated apprehension that every little misbehavior in the school yard, every overdue bill, every untimely sacrament or doubtful opinion might open a great hole in the glimmering gauze of secrets, let in one never started to imagine what cackling of neighbors, what triumph of enemies, what *malocchio* of every child who had grown up reciting an uncuttable silver ribbon of lies and happy inventions while mysteriously unable ever to stop for a moment and enjoy the evident beatitude of the composition.

The cemetery, the big cemetery of Calvary across the highway from where I grew up, used to be my favorite place to wander. Last night, I dreamt I was guiding people through it, pointing out the fancy bronzework glistening with polish. It seems a plausible image for the stories I'm telling now. Even though so many of us are still alive, these passions of rectitude and loyalty lie mouldering in the grave. If they were still to evoke responses, they would require an imposing, an impossible, degree of resurrection. They can no longer produce the feelings they once could, not because we no longer worry as we then did about sexual or political shame (my grandparent's boarder in l'Astoria was a Communist, for example), but because the conversational glass pyramid has fallen from the airy delicacy of vibration that it long occupied, quivering but stable, as we sat, night after night over coffee and cake, and kept it in place, repeating our stories of one another to one another, arguing about some change in detail, comparing our recollections of a picnic afternoon in a park in New Jersey or a cousin's fiftieth wedding anniversary party in a backyard in l'Astoria when a certain spectacular joke was invented or a certain subtle insult was perpetuated, events we were sure had infinite iterability in them, things we would expect our grandchildren to know, as we knew them, better than the names of the presidents or the capital of Montana, not foreseeing, on the one hand, that television and the automobile would collaborate to make this form of conversation appear as quaint and impracticable as the contredanse, or, on the other hand, that I myself would carry all of this memory around the world paying it every kind of lip service but getting less and less use out of it, finding it inside a hard leathery shell of desuetude that puzzled me where it did not simply bore me, and suddenly having it break open like an old *piñata* that slipped out of my hands when, one snowy morning in the Rue Sainte-Croix de la Bretonnerie, hurrying to keep an appointment, I lost my footing on the unplowed snow-slick granite pavement and saw all my papers scatter through the air as I was landing painfully on my right shoulder, and knew in an instant of irrefutable illogic that Paris, the cemetery of a dozen revolutions, would be for me the museum of my own spectatorial childhood, where, alert to and acquisitive of every possible meaning in every raised bushy grey eyebrow, I had been watching the pathless progress of the Italian migration to the United States, a bouleversement in the lives of its protagonists not, despite its complete failure to produce on the instant even the rudimentary philosophical circumnavigation I am now attempting, one whit the less a total change in the meanings of every move a human being might make than any revolution, not one bit more impermeable to paradox and the columbine-like double tropism of time.

To see these effects at home (and I can), one must (and I can't) constantly pay the price of the practicing visionary. America has almost no museums of its struggle. Our antiquaries can only show us cases full of trophies that have completely changed their meanings, as we did, by the simple act of being transferred to the other side of the vast magnetic planet, but in ways we have not yet begun to understand except by the dumbshow of dialectic, which has moved us, for the space of the present generation at least, to pretend that nothing of interest stands between us and a handful of universal principles that can be applied with perfect confidence by any jackass docile enough to spend five minutes getting them by heart. It is just as easy, God knows, to play the atavist in Paris, but the city is festooned, nonetheless, with the immovable corpses of its enthusiasms of the past two centuries, so that nowhere in the world can you have so painful a sense of the utterly dead vivacity and persistence of what, though only as old as yesterday, can never return, in the midst of what, though completely lost to understanding, can never be forgotten for an instant — a counterpoint of lucid confusion which moves me to an eagerness I almost never feel in less depressing places because, for all the mustiness it makes you suffer, it offers you at least the chance to see what only drugs and poverty allow you in the United States, the growth of decay that Americans used to call the Shape of the Future, a natural boiling and blossoming, under all, to which I passionately fasten in the hopes of seeing the prospect of my past and the immortality of my mother, aiming by this act to save her recollection, as well as those of her parents, her husband, his parents, their children, all of us, from the flattened identity of a fingerprint or a jumble of digits at the same time that it becomes possible, delicately, to lift them from the cloudy amber of those speeches which inevitably accompany the birthdays of monuments in New York Harbor. The glory of the immigrants, as of the Revolution, is in what they did that no one knows how to mention. Like the Terror itself, this has parts that are obvious and parts that, being parts, appear to be nothing but are in their very incompleteness the one assurance that history may turn out better than expected, that there might come again, as there occasionally will to me if I am lying very still and a hot breeze blowing through the leaves causes me pain, revelations of la storia or genuine youth, even in the age of the millennium, but the obvious parts must come first, if quickly: the abandonment of parental conversation, the enforced sexual anarchy of boarders, the experiments in the politics of capital and communism that came with these womanless strangers at the table, the rendering unpronounceable and nonsensical of ancient names and associations, the growth of secrets that a new invention or a new regime would render pointless in an instant. All clear then for what's not so clear. Why did we choose l'Astoria and not Sunnyside for our heaven?

And even part of this is plain enough: l'Astoria aimed, having nothing, to *be* heaven. Sunnyside, with plenty, thought itself adequate. Or did it? The Terror arises, as the historians almost say at every turn, from the incapacity of the bourgeois revolution to represent itself, thus giving rise to its obscene liturgy of human sacrifice and the liturgical hum of obscenity that, taken together, constitute the most newsworthy features of that period. Similarly, one can see how Sunnyside, where we lived in the bowels of petit-bourgeois production, whose means we thought we owned, required l'Astoria, where a constant refabrication of the old ways was conducted. Subtler than Robespierre, but equally effective. L'Astoria in its turn of course required Sunnyside, but — and this is the mystery of my own paternity no doubt — the two could never really touch except in the intercourse of marriage producing children with parts so inelegantly matched that when I write of the multiplicity and intricate inconsonance of the first person singular, the theme appears to be philosophy or grammar but is in fact a simple exuberance of relief at having discovered in these supposedly arcane inquiries a general machinery of agreement that could corroborate what I always expected would be greeted, indeed often even in learned conversation has been howled down, as a naughty paradox, or at best the phantasm of a boy who was too clever by half, while for me it always had had the stubborn reality, impossible to ignore, of a broken toenail or a farting mule. Not, that is, anything so comfortable or final as a pathology one might freely choose to treat or to imprison or to destroy with an applicable rhetorical Gatling gun. Not just a mess, either. Merely the stubborn liveliness, yet another cockroach in the wall, you might want to call it, that keeps theologians in business by taking the dictionary apart when no one is looking, and scrambling all the definitions, and I want, or *I* at least wants, some map more susceptible of complex registration than the handful of waterproof playing cards that the social psychologists hawk on the streetcorner outside the police station. When one says *I*, there is no reason to suppose the referent less peculiar or, conversely, less workable than it might have been had one said *Paris*. Paris might include a spindled schizophrenia, might be the multifidous site of a flowering avalanche of paranoias in fifty original shades, might even offer certain pedantic vistas that would appear to give a spuriously innocent or divine substantiation to what you had just been reading in *The Phenomenology of Spirit*, even if that had not been, as in this case it had, the architect's favorite explanation to his wife of how it was that one celebrated Égalité with a cavalcade of tortured nymphs relieving the shadow of a cornice heavier than grief. Paris might do more, and every several act might have its nutcracker nomenclature, without the place's having ceased to do what it does or to be routinely discoverable by airplanes in a rusty fog.

— Oh yes, she said. Transgress!

It was again raining. I looked up from the page. All I saw at first was the overflowing ashtray.

— It's easy enough, she said, to violate the language of the clerks.

The car was waiting under the gleaming lights of Châtelet. My friend had gone to the bathroom for a month.

— I was about to say, I said.

— You were, were you?

— ... about to say that this: that...

— Say what?

— ... even if you show or has been shown...

— You is showing nothing yet.

181

— ... a certain respect, a certain doubtful reliance upon the negative valence in...

— Yes, yes...

— ... the jargon of epistemology, phenomenology, ontology, and deontology...

— De very ting or willah-wallah what that you seek, you say, says she.

— ... of sociology, of depth psychology...

— Of priests' apology for Mariology, you pray, she says.

— ... you will not, no, nor never...

— I've noticed as to how you won't or won't want to.

— ... be able to pause, stop, breathe...

— You don't seem to be having any trouble.

— ... without incurring the risk...

— ... and bravely, no doubt...

— ... of interruption.

By which he meant that when the Parisians, by whom *I* means mostly Lacan and his interface Professor Derrida, tell you that the unconscious is more or less continuously something like an interruption, they is right if he are wrong not to take it the further step that would allow for the explosion of a field of trashy metaphors enabling us to understand, before crumpling the paper and tossing it into the filthy, handy canal, how the *I* is a telephone book full of dirty pictures, a crunching of deep plates that supports, among other its epiphenomena, Paris, l'Astoria, Sunnyside, Rome, a bottle full of green jelly beans and little marshmallows, a dead buck strapped across the fender of my uncle's 1956 Chevy, opening wide the double doors of the Amphithéâtre Richelieu to the assumption of the Chair in the History of the French Revolution by a quintet of entertainers chosen at random one Friday night in Les Halles, a juggler, a gymnast, the fellow with the Hurdy-Gurdy who sings like Aznavour, the Living Mannequin, and of course, the Storyteller with the Yellow Buttons, who, given two hours for an inaugural lecture before a congregation of legionnaires, could succeed but poorly in solving the equation that sets forth the ongoing relationship between the collection of the *taille* in the Vendée and the figure for the circulation of *Le Père Duchesne* in Arles, but the five of them, moving freely through the audience, climbing onto the lap of the limestone Pascal and smirking into the startled alertness of the great Cardinal, might mark a beginning of the very necessary investigation of how the French Revolution is and is not like a jazz band, a professor of the history of the French Revolution discussing a jazz band, and of the value in such a comparative method — how, that is, not only is or is not the French Revolution unlike or like a method of polytonal juxtapositions in the interests, or at least the masquerade, of comparative analysis of modes of comparative analysis, but also is or is not to be regarded as still what it was, apparently, once upon a time, a carnival occurring mysteriously out of season and falling, by a law of mathematical propriety long familiar to students of artillery, into an abyss of recursion — allowing, as it almost seems actually to have been the case, for the same persons to be killed again and again and again, a glove-effect wherein the multiplicity of any given individual's individualities becomes instead the multiplication in individuals of one individual's (roughly) infinite seriability.

— So, she says, the Terror.

— Exactly. So the Terror continues its utility, making for its old Sunday afternoon sloppiness a very wonderful and wonderfully verisimilar image of how the *I* is forced to behave if it lacks the image of itself as the Terror itself, not the only image it needs, let us hasten to say, but an especially useful reminder of the remorseless character of arithmetic.

So it all comes home. But where is that? In the 1950s, after my grandmother nearly died, for a while, the order of l'Astoria began to disappear, and my parents, now well established in their house in Sunnyside, across the street from my father's parents, began to become the center of the clan. But this move — was it because I lived in its backstage? — seems, at this long retrospect, to have lacked power of impression. The old food was gone. My father used televisions as a temporary replacement. He put one on the porch so the whole block

184

could watch Milton Berle together. That was a stirring moment, but soon everyone had his own television.

I opened the door. A large expensive room full of prayer books. A double folding door of walnut on the far broad side. I opened it slowly. A man with a red beard stood in the semidark at a lectern. Were there others? I knew I didn't belong and started to leave. This was the wrong place. They had not called me.

— Come in.

They sat me at a table. I had my portable keyboard at my right hand.

— Play, it's all right.

— What?

— Whatever. Play. He smiled.

I began some kind of tune, more or less making it up, phrase by phrase, in response to their reactions, until I began to weave it into a song they were moving and humming with, something of theirs I had discovered by following their faces. The music went on, tune after tune, a long time.

— So who said your rhythms are no good? the host asked me.

— Come back next week?

After a few weeks a check for a thousand dollars came in the mail. After that they called him Moshe Augenblick, and he played in the shtebl every week.

It was in the library in l'Astoria that I discovered the Jews, in a little book about the

185

Seder ceremony. From then I knew that they had what we had but they had learned, as we had not had any reason to learn, how to carry it with them from country to country. They had, they have, an entire world devoted to keeping everyone together, within walking distance of dinner where the telephone and the doorbell cannot intrude on a day when no one can work and only God in his friendlier postures can be the object of effort, every man a king, and every boy the son of such a man. So as I watched the improvisings of my parents and their brothers and sisters, my sisters, my cousins, myself, to make a way of being together in America, my eyes kept turning to the Jews, and when I bought a house to raise my family in, I bought one in their midst, not to join them but just to feel around us the peace of the Sabbath that we had lost. Of course it only partly worked. My sisters, seeking only the same thing, have become Baptists. My uncle is a pillar of the church built on the site of my grandparents' house where he used to sleep late when he was a young ladykiller. I have a cousin who was so lonely as a boy that he had ten children, whom he taught out of McGuffey's readers. They, my sisters and my cousins, move more directly than I do or can.

Before you join the lady in the café and make a hash of my sentimental innocence, consider that you cannot yet, any more than I, know for certain that it does not in fact open some double doors into the real object of the search, nothing so elaborate as to require even a sentence, you might think, but so simple in fact that the Jews have only sustained some purchase upon it by never talking about anything else. A drastic step that we are going to have to take in our own way in our own time. Because nothing else has worked? You might ask, to which I might answer nothing has been tried. When I look at l'Astoria, I see now Paris, a prison of ghosts. Not the Paris of the Parisians, you remind me. No or Yes wouldn't matter here, however. We slipped into l'Astoria like the nymphs in the cast iron fireplace, each of which had a little pin you might remove it easily from and upon which just as readily set it back in place, always the same place, gone when the house burned down, gone even sooner when my grandfather died in 1959 and my grandmother came to live with us in the Italian-American 1960s, which were years of all meals in the finished basement, a house full of studio couches and an upstairs kitchen on the first floor, recessed lights and formica and stainless steel, only for occasional use because not nearly so comfortable as the big, cool, clean all-purpose room in the cellar, color television, long hair, sex, and my parents planning their escape to Florida, which came at the end of the decade, all of their tentative gestures of the fifties, the Sunday dinners that were so boring and the infinite nights full of comedians on the tube, the discovery of the stock market, the house they bought in the country, all these little and big acts of independence and purpose moving them and us into a sort of broadloom and rolling-stock universe that one hailed, with each glistening new acquisition, as a marvel of refrigeration engineering or mortuary cosmetology, loud with congratulation upon the miracles of America, without seeing, without being able any of us to be seeing, any of it from a point of view we could have in common, so that when the crystal bloomed in 1970, they moved to Florida like General Booth entering heaven, while I moved first to the Bronx and then to Brooklyn, looking in the one place for Edgar Poe, who would teach me to console myself with opium, and in the other for Walt Whitman, who would teach me to die in a productive manner.

All of this came about so gradually that when the point of it became clear it seemed not to have happened at all, but to have been there all along without my taking notice of it. Neither of these seemings answers now to my sense of what must have been going on, but I was enduring the kinds of feelings for which the names that grief-therapists use must sound, to the sufferer, like bad jokes, full of the grisly accuracy witticisms need, since they are hopelessly flat and clear when one tries to map them against the shifting sandbars and floating islands of what is unpleasantly taking place under and from under his feet. So, how does it go? Denial, guilt, anger, depression, acceptance. Or is it anger, denial, guilt, depression, acceptance? I have the book here someplace. It's helpful, as when one says North Carolina, South Carolina, Georgia, Florida, but it's not helpful enough, especially if your car is stolen while you are eating breakfast in a truck stop on the outskirts of Columbia. When they took my tires I was in the state called anger, and I stayed there a long time.

Thus, possibly without your having received the hospitality of a flag announcing the hole's number, we have arrived at the point where it grows easy to answer certain stubborn questions that have been arising frequently here, such as *Is the Terror a shift from the first to the third person?* and *Why l'Astoria instead of Sunnyside?* The answer is a story inside a story referring to another story including the same story inside the first-mentioned story, though the third-mentioned story is prior to the second in order of occurrence and the first-mentioned is prior to the other two but comes third in the story I am about to tell.

— Do you remember what I told you last week, I said, about the fight you had about the record player?

— What are you talking about? my mother said.

We were in the living room in Sunnyside, 1969. The fall before my parents left. I don't

189

remember thinking of the room at all under
the glamor of twilight ultraviolet that places
have if you remember some time you were in
them before they were dismantled, but I remember that room as the violently compacted
center of the absolutely ordinary and as the
glimmering stage set and groundwork of our
entire life as a family, picking out readily the
texture of the couch, its arms different from its
back different from its skirt different from its
firm square cushions different from the top of
its back with a triple row of piping in the rough
brown linen like sailcloth, able to show you, if
you could be wired to my memory screen, exactly where to find the lightswitch, the telephone secretary with the button that made it
spring open, the statues and pictures and who
bought them when for whom, the porcelain
tracery on the Chinese lamps, the three-legged
table with the marquiserie border which is now
supporting a vast Wandering Jew under a long
thin mirror which shows you yourself framed
by trees and in the background the country
house my parents used to own as you step into
my sister's house in Putnam Lake, can see precisely the angle of the armchair that was the
only survivor of my parents''wedding set' and
my mother in it and behind her in the dining
room from where I stood the chandelier, now
in my other sister's house in Highlands, New
Jersey, then hanging over the Duncan Phyfe
dining room table on which I am writing this

page the morning after a party, one of my mother's old linen tablecloths still on it from last night so that as I bend over the pad to write I do so in a faint air of Parmesan cheese and what we used to call *gravy* and later *tomato sauce* and now *ragù* and next year when we come back from Italy will call *sugo* though we will never stop eating it as long as we live, even if our children come to regard it as tiresome or shameful or merely another ethnic badge like matzohs and watermelons because the senses of smell and of taste, the dumbest, age the least, always trigger the same freshness of response, can feel the air in that room, see it in the huge mirror of my grandmother's (now in my cellar) over the Baldwin Acrosonic (in my dining room now), sparkling with the flash of purchase or a collector's pride in a stampbook where all the indicated rectangles have been filled, dusty at the same time with failure or catastrophe, a family altar painstakingly assembled through decades of labor, choice, harmonization, only to be scattered recklessly on a whim, deposited indifferently here and there like quarters at toll booths and candy wrappers along the shoulders of the highway to Florida.

— I told you last week and you didn't remember.

— And I don't remember you telling me anything last week. I don't know what you're talking about.

So she didn't remember it or even remember that I had spent an hour in this room the week before reciting it, so I told her again.

— In 1948, the year after we moved into this house, Daddy brought home the Maguire record player.

— Yes.

— And the record of the song 'Linda'.

— Yes.

— And somebody put the record in wrong, which was easy to do, and it got stuck in the changer.

— So?

— And he made a big deal of it.

— Yes.

— And you had a fight with him and threw the record at him and threw him out of the house.

— I don't remember that.

— He came back after five minutes.

— Oh.

— But while he was gone and you were hysterical, you said to me if 'I thought you were going to grow up like him, I would strangle you right now'.

— No.

— Yes.

— I don't remember that.

— You wouldn't. You were crazy.

— So what can I say?

— Nothing. Just remember it.

— I can't remember it.

— I can't forget it.

She never did get it all clear to herself, not, I mean, just what she'd said, or not to me then, but how to live in her marriage without these spells of violent longing to have it all otherwise, to have *him* all otherwise, and, as I learned that evening among the fragments of the phonograph record, to have *me* all otherwise, making it hard for me to accept on other occasions her extravagant praise of so much that I did and was. I never really believed her, was always looking for some corroborating testimony to reassure me that the looks or wit or generosity or whatever she had found in me was actually there for the general public and was not merely some badge of maternal influence that she was pinning on me as sign of a victorious skirmish in the war between l'Astoria and Sunnyside that raged on year after year, up and down my legs, back and forth across my chest, still able even now to stage a major spring offensive if the tensions get high enough. For as you may imagine, a child once let in upon so tremendous a secret will find its key in every lock, with the predictable result, for example, that all his desire to duplicate his father's strengths would now go underground and take the paradoxical form, in the boy's need to survive the deadly threat, of what the father would oppose, although, at the same time, the boy's resentment of the mother's interdict would lead him to seek a plowed field of parallels beneath the foliage, a structured sympathy of coded replication joining him to the father's forbidden nature that, as he well knew, he must bear in any case, however doubtful of the appraising glance, however industriously concealed or persistently troublesome to the public face of, in my case, maternally acceptable charm, frivolity, bravado, and sexual conquest.

These conversations took place during what presented itself, even at the time, as the great watershed moment of my life, when my parents were planning their escape, when I was talking a mile a minute in and out of the shrink's office, unable to pursue my career in any way that promised a good result, chasing and chased by women, startled by a dose that summer, twenty-eight years old and sure only that the set of compromises and rescriptions under which I had managed to thrive, after some fashion, was no longer going to hold, that all these pieces having begun to fall apart of their own inadequacy to the need, I suddenly discovered an appetite to rip all of it down, laying the pieces here and there on the flat surface around me for inspection, for reconsideration, for the beginning of a simpler, or at least less painful, concoction, a better plan. It turned out not to be so easy as such a metaphor would suggest. The principle of composition that supports the Terror is nothing so obvious as the rules of harmony or

counterpoint but something simpler and subtler, the principle of infinite variability. Antique
conflicts that write mother against father or
king against people can rattle along, it would
seem, forever, never really running out of
material, because the politics of perception will
draw directly from such conflicts and provide
them in turn with new configurations, new instruments, whole new orchestras with fireworks and summer costumes as modes for new
development, fresh diversions, inversions, new
blood for old bottles, new wine, new bread,
new heroes, new victims.

So, though there is plenty left, and always
will be, to be sorted out, this much is clear.
The Terror in which I moved taught me to
make the most of l'Astoria, to 'favor' my
mother's family, even as the Terror inspired a
double desire to obliterate it or at least avenge
myself upon it, a crossfire of contraries and
contradictories in which I learned to dance
upon piano-wire tensions as if they had made
me a trampoline, earning me a reputation for
bottomless sarcasm, and leaving me wide open
to any theory that might, in slipping the moor-
ings of the referent or dividing out the personal pronoun into a vast spattering of fragments, generalize my condition. The project of
the Terror, to give to the first person the
smooth shell of the third, subsumes the impossibility of the single *I* but does so in a way
that eludes its protagonists.

It had to be thus, for the opposing sides of a square only retain any sense of themselves in relation to one another and in relation to the field of forces where they play together, and they are none of them likely to realize that an escape might be possible. Paris, of course, all parallels and radii, does not encourage such a realization. Nor did a world like mine, at any point in the early years of life. Nor even now, when the professor of immigration studies only too probably is waving the banner of his grandfather's imaginary vision or his grandfather's imaginary truth.

The case is hard. Terror comes unbidden as you try to be your mother's voice while it is only your father's lost speech that can utter your desire, inventing a machine that deprives you most thoroughly when it most fully does your bidding. Everyone has had a crack at this, according to Lacan — Hegel, Marx, Nietzsche, Freud — leaving us only the option of recognizing that all schemata have their elegances, and all of them lead you to a contemplation of these beauties without necessarily helping much in the real project. You may wander forever between the workshops of Sunnyside and the processions of l'Astoria, unable to find any connection between them more convincing than the great blank expanse of the Long Island City yards of what used to be called the Pennsylvania Railroad where, as at the foot of the hill Thirty-Ninth Street becomes Steinway

Street, there rises a long high monolithic warehouse with glass brick windows and castellated with little silver-hatted tin smokestacks as if it were San Quentin, reminding you that the American 'promise' led through these places that only some children and grandchildren escape, while the migrants and many of their descendants live whole lives in the terms of the old bargain, fifty hours of murder every week for a Toaster Oven in the Hollywood Kitchen. Harder than anything is to climb down into the yard and hop a freight train out of there, realizing that the two horns of this dilemma might, for all their sharpness, permit you to avoid the whole business and sit, like Mme. de Stael, in Switzerland or Italy waiting for it all to blow over.

These people had an intense attraction for one another and for me, however. Their map of possibilities, small as it was, had been lovingly carved and had, moreover, mammoth warning signs over every exit. One early gave up hope of leaving, imagining instead a life lived simultaneously in five or six places, l'Astoria and Sunnyside never yielding pride of place to Manhattan or Washington or London or Oxford. No surprise in this. Robespierre did not tear down the Louvre, and after they had desecrated Notre Dame, they were perfectly willing to go on using the building for their own purposes. Regicide is a self-limiting act. Having killed the only King, one was left with all the Kings had done, spitting into it, sleeping upon it, drinking it, cataloging it. Terror, it turned out, ignored this stubborn truth as my mother chose to ignore the profound meaning of the choice she had made in marrying my father. In neither case could any confection of l'Astoria get in under or behind la storia, the place of passionate attachment. France can never not have been a monarchy. *I* must always include the site of this blinded passion as the mystery of its incarnation, the place where it recognizes the rudimentary resemblance of human beings to food, which exists to satisfy an appetite. It is true, perhaps, that such things can grow distant, muffled, healed, scarred, calloused. Twenty years divorced can be tantamount to never married. *Can*, not *must*, be. But of the things I recall here, even this may not be said.

You do your best when you see them, these opposing worlds, misaligned, trying to meet in a knifeblade when in fact they never really find one another at all, so that the plains of their marching and shouting, shooting and bombing, might allow them to go on, as they will in your revery, forever in combat without actually doing any more harm than a couple of three-year-olds with a pile of pots and pans. Comedy, however, takes much harder thinking than tragedy or melodrama, requires of you that you erect some theoretical telephoto lens in which by careful framing and lighting, you may render the dullest objects delightful or transform a murderous agony into a kodachrome rainbow. I have attempted to make the sorry hilarious and the horrific at least picturesque if not downright ridiculous, and this many times, but found I could do no more than pull at it strand by strand like a baby emptying a bowl of spaghetti, an act they call analysis or intellection, though it has more in common with everyday biting and chewing and swallowing. That is, I cannot rise to comedy *or* tragedy or even to melodrama, but have had to learn to content myself with the essay, which is literary digestion, the only form at the same time straightforwardly beginning, ending, and infinitely flexing, where, as the king goes his progress through the guts of a beggar, the beggar himself operates at the cellular level quite as efficiently as a King or a shark, and completes his meal, as we all do, quite willing not to have rebuilt China in an afternoon.

For a Terror can spend itself, finally, and for the space of two or three or perhaps many more lifetimes need not go relentlessly hand over hand, though it is easy to see why one might suppose it would. Even an hour of peace is sometimes a victory. At the moment you read, someone's arm is being torn off, a heart pierced, slaughterhouses of vindication and purification are going up, brick by brick, furies descend upon children, and, from a certain not-so-narrow coign of vantage, the human world shows a nested perspective of scenes you do not wish to look at and cannot quite forget, whatever you do. But even the Commissioners of Public Safety, taking this as their ground, thought they might someday escape it, there might eventually be a genuine revolutionary peace. How mistaken you think they were will depend finally upon how you estimate the evil in the midst of which they took up arms — an evil, it is fair to say, they neither eradicated nor escaped for a moment, caught as they were in its own way of seeing and, though conscious of the poison of language, not able to replace all the words and all they meant, not able, after all, which would have been the only way, to rise from the dead and start again as often as necessary. Generations deposit their thin lines of weed on the beach and subside, saith the preacher, in a fair approximation of the plutocratic extravagance of nature, which will give fifty men each fifty years to do what could have been done better by one who stayed in his prime a single century, making well the case that the *I* knows itself not merely to be fragmented and splintered and self-opposed in its waking and sleeping, but to feel long thin nerve-lines popping like high voltage wires deep into the past and long into posterity, the one dimension we are able to understand not by an illusion, if that's what it is, of perception, but boldly and only by inference. Indeed, the whole Derridean argument against perception seems a mere quibble when you consider that, even if we actually did perceive the things we suppose we perceive, our mathematics have made it plain that there is an interminable series of extensions and that all of these must hypothetically be assumed — not as something upon which we may necessarily stand pat but certainly as a resilient barrier to unification, to the project of any ideologue. You can leave everything on a shelf in the attic, can you?

Not exactly. You know better. You know your battlefield by now as *I* knows his, and we know the old blue-and-gray armies that keep reappearing in new wigs and masks, every boulder seeming to reveal a fresh devil that you must encounter and strip bare even though before beginning you know it is sure to be the same old Scylla or Charybdis, chewing tobacco in Tennessee, *pâté* in Paris, before you can move on to the next boulder where the play repeats itself in a fresh set of costumes, always equally transparent and convincing, in the hope that you may someday find either the way to the hills beyond or else — and is this more to ask or less? — discover the formula of an enchantment that might do with a half dozen words that which you have so far only been able to mimic by dint of constant losses after committing to battle untried troops and always too much ammunition badly placed, causing plenty of damage but gaining no ground.

— You can close the book?

— You have to just turn the pages one more time.

— There you are in your Eton suit.

— A charming smile.

— There you are as a babe in arms in the head-on sunlight over your grandfather blinking.

— A huge head glowing like a rock.

— There are your mother and father and your big sister and you in a canoe on Beach Lake.

— Who took the snapshot?

— There you are leaving for your first day in kindergarten.

— Do you know what became of the plaid schoolbag?

— There are your father's mother and stepfather on the wooden bench in front of the house in Sunnyside.

— They smile, too, very sweet smiles.

— Why?

— I thought I'd ask *you*.

— There is your sister and your cousin Judy with a dog behind her.

— There they are in l'Astoria.

— There is your uncle home from the Navy.

— Flip the page.

— There are your mother and your aunt in

beds next to each other in the hospital. Two sisters, two babies, one day apart.

— Flip the page.

— There you go to your high school prom.

— Close the book.

— Close the book?

— Close the book. You need so many monuments, and no more. You need to regard it as done, edited, published.

— There is your mother's cousin with a plate of spaghetti he's holding up to the camera.

— And then what do you need?

— You need to close the book.

— Yes, that was a story.

— So?

— Close the book.

— Is this you in your altar boy vestments?

— And this is Kenny and Joey and Tommy and Mikey saying mass in Kenny's backyard with a cup, a saucer, a tablecloth, and an unabridged dictionary.

— And who is this on the Eiffel Tower with blue Paris stretching off into the distance?

— That's me. Close the book.

— Why is this in the same book with the others?

— Because the book is open.

— What did you think of the Eiffel Tower?

— It's big all right, and it's an illusion.

— How is that?

— It makes an illusionary Paris seem real,

a Paris no one can live in but everyone can admire.

— And?

— The worst food in Paris.

— And?

— And close the book.

The album is slipped into its place on the shelf. Suddenly, the Terror is a tennis game, straightforward opposition, expensive tickets, but in no way mandatory. Life loses no sweetness if you stay outside and watch the boats rumble by. How did he do that? Napoléon used to imagine each of his problems in a file drawer which he would close in his mind, one after another, till they were all locked up and he fell asleep. You may do the same. You may open the drawer and work out always more of who meant what when how to whom, and you may like to do this often as years go by, but you will only think of it when it will seem worth the trouble to drag out the file, look through the album, seeking the terms of the necessary transaction. For you would never have known that this — these yellowing color slides, these secrets in rooms with open doors and windows — could be the Terror had you not already, much of the time, outlived it, outrun it, constructed a string of forts along mountain ridges, places that show you those ancient giants as pygmies.

When my mother was dying, there were my father and I talking to her about my faulty carburetor. Yes the famous carburetor dream came true. When I was six, we moved into our house. Between it and the house next door a narrow alley led to two backyards. Theirs had a birdbath in the middle, waist-high. In my dream one night my father lay my mother over this and chopped out her heart with an axe, showing it to the man next door as a form of faulty carburetor. Only after her heart gave out, almost forty years later, did it occur to me that the angry person in the dream was myself and that it was not only my father's analytic dominance that appalled me but the fury, altogether mine, that drove the axe. A reasonable dream to have about a mother who threatens to kill you. I never quite got the book closed with her. When I told her what she'd said, she couldn't remember it. Telling her again, I heard her say I hadn't told her before. Then she decided to tell me about other things. So I never did tell her the dream. So I felt guilty when my carburetor failed and she died. So.

So, the Terror is the book they couldn't close. How Paris must have seethed for them, every file of traitorous bastards only dying so that their place could be taken by another set of schemes, subtler, more terrible, yet more necessary to root out. From Louis all the way to Danton, and beyond, and nothing sayable, really, about how one felt, no way of thinking it, in the, or through the, tubes running between the screaming of babies and the printing of placards or the debating of principles in a human terrine of sawdust and wine.

— I could have kissed you instead, he said.

— Instead, she said, you insulted me, covered me quickly in condescension.

— He said, I said, you said what you felt but was it all you felt?

— No, I said, some of us, as you said, felt otherwise, but how does the one who said what I said get to say it when the rest of us (if us is the right name for *I* and *I* and *I*) might, would have, said, or done, otherwise?

— Yes, she said, how?

Around they went. Things never seemed to get better but were less frequently bad. (He said.)

— Is that 'better'? they asked.

Down the avenue of London plane trees rolled the Prince and Princess, Their Royal Highnesses the Duke and Duchess Andrew of York, while on either side the royal road of Roman straightness mobs waved flags and turned gaily heads in party hats bearing Royal faces in glossy four-color separation photographic reproduction, signifying as they rumbled across the television screen the imposing maximum of marriage, that monad of mingling tribes which teaches us, as my grandmother said in l'Astoria, that what you do in private you will do again in public and, by corollary, what the public does in public it will do in private, filling your face-to-face with not

206

a quartet alone, as Freud suggests, but with a battle of the bands, a flooding and streaming of persons known and unknown to the memories against which, as they move, the faces seen thus intimately are seen, giving the *Iliad*, as the shaft of analytic sunrise reads the page, an aspect of plainest social realism, all those ships and wombs like subway cars seething for you as the merest café conversation between adulterers, not even as Joyce would have put it but yet more photographically previsionable, just what the video so readily gives you over your shoulder along the Avenue Foch. Which has been my guiding, my supporting, notion all through this peculiar investigation. Moving backwards from the victims of glory through its monuments through its actual bloodiness, I have seen at every point the reenactment on that stage of Paris what we silently fell heir to in Long Island, so that its very process has been filling for me all along the liturgical function of a history never written down or even experienced as what it was. But this all is to bring us to a point you will recognize as one of hilarious simplicity, the Revolution itself, which even in its maturer days had something of the same shapeless quality, no one really being sure just when it had started or how it was ever going to be brought to any kind of satisfactory conclusion, and so, in my parallels leaving me to jump off the parade float and from a point on the ground to look as directly as is possible, with all the aids to reflection a person of my disposition is likely to have to hand, at the small dust-raising crowd in which I myself am walking.

III

The Revolution

— All of this was supposed to prepare him to go to Italy, where he was going to use the French Revolution to explain the Italian migration.

— Idiot.

— Perhaps. His idea was that the Italian migration was not very well explained.

— The libraries are full of books.

— But not books about his question.

— Poor him. And what *is* his question?

— Down below in the Louvre, he saw himself in Michelangelo's slaves. Down below in Les Invalides, he saw his mother in Napoléon's tomb. Did they belong there? Did they belong to that, did that belong to them?

— That is his question?

— More or less.

— He expects to find books in the libraries to answer this question?

— Well, no. That is why he wrote his own book.

— He must have had some hell of a time in Italy with this project.

— Nor was this the end of it.

— What more can there be?

— He had another — an official — purpose

as well. Just as he had gone to Paris to teach, so now he went to Italy on a grant to do specific research.

— To research this famous question of his?

— Not exactly. I am a professor. I write papers. While my mother was dying I was writing, and after she died I completed successfully, a paper about the body of Italy as it appears under the not-so-gentle hand with which Robert Browning composed *The Ring and the Book*. Sometimes you can write a hole into the sky, which is more or less how that paper changed my life, for thanks to the reception it found, two years later and all the while the Parisian sidewalks were giving me frost in the toes, I knew that, safe in an envelope at home, there was waiting the award of a grant that would allow me to go to Italy for a year, my family with me, following the extravagant path of the dangerous Robert Browning. And Italy. Browning and Italy. A rich subject full of unanticipated reversals and false motives slipping down the glaze on the porphyry pyramids at Santa Maria del Popolo.

What do you read during a tragedy? The hospital offers you a glistening collection of offprints from *Reader's Digest* and *Guideposts*.

A mother died young. Her eldest child consoled himself remembering how she had called him to her bedside and said, 'I must tell you a secret: you were always my favorite child.'

Her second child consoled herself by recalling how mother had summoned her to the scene of what was about to be her final moments and said, 'Don't tell the others, but you were always my favorite child.'

The third child — but let us draw the veil across this comedy and merely report that in like manner had she treated with this one.

Each child went forth after the (we may be certain) horrible death of the beautiful young matron and was not the brokenhearted orphan the mother had feared to leave behind but instead was whole and confident, happily reborn into a world where his/her status could never again be revised, called into question, where he/she was freed forever from compromise and from the unwelcome triumphs of siblings: a favorite — signed, sealed, delivered, dead, and buried, a favorite for good. But, according to the article, afterwards each one of these children told the others what mama had said, and all of them marveled, praising the deep love of the dead mother who had shown herself willing, in order to placate her wailing babes, to enter eternity a certified hypocrite. Danbury Hospital was well supplied with copies of this article, and I seemed to read it every week.

It never stopped puzzling me. I never told my sisters the things my mother had said to me in the hospital before she had the stroke. No more did they ever tell such things to me. You might say it was a pact of silence between us, but you would have to add that it was a pact made in, of, through, by, with, for, from, and to not even silence but some enabling condition that, of its very nature, cannot have a name. An old habit and nothing terrible. We would give ourselves a lot of trouble on its account afterwards, of course, when we tried to decide who should get what and why. But to us, it was a quite usual something, after all, that came naturally, wasn't it? A rubble of stumps and broken fountains through which we bustled thoughtlessly like the old ladies who used to feed the cats at Porta Maggiore.

That vast ugly gate pierced by trolleys and highways and wires, rotting vividly like a permanent act of aggression.

So I was reading about Robert Browning. His sick wife with her morphine. Their elaborate son whom they called Pen. And I called him Italic Pen. Roman Robert and Italic Pen. That was the plot of my book, and I was having a hard time getting along with my son Robert. It was a hopeless mire of paper mirrors. My brother-in-law kept saying, ' Why can't you let her die?' But you know in a hospital corridor it is possible to read with an almost unadorned efficiency, since you have come there to be helpless and ashamed and so find yourself free more time than not, with no other distractions, once you have digested the inspirational literature, which is why you find yourself breaking through an arctic wall of boredom into the indifferent hills and dales of literary criticism as if these were the great vaginal chasms of your secret paradise.

I abjure nothing. Everything I discovered about Mr. Browning was true because I was in that heightened state where you are dying in order to be more accurately deadly, dark to be lighter, meek that you may inherit the earth, the bedside school of inverse sincerity that can teach you in a single term, if you study hard, the inside of a motive contrapted like a cardboard campanile. You can climb it, write the map of the prospects from its fourteen windows. You can do these things without effort. When you finish, no one will love you any better for it, but perhaps you will be by then such an anthology of aches and pains and incipient chronic conditions that you will have forgotten that this was why you started. You were in that state where your every glance carries a visible wound. She looks at you with her eyes full of what you know has always been solicitation, but she spells it out blinking at the blackboard HAPI BIRTHDA.

Hapi birthda to who?

She can't remember.

As the moments become months of this, a broad thick corruption spreads throughout your vocabulary of gestures. Your eyes can only mean, even when they are loving, that they are turning away, that the rain is going to drown the world in a deep wide subterranean well where you won't even think it worth the trouble to say that all this water used to be tears. You will no longer be sure of that, in any case. You will come to regard your tears as one of the ways that moisture occurs, somewhere between sweat and a hurricane. The neighborhood will have become comprehensively empty, and it will be too late to run away, since there will be no one left who cares if you decide to stay home.

My head was full of revolution, I thought, when I arrived in Italy. *Was there an Italian revolution? Was the migration a revolution?* These were the leading questions. Under them were arranged huge families of others. Did Browning really believe in the Risorgimento? Was that or was that not a revolution? And Elizabeth, whom the very word could inspire to fill a folio, was her revolution political in the sense that at last she had escaped her monster father, or was it political in the sense that the Italians thought it was, that she was a heroine of their unification? What was the Risorgimento? My grandfather believed in it. He taught me its music, its poetry, his walls were covered with its Garibaldi and its Mazzini. But why then did he leave Italy? The Risorgimento was a revolution that emitted hungry exiles in the millions, was it? There were all these questions that were only one question that I could not put into words, but I thought that Italy was the body of my mother and my grandmother and that I would come back from there, if I came back at all, whole again, or else that I would die there into one sound and conclusive shape like some travertine Dante whose second life, feeding the moss and calcifying the fish in the fountain, could last beyond imagining. My question had these strings of subsidiary inquiries, they were a catalogue of catalogues; of course, I would never shut up, but in the first as in the last case I wanted to know only one thing of Italy: could I have her back?

I would take Italy as a replacement, would I?

Italy might have been only too ready to be my mother. Accustomed as she is to the obscure, insane sabbaticard, the *professore universitario statunitense in aspettativa*, as it said in my visa, entering the country for an uncertain period *per ragioni di studio indipendente*, accommodating to the phantom-seeker, Italy might happily, upon hearing my request, comply. Her first response would be to recognize another anglophone lunatic with more money than sense. I might never get beyond that. I was to be there a year before anyone uttered in my hearing the expression *americano in vacanza*, a category of the totally contemptible from which you know you can never entirely escape, no matter what you do, even if they give you the keys to the opulent tomb you are seeking, bursting with silks and bones, and you go in, happily chattering in dialect.

217

I couldn't find my way around Porta Maggiore and always came out driving down the wrong road from which it seemed impossible to turn in a productive direction.

It was stupid, my plan, after all, in an entirely different way. I was not Columbus. They had seen my kind before. They knew all about it, even if sometimes only in theory, or, to put it more clearly, they had known about it so long it had receded into the abstract space of what is no longer worth talking about. Of course you can have it back. Or her. Let us call it her, since you prefer it so. No need to be boring about it. Here you are, this is the list of prices, and of course there are others should you care to see them.

Suddenly everything lost its tongue. He thought, stepping on and off airplanes with mounds of notes and sacks of books, that he had brought with him, if nothing else, at least the secret of talk. Paris, which explains everything, would be the key, the prolegomenon, and the concordance to Rome. He had walked straight backwards, this is what I said, through a paper cemetery whose leaves fluttered in ripples as he passed, and it was a long walk, that would take him, as he supposed, directly to the gardens of the Palais-Royal where Camille Desmoulins stood up one day and made the speech that led to the Bastille. Italy would be the garden. Italy *was* a garden. He had seen it before, and he knew. But it had nothing to say, it had not heard any speeches apparently, it was roaring back and forth across the lanes of the highways at a hundred and forty kilometers an hour, trying to avoid the uncertain wobble of the double-trailer trucks under their loads of mineral water as they came tumbling into the sunlight out of tunnels down mountains, or shot like arrows into the receding target past factories plated with ceramic tiles in primary colors that alternate with terraced hills of grapevines all the way from Milano to Verona, and up into the Veneto, the towns cresting the hills, compact, certainly old, but still intent on business, a blizzard of messages, everything written forever, everything getting ready to gleam at sunset as you step out of the car and come into the house.

They stumbled up the stairs of a huge villa. He was no longer traveling alone. His wife, their children, as if for a long camping expedition, were bristling with impediments — books, computers, cameras. Where had he brought them? This was not their ancient homeland so much as it was the universal nostalgia for order, so intense he felt they had come to the margins of the known universe. Somewhere off in the distance lay the Adriatic where the smoking mills awaited the stragglers of the Last Crusade. He had not stepped into just any garden, it soon emerged, but the simmering grave of Italo Calvino instead, a stiff, polished underworld of millionaires where one actually lunched with the baron who never touched the ground and the knight who — while faithful to a certain military lady and himself walking about with a great emphasis of clank and crash as he displayed the interminable excellences of a would-be Palladian library — in fact did not exist. People had died in this part of the world, it seemed, but only at the hands of the Germans. God, though he had retired and was now a collector of pictures, continued to drink wine on the terrace and to argue with the gardeners, as of old. The great fear was the mountains, where the Austrians and Prussians and the snow originate. Down below, in the abundant plain there was a blue haze over the canals obscuring the vast, dusty, deserted cattlemarket of Castelfranco Veneto. They were living in a house where Robert Browning had reconsidered *Pippa Passes* ('God's in His heaven, /All's right with the world') and, in his decline, wrote a poem about the view, filling it with that tortured obscenity of which only men near death are capable. This was all very edifying, of course. Very pleasant, everyone had a job or pretended to, new cars everywhere, good weather. Not, in short, what he had been thinking of at all. Instead, mere civilization, prototype virus of. Bassano del Grappa, a resort town for the Viennese frame of mind, has a Piazza Garibaldi, but the only reminiscence of war or of democracy is the way people drive in it. For the rest, an overpowering easiness. A plaque indicates which palazzo lodged Napoléon Bonaparte in the winter of 1796. Inside, a vast bookstore full of toys, art history, and, in the back, a garden. The wrong garden. Napoléon did not exist, either. The books the leftists publish are all gorgeous. You stand there feeling the subtle ridges of rag in the paper covers and drinking in the astonishing colors with the same systolic squash that leads you, like a barbered Pekinese on a silver tether, down the piazza to lick a cone in three tastes of gelati and a thick plop of whipped cream.

He wasn't, this was the worst of it, in the least displeased. It wasn't that nothing had happened, he reasoned, only that it had moved differently and it wasn't talking at all.

— These ugly factories, she said.

— People are earning money, he replied smugly. Who can argue with that? But even this had a theoretical backscratch in it he could not ignore. A tourist looks at monuments first, and these advertised only the prestige of the prestigious and the blood of their victims. That familiar effect does not quite break the crust of pleasure. You have already forgiven Italy everything you never knew about it on account of Giorgione and Michelangelo Buonarroti, on account of the dozen different guilds it took to make the amazing scarlet cloaks and hats, on account of sunlight and color that touch you all over, but courteously, never wanting to fall on your head howling with rage as in Paris, never either interrupting or even placing some seam of parade-ground importance between themselves and your Campari-soda under the striated parasols in the breezy shadows. It is working very hard, you sometimes see, but it will not say anything about that, wants to enjoy the fountains too, the castle up the hill, the Easter egg of heritage with fading snapshots annealed to the tombstones and wedding portraits posed at the cemetery gate, gently like a smooth gold bracelet with heavy links slipping and caressing in and out on your wrist as you hold it up to the reflected light of the river out the jeweller's window, printing itself, this generational flux, into your letters home as if they were so many cunning olive oil labels, prepotent forever afterwards to give you a taste of *tortellini in brodo* or a whiff of pork on a brazier even if your eye merely falls by chance upon the opened page of pictures while you walk past the disordered bookcase, or fills the folds of the cloak with shadows of venereal splendor, simply reconsuming themselves and stepping forward later on, in a restaurant in New York or on a hill in San Francisco, to graze your arm like a large soft begonia dripping wet.

Which put him more impossibly aside than he could have supposed possible. This was the *ancien régime* — with an infinity of adjustments and complaints of course, it was not to be doubted, as when the contessa one day opened her arms to indicate complicity at the swimming pool and lamented the *piccola gente* down in the plain building villas with bottle-bottom windows ('But, contessa, *I* am of this *piccola gente* myself') — considering itself at random, as if it were its own portfolio of shares to be sifted and reordered in the arbor, Italy having stepped through some perfectly-lit restoration of a romanesque convent into the photographer's dream of six-o'clock luminescence and, as it did so, emerged not any more or less visible than before, still smiling, and possibly, it was hard to see clearly in the artful green mist, paring an orange, but suddenly *large*, suddenly, as if merely to remind you through its quiet dribble of goldfish fountains, all around you very remarkably solvent and solid and still and full of unsuspected extent, so many mountains ballooned above ice in the schist, so much vertical kilometrage and falling heft to be added to the slender anatomy of a duchess's riding gear that lay, as usual, scribbled flat across the folds of the map, but now unforeseeably, undeniably, *full* — full of dogs and walls, electric lines, patiently restored, rebuilt, replayed, no noise this time, just the regular haulage of goods, expert gleaning of tips, slow accumulation of tariffs, pyramids of glove-leather handbags, olives, pigs reinvented at a hundred times the cost of the feed.

— And this is another of those sentences you can't hear.

— And what is that supposed to mean?

Here was a conversation involving nobody at all. It can't be written *he said, I said, she said*. No bishop, no viscount. Appalling and, in the language, silentious. He was, first of all, completely used to being naked in Italy. You couldn't know enough, though he meant to try, to see past the false perspective painted into the sky outside every bathroom window — there was a crumbling perhaps, but entirely subsumed as it was in the metaepistemology of *ut pictura poesis* writing newspaper essays or, if you like, the art of helicopter navigation perfected half a millennium *in anticipo*, it was easy to resist any attempt you would make to wash it down in the rain. And, though you might never succeed, on the other hand, or be able to imagine doing so, you could always be frightened by the suspicion that if you did, you would be left with just another bankers' suburb full of abundant money that you see cascading down the empty meadows or in a masquerade of trees lining the ridge of the hill like international flagpoles vaunting great big bags of greenback dollars. Thus, from the outset, he felt himself trapped by the requirement of not seeing through a thickness of texture that had, in any event, no intention of allowing the geologist more than the appointed daily jug of milk and the cryptic liturgies of sunrise, where the mountain, opening between the bees and the knifeblade grass into some promising crevasse, only takes you as far as the next, the definitive, rise of water over the rims of your boots. Then, as the splendid cheeses, the wine a drama of selection, the day drawing the sharpened pencils of the blue cypresses across the town, were all prepared for your, or *the*, return, it would always be, had always been, the stranger's option to allow this flowering its habitual discretion, not to say unwillingness to give up more than a virtue it had never heard of, while keeping to itself a set of purposes quite as extensive and intact as the unimaginable mass of the Dolomites, still there next morning, cheerfully fresh and unexamined, precisely as you left them behind and turned, the night before, with relief to your book.

— No, wait a minute, I said.

He couldn't want to see this plainly, there is a limit in things, you know, people die and things are for sale, even precious things and beautiful ones, and even in Italy. So you seek pleasure cynically, torn between your rage at having lost it and your rage at having it so noiselessly fall into your outstretched palm. It was only money all the time. It was they had it and you didn't. It was you had it and they didn't. It was money. It was extremely money. It was money like a wall, a palace wall, a mountain of truffles, a gate with great bronze studs in it, but you can't fool me any more, it was money, I saw it was money and it was money, you could smile at me and they opened the gate of the villa, the one you rented, as if you had been born in it and you were only now returning, which would have been money too you began to understand, and who were you after all, you an American of all things, to be shocked or angry or disillusioned because it was money, because that is what it always had been, it was money, all of it was money, and weren't you anyway glad of that?

And did you trust this Shakespearean twitch? Despite the crystalline air, it really was not so plain what you were seeing.

We were in it everyplace and noplace. L'Astoria in any sense you could extrapolate. *Cento ignoti italiani*, one hundred unknown Italians, it says on each of many bronze doors in the monument that sits astride the peak of Monte Grappa. One of those hecatombs should have included my mother's father, who, like so many of them, came down from the heights and disappeared into the ocean to America in order not to fight in this battle. One million uncounted Italians. The monument is a circular ziggurat big enough not to be dwarfed by its site, adequate to the bones of three years' ditch-fighting in the snow and tunnel-digging through the stone, shaped on a scale to be inserted upside down like a plug into the pink Roman arena in Verona that on a good day you can make out from there with a strong pair of glasses. We did not die in the wars, but we died in the peace. Now we could light a candle in the chapel if we liked. Which Madonna was considering our request, and what did we want of her anyhow? This disjunct familiarity of my grandfather's nostalgic architecture invested every little garden shed in the uplands, the hoses and buckets, the tiny doors abutting narrow streets, ossobuco and polenta in a chalet where you could see it snowing in August, with the delusive glamor of miracles the Commission is certain later either to define as false or to postpone evaluating, again. We went to bed every night rosy with recognition, like cut flowers in a copper vase, everything that fed us having been in the course of the day obviously poured first into the pail for strangers.

Every person we met was, of course, perfectly conversable. They told you everything except what it meant to tell it. I grew lonely for my professors of the history of the French Revolution and their lucid, mistaken, suggestive prolixity. At the end of a month we packed our bags and kissed the housekeeper who had guided us like a grandmother and came to Rome where there was, if nothing more, the chance of a productive confusion. But the same thing happened. Paris had produced a vibrating field of its history. Rome only more thoroughly than the rest of Italy devoted itself to cultivating a skin so deep one could never remember, having lifted it at last, what he had been looking for in the first place. Even the horrors are comfortable, the paper-shuffling in the questura allowing you time to consider the carabinieri outside in the courtyard as they throw back their splendid cloaks to light each other's cigarettes. In a lifetime, you might aspire to grow expert in the distinction of not just wines or paintings or breads, but, given at least a momentary breaking of the circle and a consequent taste — acquired during a semester in London, say — for moral sociology, then of, then in the distinction of, then expert to exquisite degrees, agonizing to consider, in the detection and classification of, silences: those that fall in solid shafts of brilliant noonday sun into the alley where the racket of mothers and sons is symphonic; that famous one which scratches its chin while computing the check in the restaurant; the hard quiet you find in stone houses and lawyers after someone dies; the incoherent rumble of well-regulated traffic, which must be the father of tourist Italy Italians themselves cannot tell from the one they invent; silence the white smoke of supper; silence the notorious kiss, in church, of peace.

I was not their scholar. I could not hear, could merely hypothecate, their presence, could not dream of beginning the fatigue of winnowing long from short. I was lost among the empty lines in my agenda. I was sitting still in the loggia with my copy of *L'Italia come problema storiografico*, trying to remember what was which. (Imagine a great water balloon in the shape of the Queen of England, six feet high, someone has stabbed it with his pointed shoe and she has collapsed into something that will need to be mopped up all over the house. This is what had happened to the Robert Browning of my project. I was hopelessly embarrassed. When he called himself Roman and his son Italic, as I said, he had grafted them onto a system of separations joined at the roots that stretched back under the wall of Romulus, where they poured the blood into the ditch.) I was sitting there in a mound of books and cards and hardly the man I had been in Paris. I had changed modes and was no longer the owl-eared student of the radio. It was evident in the children right from the start that the double-edged letter-opener of solitude, which I had trailed inconspicuously scraping along the lines of masonry in Paris, would be replaced now by the disheveled calculations of Fagin, the pensive daddy in the dark hole, attending, ascribing, advising, he that has for fingers a thousand hands and sees through the eyes of innocent sentences into the markets where daylight never finds him. This was no constriction, he knew. You might collect, this way, enough secrets to draw a genuinely usable chart of Italy. Alone, you might only be ravished, you could possibly sicken and die, but you would probably never know it was happening, like the aesthetic Italian in Peking who got up in his bed and, looking out at the Forbidden City all red and graceful, exclaimed *Che bellezza!* and fell back dead, whom I encountered, he was naked to the waist in bronze in the Campo Verano, his narrow hairless shoulders far more present to that monumental freshness than Garibaldi's beard which you could only infer from the nearby tomb with his name on it (whose is it?), seeming as it does to be the foundation of an unfinished warehouse — supposed, no doubt, to be eloquent understatement, but that is a category of elocution with slight effect in this carnival of tribunes, as I was from the beginning entirely aware, buried as we all are by the sheer impossibility — even at the cost or as the profit of a youth spent altogether otherwise than mine had been — in what I now realized was going to seem more and more a clinker-built dinghy trolling daily among sandbars that produced clams and oysters you hardly had to bend over to reap — of ever making heads or tails of it all, Italy just past the velvet rope of the grand saloon, where the television crews were concentrating, apparently with perfectly straight faces, on a panel of experts in the history of *trasformismo*, one of the hundred synonyms for what, looking like corruption but also never less than necessary for survival, is always receiving new coinages as the years go by, a way of keeping distinct each one among a set of recurrences that surely deserves, though as a group it has never had, its own political archangel, Machiavelli coming no nearer this particular polymorphology of deltas in April than do less disillusioned prophets like Croce — a phenomenon, as they perceive it in their estimable journals, requiring that you hold simultaneously in mind the names and positional chronicles of, during any ten years, hundreds of politicians, almost all of whom kept changing their minds with the morning's headlines from Paris or Berlin or Palermo or Vienna: an imposition, as it were, at the entry, certain to exclude everybody not somehow or other born into it or what I saw must be the generally acceptable facsimile of it, or else those willing to content themselves inside the warm, dry permission of some Papal duke to pass the best years of their lives preparing for publication the checklist of an old, large, capable correspondence or the *catalogue raisonné* of some great ecclesiastical miser's accumulation, most of it long since disappeared by night across the border, although my uncle told me, *caro professore*, that your colleague from Harvard, who taught me croquet when I was small, did, long ago, have a letter from Professor Trevelyan relating a conversation with Giolitti which shed considerable light on this matter. I have no idea what has become of it, no. Italy, even when it wanted to, could tell you nothing that didn't drag along with it,

all hanging together like the interminable in-
testines of a dynasty of prize hogs famous in
some town of the Romagna, the trailing stains
of genealogy, these prodigiously rubbled collections of crested china, a complication of
generosities adding up to a formidable blankness, confusions of musics in noise, though I
knew, sitting in the kitchen as the children repeated the teachers' instructions and what
Gianni did and Stefano said, that the real
silence in question, just as much as Italy's, was
mine.

I would give, I gave, as I was given, everything amounting to nothing. This was the
original or sterile Revolution, where you constituted yourself an irreducible and unrepre-
sentable monad of will, what otherwise was
called the Terror, but only a little later, a little
outside, a little for the newspapers, a little
compromised, that is, by its desire to share the
limelight on the hook in the butcher's window,
but, before that, the sudden pulse of logic that
allowed you, the very first time in history every
time, to step aside from the procession, to
gather up the skirts of your acolyte's cassock
and walk off the altar straight to the bathroom
while the priest was hissing, a syllable at a time,
the consecration of the host (it had been my
specialty, this version of it) because, I suppose,
from the start I saw that it was (tradition gave
it to me just the way the baronet inscribes the

232

family gryphons on the baby's cradle) the politics we made.

When the cheerful, plausible curate hung the slender purple stole around the collar of his plaid shirt and my nephew turned off the television, my father escaped to the patio outside with a cigar in his hand, where the rest of us, all gathered in the living room, could see him through the walls of plate glass as he recognized Joe Notaro up the hill and, relieved to have something to do, climbed the steep lawn to assist at the installation of a new electric pump for the well. Then my sister came out of the kitchen carrying a large green glass jug of California wine and two loaves of Italian bread from the local supermarket. When Mass was over, my mother told me that this piece of Lazzara's bread dipped in Gallo burgundy had been (she was almost sixty years old) her First Communion. This landmark event was a Marriage Encounter Mass, celebrated in the living room, part of my sister's long project to find a way of practising Christianity, but I was thinking of all the other ceremonies our mother had sat through. Had she really never taken communion? Of course, in the old days, you didn't always, even Protestants, the way they do now, to show respect.

— This is why I never would tell you my middle name, she said.

My mother had a pin, I can't say where it has got to now, with what appeared to be the intertwined letters VMV picked out in brilliants. Vera M. Viscusi. She always claimed the M was for a name she disliked, and we would guess, sometimes raising a laugh by alluding to a neighbor she held in low esteem.

— There was no middle name, she told me now, I was never confirmed.

— But we all had middle names and confirmation names, I objected.

— They didn't do that in those days. Middle names were for confirmation. It was Tomàs, she said, they listened to him.

Tomàs was the communist with his own bedroom in my mother's parents' house. I never saw him, so far as I know.

— We used to go to Trowbridge Street or Astoria Square and he would make speeches on a soapbox.

— What did he say?

— You know, communism. Nobody had work in those days. A lot of people listened. You have no idea, she said.

We were walking up the hill past the Notaros' house. My father came out, laughing with Joe, who had given him a present of fish caught that morning in the lake.

— You have no idea, he repeated her phrase, how close they came to revolution.

I had no idea. Back at my sister's house, the priest had left. I searched through the piano bench for the music, I knew it was in there someplace, for *Which Side Are You On?*, an old union song. I played the piano a great deal in those days. It had been as if, every time we had an argument involving politics, I found a fresh motive to play the piano. And the politics would be safely folded into the melody, roll after roll of Grandma's *bastone* as she slap!, roll, spread and spread the flour again and slap!, roll, roll, rolled the dough, humming a certain lullaby, or her quiet, red-faced husband, coming in and pulling off the heavy gloves he swept the street in, whistled an interminable falling tune in one of those modal Arabian reveries you hardly ever hear in Italy any more, his signature like a character in *Der Ring des Nibelungen* that alerted you, filching a cucumber or playing with his wrenches under a bush, his way of making certain never to catch anybody at anything again, a tremendous racket of music we made, all of us, one way and another down the years, so that I can index the stink of the Men's Room at the Bronx Terrace by the sound of the imitation of Tony Bennett that was asking the wedding guests *Must I forever be a beggar?* when I went in and, pissing as quick as I could to get out of there, it was incredibly vivid in June in that little space, was still imploring *Open your heart and you'll open the door / To everything that I'm waiting for* when I escaped into the big glittering room with its curved white staircase and the mirror ball giving the effect of the many mothers-in-law in beige taffeta as glasses of champagne. I can gauge all feelings of triumph by the Monday night, having been engaged for Devotions in order to allow the regular organist to avoid spending three hours on the subway from the Grand Concourse to Queens Boulevard and back again, I first ascended the bench in the choir loft and gave out *fortissimo*, drowning even the suspicion of sound from the mouths of the dozen old ladies scattered disconsolately in the echoing murk, the diminished seventh in *O Mary Conceived without Sin, Pray for Us Who Have Recourse to Thee*, a habit of compiling experiences halfway between sleep and reconsideration always available as a refuge, since the fiction is that, singing around the upright in the dining room, or half-listening while reading the funnies, no one pays any particular attention to the words anyway, though, despite an apparently undevelopable singing voice, I always thought them the most important part of the songs or even of the 'pieces' one lives with at lessons, entirely innocent of words as they are, which I could never hear except as Mozart's parents arguing or Bach's twenty children all playing in the next room or being put, patiently and mercifully one by one, at last to bed.

— Picture the wind in late October. It is raining and already quite cold. The ocean waves that hit the seawalls make such a tremendous roar that you will say, perhaps not realizing how truly you speak, that you can't hear anything.

— But who will hear you say it?

We would rush home from school to watch the Army-McCarthy hearings on television. Everyone was very pleased to be seeing history in action. Father Murphy recommended these programs. I am not making any of this up. Mrs. Hansen, who appeared to be German, called a meeting of all the mothers. A little girl had been run over and killed by a woman looking for a parking spot near the corner of Thirty-Ninth Place and Fiftieth Avenue, where, through some oversight, there had never been placed any stop sign or traffic light. Repeated letters to the Department of Traffic had produced no action. Mrs. Hansen served sponge cake and coffee and the mothers formed the Thompson Hill Civic Association to get a light put in. The next day the word went round that this group was a communist front, like the Boy Scouts. None of the ladies went back, and there is still (thirty-six years have gone by) no light on that corner. No one spoke to Mrs. Hansen any more.

This was not as loud a silence as the one in 1945 when Franklin Roosevelt died and another German lady, all alone, danced in the street. Or when, the same year, an Italian American G.I. came back from fighting in Italy. Or in 1943, two and half years old, I was singing *Mussolini is a meanie*. No one said a word.

Silence is cheaper, is safer, than debate. And there was really no way to remember, as the song says, what there was to forget.

It was another wedding, this one in a dream. Among the guests were my mother's cousins Margaret and Rose Giardinelli who, it turned out, had grown up with a girl (my mother said she had known Tony Bennett in l'Astoria) who had written a famous patter song, which for all I know really exists though I only remember it from the dream, with a big chorus. The verse begins, *Oh the Irish hate the English and the Turks don't like the Greeks,/ The Germans hate the Frenchmen and Americans hate geeks/, But (dah-dah-dah, everybody sing) Italians Love Every Body, Every Body*, and I was trying to pick this out in the key of E-flat, but another of the guests, a flapper in a white dress with a beaded fringe, Al Capone's girlfriend, insisted on singing it without accompaniment, to my intense annoyance. I woke up with my left hand so sound asleep under me it flapped useless for a few minutes the way my mother's did after her stroke. Every research has its own methods, and you can hang a book, as I have done here, on dreams, following that theme in the *Traumdeutung* of Sigmund Freud, frequently ignored in the commentaries, which brings back to the surface again and again the interpreter's desire for a professor's chair, giving the treatise, without a doubt, its inner spring, the parallel in the pre-

238

sent case being the writer's discomfort with the same ambition — this time, however, achieved, but, as he supposes, at the cost of a measure of fertile self-interruption, assumed as a burden in lieu of military service during the Vietnam War, and pursued, as seemed inevitable, under a double burden of silence and of allowing other people to make all the effective music.

— But was it not your mother who stunned your hand? Or your desire for your mother? There they go again.

— It was my mother's hand, as much or more than mine, that was stunned.

The Irish priest said, 'I don't want to see any pennies in this collection.' So my father and his brothers, who had five pennies each for the basket, kept their coins and went to the movies where their money was welcome in that as in any other form. He never made his communion either, not until he was married, he told me. Why he did it then he has not specified. It would have been a simple enough policy just to stay away, keep on going to the movies instead, you think, but it wasn't, apparently, not for them and not ever, because they sent us to church, where we took it all in, one way or another, either the reverence or the theology, as they sometimes claim, or, as I suspect for my part, the message that elsewhere some distance back in time all this had been elaborated to a point of extraordinary fineness not to be otherwise here reflected at all once I had laid down the altar card with its measured Latin prayers, bowed to the emerald-mounted tabernacle, preceded the priest into the sacristy, removed the surplice and folded it in such wise as to preserve its pleats, undone the thirty buttons of the cassock, hung it over my forearm folded with the surplice above it, walked down the epistle aisle under the golden windows, genuflected, and stepped out into the smoky orange morning of Long Island City, where the roaring chaos did not contrast with what went on inside the fragrant and measured spaces so much as it imposed between itself and them a total scrim of disconnection, leaving you the option of carrying the ceremony with you along the avenue like a viaticum in your head, while it rendered the rest of this somehow unreal or at least unlikely, but you needed to find a way across this searing vacuum, it was your task sooner or later. My father secretly confused the simple meaning of his presented self by sending us, our heads ringing with his condemnation of the priests, to church, and my mother contradicted nothing he did or said on this subject.

— This was not revolution, or was it?

— How close they came. This may have been, I started thinking, what was called *Risorgimento*.

— *Risorgimento* meaning how Garibaldi knocked out the King of Naples?

— Well may you ask.

— *Risorgimento* meaning Cavour out-maneuvering the Pope?

— So you may think.

— *Risorgimento* driving the Pope at last into the prison of the Vatican?

— So they say.

— Was it *Risorgimento* how they felt when the priests refused absolution to the women unless they would say if their husbands were active against the Church, and when the women told, they sent names to the bishops who sent them to Rome who hung the men along the roads in hundreds?

— So may I think.

— So why did they send you to church?

— I think they forgot. I think they didn't exactly know. I think it never was made clear.

— You mean your father didn't know.

— I mean my father felt it. My grandfathers never went to church. No one went, but they sent us.

— So you didn't know?

— I felt it. I bristled at everything. But I went. What could possibly have taken its place for me?

— So why is it what you called *Risorgimento*?

— It isn't this and it isn't that. It isn't revolution, *Risorgimento*. It means rebirth, resurrection. It means that Cavour, who first used the word, was baptizing the French Revolution so it would be less frightening.

— You mean less revolution, don't you?

— That's how it turned out. We were left to lumber into the twentieth century with all our contradictions squirming together like lizards in a sack.

— We?

— A big *we*. The ones we left behind, who were in for a long diet of long speeches, mountains of corpses, medals, diplomas. The ones who came to America, escaping the mess left behind by the Risorgimento, and found themselves sending their children to the priests to be educated.

I had the unpleasant apprehension, visiting the Church of the Gesù one day, and comparing it, like a good American, point-by-point, according to the method of paragons taught to me by the Jesuits themselves, with the Whore of Babylon, that the white-haired small attending priest shuffling about on the polished pavement would suddenly begin asking me rude questions about my politics. We had a theology professor in freshman year at Regis High School who kept challenging us to produce a parent who could prove to his satisfaction that the *New York Times* was not a communist front. This was in 1954, and I am not making this up, either. The International Ladies Garment Workers Union did not know what language we spoke and sent to my mother every week two newspapers, *Justice* and *Giustizia*, of which no one read the latter but I always consumed the former with its epics of the Triangle Shirtwaist Factory Fire and the outrageous legal murder of Sacco and Vanzetti and its cartoons showing the difference between the fate of a hand with five splayed fingers and that of one which had decided to coil itself into a fist, right alongside those other regular visitors, the *Saturday Evening Post* and the *Reader's Digest*, since it appeared we were living the socialist program of organized workers in order, when the apple-picking would begin, to ascend into a Currier-and-Ives-and-Norman-Rockwell heaven of self-realized Sunday-going-to-meeting and muslin curtains in the mail from Stockbridge, Massachussetts. We only lived successfully, and it was a triumph, in this chaos of self-contradiction, by what my dream so acutely specifies, the stunned hand and the thorough adaptation of *Italians Love Every Body*, faithful according to our antique illusionless belief that, really, nothing meant anything if you didn't have enough to eat. But it made a prodigious weight of evasion, and every time another priest raised his voice, as they were always doing, against UnAmerican Activities, one found a few more things never to say and a few more places never to say them.

So, I thought, I am sure to stay out of trouble in Italy. The Italians have prepared, as people in most countries do, an avenue for foreigners to travel in without disturbing or being disturbed by any actualities of current events. You could walk securely down a path for the most part already furbished in the days of Benito Mussolini, marble maps that show the Roman Empire spreading like influenza, a street wide enough for bubbletop buses straight into the Piazza San Pietro, everywhere churches clean and more or less adequately illuminated to leave even the most avid connoisseur of paintings of Jesus and John with excuses to come back next year forever. But of course I had no intention of walking only in this valley of dead pilgrims, though after six months I could tell you more than you cared to hear about the display of relics or the astonishing bare face of what they insist upon calling *restoration*, as if one could not think of more precise terms, choosing the most notorious example, to use in describing the reinvention of the ceiling in the Sistine Chapel as a blunt Polish icon — even if that may be, as sometimes seems only too likely, exactly what the angry Michelangelo left behind, it was easy to see why there were many lamenting as they watched all the ingenious pornography and all the incredibly touching gestures of filth and misery washed away in the ample ruthless turpentine. It made itself available, in what you might call its luxury edition, to the Jesuit-prepared surface of my recognition, so that there were days I drifted in and out among the broken capitals under a summer lightning of long connections, all these Agneses and Cosmases and Damians and Mary Majors and John Laterans having forever familiarized themselves to me as part of the magic formulae, talking to God in secret mumbles in the *Canon Missae* and now suddenly appearing to my stupidity as great cracked and branching caverns of polychrome marble and gold ceilings from Peru, actual weary public works projects stained with perspiration and smelling of cats, where you could see in the dusty but busy exchequers actual people counting real ordinary money. In fact, I was experiencing the famous grubbiness or scandal of the Incarnation, an effect of words becoming well-worn stone no less startling to an avid altar boy than it would be to you if, wandering through the locker rooms with huge glass-brick walls built by the WPA at Astoria Pool, you were suddenly to come upon a bronze plaque specifying that these had been the walls, that this was in fact the city, not *like* the city, but the city itself, that Plato had described in *The Republic*. Worse than the shock would be, was, the simultaneous realization that everyone, or at least the operative everyone, else had known this all along, so that you were left equally startled by your sudden enlightenment and by your inability to claim that anyone had, really, led you astray.

Indeed — it was the price of being a father

with a family to consider — he found it almost impossible to claim anything at all. Emerging from the solitude of study or the yet profounder solitude that envelops you when you attempt to deal with registrars and bank tellers, he always came out in a scene of his own helplessness, where the need to conciliate and express gratitude on every side kept to the forefront. And this is the blasted hand of his dream, too, which I had other times in the form of a writer wearing black shorts and a black shirt, or else returning to his friends in America who said, *no, I don't like how you look*, as if the experience of living in Italy, widely envied among persons in his trade, were also bit by bit taking away his pieces and replacing them with rocks and moss, so that he would emerge at the end of the sojourn certainly transformed but not necessarily for the better. Thus he could announce paradoxes at dinner parties without being able to sustain them, every reply always underlining what you couldn't find words for or simply did not have any title to, because what could you say, *Civis Romanus sum*? or its equivalent, *As a boy I was tattooed in Latin by the Society of Jesus*?, and would saying as much take the place of all you so evidently could not begin to adduce? There was nothing to stand on in such statements. So he slipped gradually into the dangerous habit of exhibiting his withered hand, lodging his discourse on the one broken stone that

246

really did belong to him, *la miseria*, the sempiternal grinding of the poor, the remorseless conscription of Alpini, the last exit to America fifty, a hundred years ago, accepting, as he had to, this lineage as the only possible excuse not just for being here but also for taking a line independent of the one so plainly painted into the street for such as him by the Ministry of Tourism with an ice-cream cone in its hand. Which must have been, he reflected in the dream of Norman Mailer wearing black shorts and shirt, the start of what afterwards became very much of a problem, the sense, here in the stereotype factory where folio civility continues to fly off the printing presses, that all comfortabilities retained some escape clause with well-oiled hinges for the insurer, that you were safest assuming nothing, that you would need to hack your way through the palaces and pyramids as if they were the spun-steel foliage of the upper Amazon.

The black cabana set marked an appropriate boundary to the road he was thus attempting to make. That is, you had to be careful to stop at the edge of a sly fraudulence, it was a priest in pajamas, it was a rock'n'roll *squadrista* attracting girls with a ditty whose words they would either not quite hear or never quite translate. This would be a temptation on that road. I had entered the undergrowth of silence, where I found not only the mannequin, already thirty years standing in the rain but still perfectly fresh, of a Jesuit priest holding the tips of his fingers to his lips, standing on a copy of *Existentialism from Dostoevsky to Sartre* that the headmaster of Regis had taken out of my hands, *to borrow*, he said, but afterwards refused to return it until, he promised, I should be old enough to read it safely. And here it was. Pressing past this clearing, plenary indulgence in my pocket, I found behind it not the jungle they had been talking of down at the hunters' camp, but villages filled with people wearing blankets and smiling at me with the high cheekbones of my mother. And now the temptation was even a worse one, he could imagine the ravines full of the bones its victims had left behind, that you would take off your jacket and find the black shirt underneath it. You would hear yourself quickly connecting everything to everything else. You would be providing a jeep full of Beethoven symphonies and reproductions of Botticelli, and everything would be fine, you would have found the bridge across murder where people could pass back and forth as if nothing had ever happened. But really, you couldn't do this. Because, what was Mussolini, he said, if not exactly the pretence that nothing had happened, that you could make a poem out of it, a street, a night at the opera? — a lot of talk always in the end resolving itself into a dazed insistence on not facing up to the mounting evidence, so fatiguing to read in the archives, of every time you had redefined your positions, and you were left asserting that Truth was Eternal because it had so decisively changed every morning, like a password.

So I was in the peculiar fix, familiar to students of church history, of planning fastidiously to avoid committing crimes of which I had clearly been born guilty. A Medici might become Pope, but could he become a Christian? This would require virtues you only win by the troublesome and one-way narrow path of surviving despite your inability to read or write or speak in a language that could be understood three days' march away from your hoped-for two strings of grapevines, your surviving parent, your handful of chickens, your possible goat. That is, I was born to pretend to be Italian in the most elaborate sense of the word, equipped from infancy with breastplates and chain mail more than adequate to foreseeable need, and every time I removed these things, someone hailed me for how well I was wearing them. Whatever there had been in *Giustizia* of working-class solidarity, it had not been enough to get me through the nineteen-sixties without my putting on that costume again, this time with no hope of taking it off. That is, though I entered the decade in America with opinions you no longer even name in that country except as the reason you once upon a time got fired, I came out after the smoke cleared at Kent State, like everyone else,

dressed for folkdancing and looking for work.
And now I was in Italy, which presented itself
to me, despite my thorough mastery of what
the Italians still call Anglo-Saxon, not as the
familiar playground of Mediterranean iniquity
and moonshine, but suddenly as what they are
always finding in New England and I could
never see there, hiding as I was by habit behind
my Neapolitan mask of what Americans will
only too readily take for the Nietzschean Italian
who can do anything and feel no remorse —
now, here in Rome, without qualification, a
moral landscape. I couldn't help it. I didn't
want to do it. I came to Italy with elaborate
plans of walking about behind an American
smirk the same way I had played Arlecchino in
New York. It would be easy enough to manage,
I had breezily supposed.

— How do you mean *easy*? I had a letter
from my friend in Paris. He had revisited the
Philippines after Marcos was dethroned.

— Well, I can't say I really thought about
it. You know, over the years you learn when
the best thing to do is to play the foreigner.

— Yes, he grinned, they like that. Sometimes he thinks only of girls. I suppose because
we were teenagers together. When he decides
to get down to business, the change can seem
a trifle sudden.

But what stopped me was that I soon
enough saw that this was just what the Italians
expected. *Inglese italianato è un diavolo in-*

carnato, they say, meaning that the flowering turpitude the Angloamericans are always finding here is something they bring in their bags.

Elizabeth found that Italy brought her to life. She was no longer the victim of her oppressive father. She and Browning talked all day long instead of writing each other letters all day long. At night they made love. They were small people, too, Elizabeth was almost a doll, and could walk side by side on their balcony in Florence where you scarcely find room to turn around. I thought I will not let go of Italy and so I will not lose her.

Which had already brought me new life. The first time we were there we met relatives we had not even known to exist.

— What? they said, married a year and no children?

We came home and ten months later had a child. It was because they didn't recognize the peculiar way we thought we were (I was) broken. Was it? Was it that you felt like a whole man in a country where a short round dark person is president? Where you didn't feel a troll? Where you weren't clearly extraneous, full of obscure stains that only a steady practice of basketball, squash, running five miles a day, would sweat out of you? Such a regime would weary you and you would grow phlegmatic the way the Americans like. It would flush the oil out of your pores. It would narrow your waist and you would stand taller. Supposing you

251

chose not to do this or supposing you tried and found that it bruised you all over, you hurt your heel jogging, you pulled a muscle on the handball court? However hard you tried, your voice kept rising over the low white-painted barrier like an extravagant stallion.

They hid, you might say, in a pensione in Pisa. It wasn't hiding, really, but no one could get at them, and they talked all day long and made love at night. Eventually they moved to Florence. After many miscarriages they had Pen. He was born almost the same day that Robert's mother died. I made a note of that, looking out the window at the East River and wondering if it would stop raining any time soon. Somewhere down the long ward a woman as perfect as Napoléon, and not a millimeter taller, was thinking her last thoughts, which were beginning to mingle with the mist. It meant we were coming to Italy with a clear sense of revisiting a stronghold.

It meant the research was following a path not expected. From the start it would be like this. In Paris, to tell truth, I had sat down to write an essay about John Ashbery. I had carried all the books from New York and laid them out in front of me, down to Michel Foucault's essay on Raymond Roussel. Pen to paper: *I have to my account forty-five years* and so on for several pages, not what I intended but either what intended to be said or what needed to be discovered, all touched by the single expression La Storia on the sweater shop. The worst part of it having been the stillness of her hands. She once knitted me an Irish fisherman's sweater, full of intricate snakes and links. It took her, even her with her quick fingers, a couple of months. Halfway through, the whole back of it done, she realized she could not properly correct for some miscalculation and ripped it all out to start again. In the knitting-pattern book it said under the sweater that all these fisherman's patterns have meanings, record specific things. *Did his wife knit him this sweater? If so, she has woven him a story of many families, many marriages, many villages*. This must be what unraveled when I saw the sweater shop called *history* in Paris. (Perhaps it would not have come out if I had ever read the book where Madame DeFarge knits through the French Revolution. But I never had.) And opened the adventure of scholarship down a different chute than the usual. The flowered unintentional. I still have the sweater. My wife did not knit it, but she *is* Irish.

And the research, I now saw, was continuing along a pattern of treasuring that sweater as a magic gift which would allow me to choose any wonderful present, even including a bride, and pretending that my mother had done it for me. But she wouldn't. She said it was better not to interfere. It *is* better not to interfere. But is it better not to care? That is what I suspected to be really the case. But beyond suspecting, I really did think the following: I thought she had once loved me every bit as much as she claimed, but that it got to be too much for her, that she had fought for me especially with my father and especially when I was small, but that the effort had been excessive, that she had eventually tired of it, as people can, and after that had tried to fob me off with less, keeping more for herself. Even when she was dying and couldn't talk, some part of me kept saying, *She's saving it for when she gets to Florida*. So I gave myself great goods and pretended they came from her. When I decided to get married, I asked my Aunt Margaret what she thought of Nancy, and she said, *Marry this one*. Margaret is both my mother's cousin and her sister-in-law. Their mothers were sisters, their husbands are brothers. So one may say that structurally she is the same as my mother. And looks like her. I would not have tried this experiment with my mother, however. She would never have so plainly shown me her hand. So I gave myself presents and signed her name to the cards. Insofar as Italy was one of these, there was a constant slide in the research, a constant moving of one agendum from underneath by a shifting sheet of others. That is, I was interested in my English writers in Italy, the ostensible focus of my attention, but I kept learning how vividly the entities *Italy* and *English* were playing in my own personal calculus. I had two plans.

Plan One would trace Browning into the ground of Western literature, there would be ancient Romans and Etruscans and Greeks alongside medieval Popes, right down to Garibaldi and Anita wrestling together in the marriage bed inside of Browning and Elizabeth.

Plan Two began from the recognition that what I was seeing in my poets was a set of attachments and replacements that I myself was experiencing just as bluntly as ever had Elizabeth and that the investigation of this geological vivacity was necessary and proper to any so-called 'literary' work I might perform.

— Now let me get this straight.

— Is it so difficult?

— Probably not. But let me get it straight. *Plan One* was going to trace the sources of Browning's attitude to Italy?

— Yes, you see...

— Yes, I see. Stop right there. Say no more about *Plan One*. Not yet.

— Why not?

— Let me get *Plan Two* straight. *Plan Two* was going to trace the sources of your attitude to Italy?

— Including my attitude to Browning's attitude, yes.

— Fine, let's include that out for the moment. You had two plans, then. One was the sources of Browning's attitude and one was the sources of yours. Is that right?

— Yes that's right.

— But there was really only one plan, wasn't there?

— How do you see that?

— Sources, you said. Sources. When you were looking into the family tree of imperial attitudes, was Browning not full of these? When you were trying to define the power of an Italian slave, was not that Browning's question? When you wandered all over the Veneto were you not picking up for future reference the — how did you call them? — blue pencils of the cypresses that he had seen for himself in Asolo? Was not your whole agenda shaped by and through Robert Browning?

— The heart of it was what I now completely *knew*. I sat there in Asolo and looked out the fragrant window at that ravine full of flowers and evergreens and up at the distant granite heights of Monte Grappa and down at the stupendous rich plain that is watered by all the Alps and all their daughters, and I knew that suddenly, somehow, I had wrapped all of this up in a big blue silk sack and stuffed it under my arm and run for the hills and now it was mine. It was mine. I would leave but I would take it with me. This was Italy. This was all of it at once, mountain and hill and plain and river and even, from Pen Browning's tower on a clear day, you could see Venice herself and the Adriatic, the watery road to Troy, Byzantium, Jerusalem. This was all of Italy. Europe spilling over the crest of the mountains. Asia lapping at the shore. Africa blowing hot winds up from across the plains by night. It was mine. I was carrying all of our desire, carrying it so tightly it hurt and no one could see it, I supposed, my grandfather, my grandfather, my grandmother, my grandmother, my uncle Mike the day I went off to graduate school took me for the first time in my life to Ferrara's on Grand Street because I should not go away from home for the first time as a man without knowing that I too was an Italian, all of them, all those tears, all that infinite crescendo of Rossini waking me up and knocking me out of my bed every morning and this was it. I had done it.

— And you felt guilty?
— I had succeeded.
— But guilty?
— More *afraid*. Afraid someone would notice. Someone would come tell me I could not have it. But I had it. It was a small revolution, but it was mine. I had been eating for four weeks in Asolo, and one day my chemistry caught up with the food. After that things changed. I began to play with my plans.

He picked up the bibliography. Then he put it down. So much for *Plan One*.

Plan Two was to give up for the moment on the bibliography, forgetting Odysseus and his many cities, his many peoples how they lived, ingenious he, after the fall of Troy, here available in pocket form, two days to Naples, including Pompeii, Herculaneum, Capri, Grotta Azzurra (weather permitting), Sorrento, Amalfi coast, Cassino, full pensione, beverages and extras not included, or any other way you like or are willing to pay for, up to and including the villa in Cortona with swimming pool, olive groves, and the odds-on chance of real Etruscan pottery or even real Etruscans in the ground. And in putting this away, Aldo Manuzio 1520 and the rest of it on the shelf with Ezra Pound, he stood on the terrace ready to follow the second option. My father had come to visit with my aunt, in whom every relation resounds for me, she walks into my house as the queen of the floating island of l'Astoria, and I announce her titles one after another in that redoubling of trumpets that points to the corners of the horizon on state occasions, my Mother's Sister and my Godmother and the Widow of my Uncle Mike, my Godfather, who used to get up out of his coffin and tell me he was tired of being dead, only to get cancer and die at the age of forty-seven all over again, this saga of dreams went on for years in which we kept reopening his little factory in Spanish Harlem, where I used to work in the summer of 1958 and drive to the country house with him on Friday nights listening to *Volare* and *Fever* on the radio, and he would feel better and go back to the factory and then get sick and die again and we wouldn't know whether to sell it or not because he was determined not to be dead, and finally he got better. He had been dead almost twenty-one years the day they arrived in Rome, and I came out to the terrace, while my wife showed them the apartment, and stood there looking out at the Alban Hills and in the clear October Tivoli off to the left where the mountains begin, where my mother's mother, my aunt's mother, was born and once saved their cousin Margaret from drowning in the well, and then my aunt came out into the absolute morning of Italy and saw all of this at once for the first time in her life and began to cry. Of course it was a mirror. Of course you were going to walk straight into it, black shirt or not. This is why you came. *Plan Two*.

Then he picked up the bibliography again. His two plans began to blur at the edges. He would need to face Italy as if he himself were Robert Browning, as if his desires would now require this of him, and his personal research became, plainly and definitively, a general question, as when you are falling and the speed of falling objects is scarcely governed by your pocket watch.

It wasn't, there isn't in any of this, that all-purpose curiosity where you squeeze the orange good and hard and then turn the corner. You take in a great deal that way, a week here and two weeks there, but now he wants to get used to the packages in the stores and to stop seeing pictures everywhere, unable to stay on the bus, is constantly in doubt of his method, but *que voulez-vous?*, being inside the mirror is nothing like being Alice behind the looking glass, because all those neat reversals and crosses and surprises of logic are entirely the artifact of staying home, and this is not home, this is what becomes home only after you have patiently walked around it with a sponge full of acid rubbing off everything until suddenly you can't see much except what time is dinner, which now, once certain neighborhoods had disappeared from the map and he got used to the implied rule that really living in a place was tantamount to dying in it, even if you confidently planned on escaping in one piece, began to turn around in the bar and tell him things, not discoveries exactly, but the opposite of scenery or monuments, the kinds of observations you only notice after hearing them a dozen times. Thus, conversation is mostly lament, politics is a whorehouse, the bureaucracy is a whorehouse, the food is good but is not healthy, if you go abroad (anywhere) the food is terrible. Only places are allowed to be beautiful. People are mostly awful, but persons are, in Rome they say, delicious.

I was not accustomed to feeling delicious. It begins, this part of the story, as a long goodbye on the Spanish Steps, where he has to accept that in giving up the English poets for his protectors, he can no longer profit from their sacrifice and may, despite their extravagant martyrdoms, be required to write his own epitaph in Italy, feed his own delectability into the wind and the waves or the roots of the trees, as in a bad poem of Shelley's, or at least, walking around alone on the Campidoglio at night, come close enough — even where you see the comfortable lights of a priest's study looking in on itself and signalling out across the dangerous air a kind of resigned tenure — to that sensation of heavy crumbling in every direction that has made so many Hollywood fortunes and kept Mr. Gibbon for decades at his desk, because whatever has been done, clearly it needs doing again from this most intimate corner of its own corruption, or because when I speak you hear a tiny gagged and distant insistence inside, as if the broken angel were talking whose arm was carried off by Consul Smith and sold to the Duke of Cheshire who sold it to Mr. Morgan who gave it to the Conte Luigi Palma di Cesnola who had the original reinvented for the Metropolitan Museum of Art on the basis of the usual principles which years later archaeologists from Cornell denounced and taking a plaster cast brought it to Rome and it fitted exactly, and that is when I started hearing Italy, when it began to knit in my joints like grass seeds sprouting and could talk because I am yet again — or am no longer just the mottled fragments of the persistence in — my battered, shipped, chipped, sold, faked, and resold genealogy, so that if I die once more in Italy it will be to haunt it much more accurately than the last time, and when Mr. Gibbon returns he will hear something else singing besides monks, since I knew that all this marble we were, which we had died dragging up that heavy hill, stuck its thumb up out of the ground from forever, as the Italians say, glowing with that self-referring purple which does not allow you to distinguish rage from nobility, and we could kill because we hated what we killed for, just as later we could die for the same reason, splintering over the town in the forms of a thousand altars smoking to our unappeasable righteousness that continued to twitch sarcastically like Jesus in his most obscene moments of exposure ejaculating with horror, kissing the foot of the man wearing the pointed white hat, I could hear Italy now because it was inside me talking, and slowly enough that I could understand the words, which seemed to have no language of preference, but would come seeping into the dream in Latin or French or Italian or Spanish or English or Greek or German or just postcards like tourists loitering in the parsimonious shade of the bus, hardly audible at first, only a trace of green water dripping down his arm in a mildewed corner of the cloister, following him into the delicatessen on Avenue J the Monday morning after the Saturday of his mother's funeral where a girl looked him straight in the eyes in Arabic and offered that way to run off together into it really wouldn't matter what since he had to get the papers and cigarettes and milk and cupcakes for snack back to the house before it was time to take his son to school, slipping over the slates of the walk as precisely that moisture which gives hope to the languages of revolution, that one kind of feeling, philosophers call it *pain* but even this is too pedantic, which really appears on the piazza as itself, not its counter, not its insertion in the system, something irreducible, not fungible, not alienable and convertible into its own opposition, no matter what they do to you afterwards, remains serenely at the end of your gaze into the low ceiling full of bees from a garden you cannot see, recurs, once and for all any time, as the clear refutation, the complete excuse for what you intend to do next, even if it takes, and it did, five thousand years to begin.

Because we are broken. Because the mirror is a lake into which you fell in order that the green things might consume you to begin again. What frivolity taught you to dream of standing on the ground like a mailbox? *He, you, I*, all became without any weaving of the shuttle just the object of the shadow cast by mercury lamps on the Campidoglio: *it. It, that, what, which*, something so blunt has been going on here that though everyone participates no one notices, as if one of those huge

Brooklyn concrete mixers spraying water onto the sand were being praised for its subtlety of operation. By comparison with Paris, this is a neglected project. Those sudden manifestations, those lucid announcements of ruthless pawprinting on the satin walls to commence tomorrow morning at seven sharp, though they are tried, are forgotten before the week is over. *Mussolini Helplessly Reconsiders* would make a good title for a history of Roman tribunes in the hundred and twenty-odd years since the Risorgimento. Beat the drum, the angel is talking:

— We doomed or blessed ourselves, then, the angel said, to a lot of noise, a lot of photographs, a lot of speeches collecting always more echoes than they can convey, thus remaining in the strictest as in the loosest sense inaudible.

Thus Rome. I am going to love Rome when I leave as I now love Paris. Sometimes you will try to find your way from the Piazza Venezia to the Avenue Foch, certain that they ought to be in the same town, but you can't catch that bus, and Rome, tumbling ever so slowly into the ditch, refuses to make any sense at all, so that in the end you don't understand it, you get used to it. The papers are full of mayors raising their arms like Merlin over a project, but no one is, it always develops, allowed to touch the chaos except to straighten the tablecloth, and every conversation seems to draw in little wisps of Revolution, though the only form of this which is still credible here is to keep driving. All the guidebooks, with that resolute knapsack over their heads which I have finally come to recognize as their universal binocular, tell you that you must walk in Rome. Walk 1. Walk 2. Walk 8. As you stumble past the door of the church, the little car trying to park turns suddenly right onto the sidewalk and knocks you over. Or else in the middle of everything you stroll up a hill that seems unaccountably deserted and climb the steep street full of dripping shirts. You keep going but there is no exit, so at the top you must turn around and come down again. Or else, the shops suddenly cease because this is the district of banks or insurance companies or any of the usual file cabinets in what has always been a city of tax gatherers, lawyers, and welfare administrators, where the over-displayed palm trees and globe lamps of the great ministries, like the famous ochre in the afternoons, just barely conceal the permanent boredom of the Romans, who rarely glance at the fountains pretending that fresh water is the meaning of happiness, where the dust and the handbills fly along under the buses, accustomed even in their fairy tales of Pinocchio and Cappuccetto Rosso to an economy of resounding fraud, lies about older lies, teaching the children the heartless rhythm of infection, which has no logical protocols or escape clauses, integrates every single word that's uttered, so that even a promise merely to replace it with swings and sliding ponds one knows will not be honored except in some exquisitely humiliating fashion, as at Villa Torlonia, rented for a peppercorn to Mussolini by a Papal banker, now a park, with all the lavish pavilions sitting in it rotting behind chicken wire, as if to say, well, you know, it could be, perhaps, anyway, and the safest thing is to stay home and put in a new kitchen. The good weather makes you weak. You cough in the sunshine. Every story has already inspired a forgotten encylopedia. The brigatisti can kill anything except the secure recognition that a secret society is a secret society. L'Astoria has swallowed you and emitted you and must send to the *municipio* a document covered with stamps before it can tell you whether in fact you are dead or were born, not that it matters, we are very fertile, answering in a mumble while wiping the counter the epic mystery of the migration, what could it possibly matter if you left or if you came back either? It is always green in the Campagna.

Eventually, almost all of them left. L'Astoria is now a Greek neighborhood. Sunnyside, too, has filled up with airplane immigrants, German technicians and Israeli pediatricians, and more Greeks.

— I wouldn't go back there...

This is my father talking on the phone.

266

— Twenty years in Florida have spoiled me. I wouldn't go back there for any money.

Even now, his friends and coevals, at seventy-nine and eighty, are seeing the light, selling up in Greenpoint or Long Island City, and moving down to Ocala, Beverly Hills, Clearwater, Indian Rocks, Saint Petersburg, Venice, Naples, Dunedin, Orlando.

— So they were right and you were wrong.

— So you might say. You might say I clung to a meaning they had decided to dispense with. Yes, I think it is better to say it that way. I saw the beauty of it, such as it was, but I didn't want them to go. I wasn't finished growing up. I didn't expect to finish so quickly.

There he goes again. He couldn't accept it. This was not love, if they went away from you. If they did this and they told you they loved you at the same time, it was two alternating and opposed polarities. You began to spin. You began to revolve around them like an electron in an accelerator. You began to move very fast and to expect a mighty collision. You began to collide and then you woke up, rewound the tape, and started it all over again.

— So you are suggesting revolution as an image of Obsessive repetition.

That is, I was standing here under the sign of going away. Every day I think of staying, so that when I pick up and clear it out it will not seem like just paying the bill. *It is our politics to leave*. That night, I thought I heard Italy talking in me for just a moment. Afterwards it wouldn't stop. It was nothing like you expected. It was like going to one of the suburbs of Hell where the poets never come, filled with notaries who remember everything. When the philosophers, or whoever they are, raise the flags of Memory and Obsession and the Sacred, they never emphasize enough this part of it, that these are the coffee and cake of accountants and census-takers. Lean very close, and Rome will whisper to you a fifteen-volume anatomy concerning the heroism of lawyers, the eloquence of prisoners rehearsing their cases for years, and when you feel that primeval wrath of the mutilated I felt, you will also learn how straight a staircase it built to the copybook pomposities of Quintilian and Cola di Rienzo.

— This, I suppose, is what they discovered in the masonic lodges, why they painted themselves in togas...

— You mean...? There was an echo on the line from California.

— Yes, I mean that the prestige of Rome and the prestige of Italy are always at war with one another.

— I can't hear you, he said.

— How's this?

— Better. His college was paying for the call.

— Consider. Just when Italy had finally died in the arms of the Jesuits, this is when the English, the Americans, the French took to coming here to learn the dialect of liberty. You see what I mean?

Silence.

— Are you there? I hang up. Fifteen minutes later he calls back.

— What was that about the Jesuits? I think when the satellite goes around China we get cut off.

— Never mind the Jesuits. Did you get my letter?

— No.

— I was telling you about Rome as the pattern of revolutionaries. The repository of liberties, Whigs, Jefferson and Monticello, the debating societies in Lyons.

— Oh. So what are they up to now?

Every historian grows old waiting for the right moment on the telephone. In the end, you give up every line but the one you industriously scramble on the page, calling long distance like a falling star into a translation you invent, appearing in Berlin or Buenos Aires for the wrong reason fifty years later, something you read over the shoulders of the person under your pillow who is holding up, you see it but it doesn't seem to matter, a different book altogether, as if you had finally laid eyes on, rather than supposed or moralized, the fluorescent cells of dividing language, sentences that grow and peel away from one another in the vivacious slime, springtime on the beaches of Long Island Sound, little tidal pools full of mosquitoes and tadpoles, and had been granted, the way a clam might for once get to imagine an alley cat, some glimpse of the natural history that would not have known of politics or first editions, except as minor taxonomies, but would, will, display a furious neurology of words and wishes, the thing you lived in as a pool with all these professors from the lyceum and Baudelaire, a turn like the season when all of you, no doubt, will blow away with last year's inedible stubble, although it seems, despite advances and enlightenment, they are still breeding orators in Naples, growing them in their epic of fish in love, with castanets, stamping their heels on the ground in a fair approximation of a Spanish dancer defining the motive for killing a Dominican friar, plunging ahead as they do, as you do, flooding the fountain with *aranciata*, carrying the miraculous painting of Saint Francis receiving the stigmata right to the door of the restaurant where once again, seriously, you take the hand of your colleague and start to tell him how only Robert Browning got far enough into it to extract the meaning of a fried artichoke but that even he can only be read properly by someone who is willing, like Henry James, to spend a whole lifetime taking notes against his plain prevision that every staircase down comes out on the landing of yet another long descent, *facilis descensus Averni*, it's easy to go all the way to the bottom, possibly, but, more probably, less so than when Virgil made the claim, since now, in addition to the fatigue of it you are carrying with you a huge sack filled with self-advertising novelties, things you keep trying to leave on a shelf somewhere, like Alice's marmalade, but always seem to belong a little lower along this astonishing belly of re-sounding adverbs, shimmering like Mozart in the second violins, or rising at a turn of the dial as the face of your cousin, your old friend from Thirty-Ninth Street who drives a truck, here singing Puccini to a nightclub full of ply-wood palm trees and fifty chorus girls dressed in school blouses and nun's wimples, a huge howl of the vengeful past filling its chest and roaring out at you from the soprano who needs orthodonture, *'Mi tradì!'*, as if you fi-nally would have to recognize in the Revolu-tion exactly the reason it was never repeated here, that this *is* what it repeated, pure and simple, goes on repeating, catching up even Napoléon's gesture in some absolute pessi-mism of a damp cave, though caught in its turn by Napoléon's reply which you meet in the Pope's museum, hissing along the implacably fresh gleam on the tombs of Constantine's mother and daughter, so much as to say with dead Napoléon or Nero's fifty-foot basin of this same astonishing porphyry in the next room, *Fire made me what I am tomorrow*, nobility in this stone rising and sinking at once like an

271

absolute slice through any possible theory and in the end just continuing to start again all the time, as if nothing else that could ever happen could touch this mastery of the bowels of the earth, professor. Professor?

— You can't wake him up. He isn't sleeping.

— I was wondering about the price of this book.

The traveler who stops no less than the one who starts considers money afresh and must. The possibilities of confusion are instructive. Our professor's modest spiral ramble down his own gullet here illustrates this eloquently. Money is language you hold in your hand. It represents, as language does, things it really has nothing to do with. It aims to overcome the problem by printing a picture of Bernini or Raffaelo or Queen Elizabeth or Benjamin Franklin or, as on the one-dollar bill, God Almighty vacationing in masonic Egypt, in whom we trust.

Succeeds this linkage?

— Depends, one replies, but mostly the answer is *sort of*. That is, you really have no choice except to beg the question in the airplane. If you trust in God, does that mean you go to church? Can a communist spend money in England? Impossible questions except for logicians whose supper has been provided already. Our professor has the same trouble. He wants to look at spectacular Italy — which, you might say, is money as sculpture — as if it represented real Italy, or, at any rate, an Italy to which his ancestors belong, but it doesn't do so, except sort of, because after all what *is* Italy anyway except its representation of itself *as* Italy, instead of as a pile of rocks and rivers or someone's vivid dead jack-in-the-box grandfather singing *Torna a Sorrento*? And when he says he thinks he hears real Italy talking inside him, I run my finger down the list of significant noises to learn whether what he hears does not, in the end, correspond more perfectly than anything else to the profile of the gurgle that arises when, walking along a brilliant spring road surrounded by almond blossoms, he begins to drown. That is, internal speeches tell you things, but what things are these?

The blue cornflowers blow in the night wind. A man in a navy blue pinstripe suit gets out of the midnight-blue Mercedes-Benz. The lobby is agog over the theft of the duchess's blue diamond. In the bar, the blue-eyed blonde at the piano plays the blues.

— I had the feeling something was going on at this convention no one told us about, says the professor from Illinois at the reception desk in the hotel to another professor, from Texas, standing under the pink marble bust of Vespasian.

— You mean a message scribbled in the air? the Texan says.

— Something of the kind.

Our professor is listening. The government of Italy has called a meeting in Rome to discuss the image of Italy in the United States. Professors came from all over the USA to Rome. After a day or two, it began occurring to them they were not, as is usually the case, alone together. Everywhere one came upon the coded blue stripe and implausible broad-shouldered grin of the American spy. Hardly a surprise, after all. Italy is an occupied country. If an American comes here, where is he going?

— Don't be melodramatic, he says to his friend from Illinois. Doesn't it make sense if Washington likes to stay alert to what Rome is looking for among American professors of Italian, from professors of, or aren't they, double identity?

I would like to ask him, I went to sleep and had a dream in order to find him and ask, if either of us was a professor of double identity. However, neither of us seems to know. Even when you come at the Revolution this way, like an historian backwards, it's the same trouble all over again. This can be expressed in the Formula of Self-Representation:

> The problem with your double identity is that he doesn't have any way to keep track of me so that they can't give us what she needs from it.

This is so precise that perhaps it needs a little explanation. I can't for example, say *you mean?* to it without first waiting around until a dream appears and, second, he can subject it to narration, suggestion, projection, so that even ordinary political questions when they arise cannot be considered to be taken in by the so-called first person until he has consulted the miraculous travesty of my doubled identity as the colleague from Princeton who did not show up or the man in the Mercedes-Benz who did, a protocol of self-consultation prosaically, not to say exquisitely, ambassadorial in its correctness, its high formality, which of course, is why *I* went to bed early in Proust, since this research has been going on for a century at least, directly in consequence of the enormous weight that descended upon and splintered for good and all such ordinary high talents as those of the Marquis de La Fayette and Vittorio Alfieri and Henri Beyle, to name a vivid handful, by means of the new practice requiring a person to speak, as the saying goes, *for himself*, as if such a creature could securely be said to exist, as if one did not only speak in a kind of hollow echo, as to Piranesi alone in the *cloaca maxima*, of what mobs leave behind, *we* all kings and popes now, being required, as the Romans said of the defunct, *to go to the many* before opening his mouth to say good morning, since once you speak of self-representation at all, my love, you find yourself on the bridge of the channel steamer along with England and France and all other objects of representation churning the water into a complete unreachability of its own offerings, and you begin devising these new methods of self-geography, which may require a lot of hopeful haruspication before it is possible to answer questions that, some while back, no one even thought to ask, or so they say, when the pronouns slept inside their functions like gardener's tools and had not begun to break in the hands of the avid archeologists let out from school into the June air beating helplessly its paper wings against the black slate of the Rosetta Stone.

— And so, your honor, in conclusion, my client has been led to a discovery of very considerable importance, and I say this in full recognition of the reverence due your worship and of equally my own unworthiness to expound the rather difficult implications in this turn of events, which does not allow a category for either his examination or (even) his specification, since — and I think your honor will recall without a tiresome recapitulation of what I have found it, I confess, extremely difficult to comprehend in the first instance, during those long weeks in which we read into the record the Collected Works of Anthony Trollope and Ralph Waldo Emerson — my client has put forth what I was forced to recognize as a classic if novel application of the provisions in the

276

First Amendment guaranteeing freedom of worship, the argument that it has been his re-ligion's primary, perhaps only, tenet that sleep is waking and waking sleep, forcing us to ac-knowledge that at least from the point of view of this little-understood and, it must be remem-bered, vastly-unpopular sect, the variety of dreams does not verify their dreary quotidian reality nearly so thoroughly as, on the other side of this startling panorama, does the reso-nant harmony of the law signify its ontological status as phantasm, or as my client maintains, airy nothing.

This elegant defense was entirely success-ful. The question of identity's number passed into the archives with George Washington's white horse, and he was left standing outside the courtroom, dreaming, as who should say, of a rich cappuccino in the company of those familiar great bellies and forceful measured smiles and red sashes or plum jackets or lapel rosettes or little strips of green thread in the left cuff, that had been waiting, as he knew, all along for him to come to the point, since it is required you see it for yourself first.

— Kappy birthday to you, they sang.

They gave him a book to read in which all the h's and s's were written as k's. This seemed to make what might otherwise have seemed dull exposition into expressions that evoked great emotion, as if the mere mutation of the spelling had caused the book a deep wound, a lasting ache of regret. His birthday had been recoded and he now belonged to that select society of people whose mothers had died in giving them life, though he hesitated, despite the handsome generosity they offered at the lemon-smelling sideboard, to sign the document, since it would imply the more or less total recategorizing of what he had been for forty-three years, removing l'Astoria where you may say it is anyway, definitively under the nutritious water of expectation and providing, on the one hand, a perfectly reasonable way to conceive the slump of memory, still, on the other, a rather icy stiffness to the morning hours of middle life. He needn't have worried, after all, too much, since they had no trouble in taking these delicate waverings for marks of exclusion, and they tabled the vote, leaving him for the indeterminable time being with his Etruscanate text to read, so strongly reminiscent as it was of the hooded brethren and the burning cross, a clear case how safe it is not to lean too hard upon your qualifications but to turn aside, blowing your nose into the hanky bearing Groucho Marx's motto, *I Refuse to Join Any Club that Will Have Me as a Member*, or, on laundry days, simply, *Waiter There's a Fly in My Soup*.

Among the pilgrims from the Italian Heritage Club of San Diego, there was a pleasant retired dentist who said a word to his wife in Sicilian. The lady guide thought this hilarious.

Many of the guests called themselves Cavaliere or Commandante.

— They want love, smiled the under-secretary for cultural relations, showing a precision as sharp as his barber's, but what, I wondered, can these diplomats do? How much can they love us and still have time for business? Can they persuade the professor-guide not to tell us what we already know or the professoressa-guide not to giggle at the Sicilianisms? The mayor raises a toast to the emigrants. A good friend of mine from Queens, a person whom the Repubblica Italiana has ennobled, sings *Fratelli d'Italia*. Presents are exchanged. It is easy to imagine that what we want is not love exactly but trophies for sure. You conjure them up in Poughkeepsie and Santa Barbara explaining the beauties of the pots and rocks to invidious friends, though secretly relieved to avoid the rigors of these allegorical operas, simply stopping at the Italian store for olives and prosciutto on their way elsewhere, while he, likewise, lies down with a cold and takes another nap. For the pressure of the situation must eventually make us, we feel it on our mounting birthdays, prematurely second children, restless in daylight and suddenly sleepy like falling boulders.

From us these people want not love but money. Tourism, shoes, wine, porcelain. The complementary desires set up a familiar situation, where the girls at the Porta Pinciana do a thriving business, and every proud emigrant's grandson finds himself brandishing his degrees and his rosy cheeks before a calculating courtesy that rather frequently sends him home with a chill or an infection. Mutual misconstruction. The official welcoming committee is only looking for fair exchange. They have all become Americans here in Italy, while we have been waxing our handlebar moustaches for decades and have now come hoping to meet singing waiters who died in the war.

— It aren't so easy, he said.

— What aren't? you said.

— To pick the Italy in question.

— Who are it?

— The Gramscists, he said, they that entitled the such as what you are that didn't went along them ocean.

— Yes, I love them Gramscists, he said, turning on the television. Pippo Baudo, a man as seriously enthusiastic as Perry Como, was introducing some young, equally enthusiastic, deaf juggler to a cheerful audience while behind him a chorus of other young entertainers, all winners of a national talent search, were humming the theme song of the mass competition in which they had all reached that level immediately preceding the antepenultimate round of eliminations.

— Why are you watching that drivel? he said.

— Yes, it's terrible, he said.

— Then tell me why.

— Everybody watches it, he said, that's why.

— No, not the Gramscists, he said.

— So how can they be Gramscists if they don't watch what everybody watches? he said.

The car was dependably arriving when arose then like the sun on Passion Sunday the purple image of a certain Italy of the dead and the living, a blood-washed avalanche of confusion in which you found, at an angle to the street, a door inside which all was food and order and your cousins to whom you cling like a barnacle, the one word of connection you, as in their own astringent catechism, could take as still not anatomized beforehand and dismissed, out of which it might at last appear how raw all of it was, how ready to be made-something-of once again, but something else this time, quite as conceivably yours as anyone's, the road at last opening here, the way it always will in North America, onto nothing more than you were ready to paint quickly and boldly on the meadows, not that it could be easy exactly but that it could be spring, that you had shed your grandfather like a peeled tomato and your mother slipped away like the amorous bark to find in your roots the way to touch your baby's fingers, so you walked into the contractor's supply-yard which is Rome, all blocks of incompletion, with an annotated napkin in your fist outlining the project of a Christian Science Vatican, because, as the afternoon clouds come up, the blankness of the Bronx or Cleveland late on Sunday descends, the quivering emptiness, the orchestra reaching a climax like ectoplastic toothpaste, from which Americans have always known how to draw the spiritual elephants of optimism and speculation, radiating like laughter from that newspaper article where the art professors complain about the ruining of the Sistine Chapel and you reply how useful it is of the Pope to do this job for you, eradicating Michelangelo in the interests of a Holy Year booming with supplicants.

Then at last the funeral ends as the next group enters the church weeping and singing *Yes I Shall Arise*, and you go home to your new faraway cousins with their incredibly precise collections of names and dates and faces, their avid comparative sociology, their adequate sense of Hannibal and Cato as points of reference like Ulysses S. Grant and James Fenimore Cooper, their television sets the size of refrigerators, to discover that they who stayed here were also broken, just as much as you were, broken differently but broken all the same.

— In other words, you don't know.

— In other words, every meal we have is a banquet of survivors.

— Spare me the turgid eloquence.

— I'm glad you asked that question.

— It wasn't a question, was it?

— It is now. What is turgid eloquence anyway?

— *You* are asking?

— So I'm answering. Look, it is the an-
tidote to what we have been drinking in the
water. We have been radiated by newspaper
photographers.

— You mean it's bullshit.

— No. I mean it's determination. Look. At
that table is my father's uncle who fought in
two wars and was imprisoned during the second. His daughter whose husband was shot
before their son was born. That son, my age,
now goes on Sundays and holidays four or five
times a day to make sure the *malavita*, to
whom he does not pay protection, have not
been sabotaging his trucks. His cousin was a
prisoner of war in England for three years.
When I asked him what it was like, he said:

— Too foggy.

— So you answer suffering with speeches.

— No. You stand on the hill and you see
the wind blow from the four corners of the
earth. You turn away from the fragrant man
stepping out of the scented limousine with the
bangled widow just behind. No. You have been
wounded. You look at the great mother at the
table with her hair pulled back into a royal
silver braided knot. My grandmother was a
duchess of this gray hair. One day after her
husband got sick, I was walking through the

electric factory where all of us worked. In the room where ladies tie the wires into switches and screw them shut, sitting in rows at long wide wooden tables like shallow bins, I found among these busy hands a little round huddled old immigrant woman in a soiled smock, and this was my grandmother. It was like finding the Queen of England in a cage at the zoo.

— Why must you say *duchess, queen*?

— And what can I call her? And what were we left? You go read the sociology book and the political science book and the survey of migrations like swarming termites. What were we to them? What room was there in that smock for what we were to one another?

So he sits peeling chestnuts patiently among the cousins, while the children race wildly in and out of the kitchen garden where our recollections are finding each other and tangling like vines, the old uncle hugs the fireplace even in springtime, caught in an apprehension that the little ones scatter across the floor with the orange rind, the reduction to sentences at the age of ninety that a long-pursued purpose can assume, not in the least bit clear what any of it is going to have meant, and not concerned with that, because it is the morning after the funeral, your mother is in the ground with the gardenias, here is your father's cousin telling a story of your grandmother saying to her on the phone from America fifty years ago — I have never seen you but

I love you and if I don't see you in this world
I will see you in the next world.

Because what we are doing is only springtime, Italy stepping gingerly across the mined
vineyard where we were standing awash in
tears.

— So your grandiosity...

— Is pathetic. Is a slow pan-shot in Sunnyside, 1954, across a confirmation table full of
hams and olives, rolls and salads, a thousand
years of starvation. Is a voice whispering out
the window of an airplane.

— Is rather given to exaggeration.

— No. Ignores the convenience of police.

It wasn't that a real sociology wouldn't tell
you things you ought to face, the administra-
tive calculations of so many emigrants equals
so many points in the labor supply equals the
following approximation to subsistence wage
attainable in Basilicata by 1910, in addition, but
see on this appendix B, the rising curve of
remittances in US dollars, Australian dollars,
Canadian dollars, pesetas and scudos from
Latin America, with its sustained effect upon
the balance of payments and projected invest-
ment in heavy equipment, always to be considered against expected requirements in the
infantry, all of which you could draw into a
steady rough equivalence with the labor market
abroad in railroads, locomotives, steel, coal, ag-
ricultural expansion, canals, roads, so that you
can't, he wouldn't, deny the possibilities in an

epic economics, which could show the ball roll out of the mountains in Abruzzo and, shuttled by a program of decisions as many-toothed and many-headed as Cerberus the Dog of Hell, tin-tinnabulate along the rails into California or the Caserma dei Carabinieri like a roaring tunnel where it doesn't stop, since, shooting as your constant, precipitation is all, where movement keeps the map glittering and, leaving us at a picnic in Alley Pond Park, April 1954, gingham tablecloth in the snapshot and a great gassy jug of Pepsi-Cola where your simultaneous algorithmic vision of our laboring dissemination would require no more than its own sparse logic to give it light and allow a full portrait of our eyes in the glazed chiaroscuro, ready to be happy, preoccupied with the possible boiling-over of the coffee on the charcoal fire, just, alas, to the left of the margin in the photograph, it doesn't pause at all, despite the horror of Jacobin theologians standing on the dais where the Pope says mass, the shooting goes on, the motion is general and, if it turns out generally catastrophic, that seems more a kind of resonance-effect from this point of view than it can some march of saints into a Winter Palace, seems a field-painting, a wind again at seed-time, a rise in temperature, and a fall of rain.

— So, to put it flatly, you are no better off than a Jacobin.

— Than Tocqueville, if I could do what I suggest. But I make no claim to that.

— He refrains partly out of modesty, do I think?

— No, you stop yourself because they are the children of a thousand eradications, because in the end you have nothing to carve on a stone but the memory of birdsong, which you have followed in and out of Paris and Rome like a bounty hunter after a Nazi archaeologist.

— And when?

— Yes. And when you slipped into the countryside, there they all continued, not the same as ever but, more to your surprise, changed, and changed like you, they had sometimes found what you had all been looking for, and, though it didn't come any more cheaply here, also it didn't fail them except in the ways you already knew.

— You mean the houses got too big or too far apart and the daughter married a man from the Veneto.

— And did not give up her painting altogether, but kept changing her mind.

— Those were puzzles. When we were there ten years ago, the first time and only for two days, they showed us *The Good Death* which had won a prize, angels battling demons and leading the soul safely out of its body as the relatives wept. It was hard to imagine giving this theme a prize in 1977. As to its having been painted at all, the girl was young, the town was small. Now, pleased that I recalled it, they showed me her other work. An art student's pilgrimage, trying everything. I thought she must finally have settled for what she did best, a sort of crystallized landscape with churches, where *The Good Death* is included, but inside, so the painter no longer has to show it. Afterwards, I found her, I found them, doing what we are doing, working and getting on with it, two children, a little more of everything each year.

Now you can't ask, did she die a good death? She escaped like a bird. I could write about her forever, but you wouldn't know her in that, she would only be a Mother, which is as if to say, you are a European, part of the deal, passionately, but you only know her by inference, and what can you possibly infer here? In the end, we are defeated by the nobility of monuments, even when they are postcards. So your twitter only passed along for him to find himself almost able to hear someone else, his second cousin's second son, discovering in his own delighted recognition of a certain dancing speculation in the eyes often hailed the same way in his own at that age, but it's elusive and evasive by definition, will refuse to be nominated even an acolyte at the altar of Hannibal, much less Bishop of Enthusiasm, will only sit still for being felt in the passage of prepositions and the liturgy of adverbs, because it is a fugitive species, content always with less, so long as that little remaining cannot be photographed even in the vestigial likenesses of nouns.

— You can't express what can't be expressed, you mean?

— But I can slip it into your hand like a relay.

— What would it be?

— A bar of soap sealed in plastic. You know, a package of what isn't there.

— Or a package of what touches you secretly, the old brand of teabag.

— Even though you can't know what it is for me?

— One can guess. In a shower of unlikeliness, there is one good probability.

— Gradually, you gave up everything except the meals they piped directly into your stomach. She looked at the world from behind the black shoulder of God. In other silences you remembered every birthday and every nurse's earrings, but there was this astonishing roar of the making of things, things you had come never to notice anymore, that somehow were now the only honey in the hive, and to these you submitted, into them you went and over them you looked weeping at the calendar photograph outside the window, Connecticut steeples and golden domes, green trees, red trees, yellow, brown, and then the sentimental snowfalls, all in order, which I only imitated by living here in Italy inside a cellophane of incomprehension that would allow me occasionally to think I was standing on a balcony of pity where you might have touched me without my knowing it, pilgrim dreams of benediction adrift in every stirring of the air, as on a day in hot September, among the palms in the empty Orto Botanico, I kept supposing you standing with us, which I put down to the Florida foliage, but the next day I heard that just then Bill had died in America, so I might, given the reason, have supposed a sort of Gala Death, something they could fresco on a ceiling, great reunions of l'Astoria and trips to Rome on gamma rays.

— So you see your language barrier high as death?

— Not high. Absolute. You learn the language. You cannot learn a remembered language.

— When you passed into Italian, the gods had gone.

— Something like that.

— You had only attitudes, you could become a statue.

— I thought so. That's the familiar fallback position. Even that you can't defend. He has to draw a great diagram in red chalk on acres of vellum, showing the dotted lines of armies and the unbroken ruts of trade conspiring to write *him*, because he can bear neither to tear everything down nor to go on supposing him-

self simply the aging function of market research, pinned for the moment to a plastic
board, but wants to feel, to polish, the heft of
death and deposit in words as they tumble
down the chute into the cellar. And he couldn't
see anything of this. Every monument was too
familiar. How could you believe in this magnificence when it was all rotted and broken? The
great basilica seemed like a bank dreaming of
its own photograph in the newspaper. The
Campo dei Fiori was a scene in twenty movies.
Something gets worn off when you look at it
too much. There were no monuments here,
only their stereotypes, only their reinventions.

— Research ought to be a surprise, yet
you're never happy when it is. But what of
those voices you heard talking inside you?

— And who were they in the end? The lady
selling flowers. I was just a little further ahead
than when I found Napoléon's tomb. Italy, I
thought then, was my symptom. Now it had
become my disease.

— You said you would die into it.

— It didn't want me dead. It wanted me
dying. It? She? He? *There*. Can *there* be a pronoun? *There* is. *There* are. *There* wanted me
starving on *prosciutto, ricotta, crema sarda,
venegazzù.*

— This is what you get for reading the
money.

— You end up not getting the point?

— No, the opposite. It tells you everything

291

and leaves you with a chronic ill-being, just under the threshold where doctors can find it, just enough to ache and fill you with sleepy doubts and raw nostalgias that become permanent conditions, since even as you inspect this greedy green litter of failures and thefts and murders all flattened out for you in the baroque sculpture of the *autostrada*, you know that it will, the minute you leave it, start singing its choruses and serenades, gleaming and drawing you back, coming at you in the solicitations of belief, everyone will want to believe the frauds you will only have to attack in order to give them a fresh life.

Experts agree this dialogue qualifies the writer for Italian citizenship. He had learned not only how to hear what wasn't said but to discriminate, among a thousand intoxicating essences, the subtle flavor of return, the aroma you know perhaps as urine in the beer or cheese among roses, but which Italy reverses, teaching you not the theology, but the very odor, of hope in the rotting carcass, babies born in butcher shops, intricate dilapidations complacently caressed by socialists as excuses for new empires of construction — in other words, what it has always been easy to call decadence, but what, after sixteen hundred years of triumphant practice, surely deserves recognition as the philosophy to which even despair is sentimental, a sort of bottomless optimism that even the most extravagant American preachers have never had any need to imagine, that looks inside itself not to find all the great sages at a Concord seminar but merely the firm reassurance that not too much in there has yet come alive, that though we may be young and beautiful or old and gentle we have never stopped being made out of stone, can still crush cheap hard fruit between our fingertips, still scrape the ruminable moss off the venomous cave, still smile at Japanese and Germans and Americans without it ever crossing their minds what we think of their food or their wives, still dream of carrying ourselves like salmon far away to die or like Chinese eggs to crack and fry on the slate sidewalk of Trowbridge Street. For, make no mistake, my grandparents told me to be Italian only because they knew I was already indelibly an American. Had they seen me here talking this way, they would have laughed at how clever I was without supposing it possible I could in any way mean any of these things, since I was their millenary omelette, their pearly-toothed monkey, their unimaginable release into a flood of golden tigers leaping out of windows, I was to carry their recollections like a bibliography, but I was hardly to come here and be infected in the Forum with the bacillus of servitude or to sing a hoarse ballad of dead lawyers. And of course I knew these things. But, you know, I was something worse than disillusioned. It was not in the program what I was. I was simply lost among the dead there in America. You couldn't suppose that? You would think, no, this is the cemetery, here, Rome, Italy, Europe. But they traveled tighter than they knew. They brought all the ghosts with them to New York. Their graves — go see them in Long Island, in Westchester — are rippling like oiled muscles. They have stabbed themselves into the lawn like daggers the size of the silver Chrysler Building with the hook-beaked eagles at the corners. And they give off their polluted light, you can't escape it, you go blind with it on the Tappan Zee Bridge. No, they didn't mean to do this. They meant to fade into the fescue like fodder, just as the gospel advises, but they didn't know how, they had no acid, America had no acid, powerful enough for that. For they had become everything Italy was supposed to be, but without the choking rubble and godawful mess that in Italy always remind you how long a ruler you need to measure a lie, they became the subterranean Italy of the etymological dictionary with its toes in India and its cock laid out across Greece like a slender marble salami, with a pair of eyes blinking away the sunrise water of New York Harbor as they looked about at the raw new fury, dignified as they were by all they had either almost been or never been, it didn't matter which, and sanctified by having had to leave it behind, and, further, endowed with the prestige of martyrdom by having lost America, first discovered by them, before arriving in it, so that they were from the start great gods and filthy crucified beggars all at once, and was it any wonder that when they died America suddenly became for me what Italy had been for them, impossibly full of prepossession? — and that Rome, after I wandered in it half a year, revealed itself to me as plain as a glass of water in Springfield, Illinois? There was no Italy here any more. Not that great Italy of the double-dealing pope and the suicidal opera house. They had taken it away and made it better and planted it like a dogwood tree in Valhalla, County of West-chester, State of New York. Compared with that glistening mystery I knew as a boy and put in the ground with my mother, this, this Rome, this old welfare-distribution-center, smelled of oaktag and binder's glue. If this is Italy, I thought, I must be an Italian.

— Now I followed you right till the end there.

— I mean, I must be a fugitive. I must be running away from it.

— Even though it isn't here?

— I'm here. Italy is in America.

— Then what *is* here?

— My guess is they themselves can't decide. They know it's dead, or gone, or something. Naturally, they don't like to say so, and I think it never occurs to them what really happened. They blame everything on Mussolini or

Togliatti or DeGasperi. But the real culprit was my grandfather.

— Or the hero.

— Aeneas, whatever he was. The one who took the sacred fire and the household gods away. In Italian New York or California, they burn candles to an abstracted Leonardo who sings Bellini and dances the tarantella. Italy for the first time has become one thing, a wine-dark sheet of watered silks, the object of simple devotion so intense that the actual Italy, where everything is doubtful, and almost certainly a reproduction, just disappears in the radiance we bring.

— So how does this make you an Italian?

— It turns out that this invented Italy, which drove me and became the mark of my insincerity, since I could see through it just as much as I could not escape being its clay puppet, is the same one they have lost here.

— So you are Italian because you are insincere?

— About Italy. Just like one of the locals. The great glass shadow of America descended on us all. We became what they call here *ceti medi*, the emerging classes, not poor not rich, not bourgeois, not even petit bourgeois, just the automobile mechanic with the marble floor in the kitchen or his son the grammar school teacher who takes the two-week package tour to Scotland in July.

— Not much of a Revolution.

— Maybe not. Maybe it's nothing to give the gods leukemia. That is what we did. We were less bold than the butchers of the Faubourg Saint-Antoine, more patient, less articulate, but I think more deadly. The effect seems thorough enough to me, when you cannot stroll down the via Montenapoleone in happy Milano or admire the cornices of Palazzo Madama, where the Senate of united Italy sits in peace, without turning and finding a fellow with a machine gun visibly estimating the amount of damage you may be planning to inflict. This slow death is messy and confusing, but it does not stop its operation.

— What is its operation?

— You go to church and you only have two children and the priest cannot convince you to have more. You are aware of the money in the bank even as you are sweating in the barn.

I don't know, I still have dreams of Christians, but I have come to see that death is only the name for when it begins to grow dark in your sleep and sadness occludes the depths of light, and I will sleep now a very long funeral that may last forever, which will open to me, like a flaking eggshell, a second skin, not on the great monuments, which always seem either too new or too old or too noticed, but on whatever offers itself as not looked at for, or not meant to reveal, this quality, the gleaming page with the photograph of the young beauty or the young beauty in the brown picture on the headstone being only the expected or Edgar Allan Poe versions of a universal rain I keep finding myself in at the tobacconist's, in a crowded streetcar, and I can't quite get used to it, not that I have forgotten the secret of how to be cheerful and not that I have grown wiser either, but that, to all my doubled images and fractured histories there has been added this great moisture, this grief which is all scirocco and dark clouds on the mountains, filling me, I can't really understand why, with a direct desire to summon flying sprites and roaring diesels like a magician, to portray this Italy I see from my terrace, this long fireworks display of disappearance, as if too much history had jaded me, nauseated me as it can and then slain me with unembarrassed fishmongering of dead and dying helpless creatures, the crack of the hand on the slave's teeth, then waking me up again, so that I had paid like Oedipus, who knew his mother too well, and could no longer look at a heap of acorns or a cube of tufa cut like candy without hearing the low choked murmur of ragpickers lamenting the garbage. Happy Easter. Because this fraudulent Italy of ours, this bible much studied by folklorists and family counselors, burdened and marked and soaked us while we were waiting for the Sixth Avenue train, filled our fingers like stamping pads. We could touch nothing without staining it with the blood of ancestors whose names we didn't even know how to discover, so that

when we arrived in Beverly Hills, the swimming pool was full of old ladies in black
dresses. You might say *I*, but they would say
he, which means *you* (as the grammars explain), or *you* which means *we* (as they don't
explain), and a third faucet running Coca-Cola
that you installed in order to make it easier to
get through your study of real estate law or
the metaphysics of Wallace Stevens without
ever needing to get up off your big fat ass
rapidly developed a sort of miraculous reputation, as if it could restore youth or cure cancer,
and the house gradually spilled over with cousins and nieces and nephews who treated you
with the profound tenderness we reserve for
our own recollections of pleasure, whatever it
is we possess most entirely without question,
confronting you in your glossy studio like the
glare of the window with the sad smile that
sooner or later appears in every exile's bathroom mirror when he sees how all he fero-
ciously escaped he ran away from only because
he had never found a way to lose himself in it
at home and, thinking himself free of it for
good, finds in Rapallo or Trieste that it has
begun ever so delicately to tickle the back of
his neck, has at last allowed him to taste the
intimate sensations that continuously ripple off
the local names for ice-cream sodas in Denver,
or the salt of tears in coffee or the smell of
your aunt at the grocer's, opening your skin
as a terrain without maps and revealing in

every dream the mere silver wrapping of a gift
you do not open except to fall into it, but do
not write me any letters about how you kept
this from happening by pretending that it was
all an illusion brought on by careless use of
stimulants, since I have myself only just this
morning emerged for a few hours' liberty from
the palazzo where, all day long, they come for
my signature on heavy creased sheets of paper
that bear the interminable record of all the
little things you did and loved before the moment, in leaving, you exempted them from the
rule of the wind and endowed them with the
interesting stress-lines that belong to evidence
I am now forced to read very attentively,
against the moment of the oath in the tennis
court or the trial you know perfectly well must
repeat itself, this time no doubt without reporters present, but must take the form in your
new age of a million hints concealed in the
electric bill or the sentence of death coded in
the classified ads no one can read but you,
because this is a new kind of Revolution,
brother, in which the *ancien régime* may
spring into existence tomorrow on the beach
at Fregene or like a glory of rose petals cascading out of a window onto Forty-Seventh
Street precisely known to one person as the
announcement that all these years of speculation and wandering within the parentheses of
guided tours and annual bonuses had not carried fruitlessly this other possibility of turning,

with a grinding roar displacing mortar and beetles below, and revealing itself as a single stone, a part now coherent because we have decided to put an end to all that, my friend, which is where this flight is landing, and one is familiar with those famous tearful scenes of revisiting the big stinking room at Ellis Island or the innocuous spring breeze over the Lager, but you must not worry that we are going to rip you down the middle like a bank note chosen at random by the counterfeit police, because, really, we have gone beyond that now, our only interest being how to control the flow of traffic, avoiding the equal disasters of under-utilization and of insane mobs squeezing into the cloister together, old people dropping dead in the Borgia apartments because there is no air, and this crisis of swollen parts, this open-air surgery that so worries you, has to be seen in the context of the unending battle we are forced to wage against confusion and emptiness, our natural desire, which you certainly share, not to see the words in the dictionary follow into the mist all those things they used to mean.

Here had we arrived before the great garlanded arch at the end of the Revolution which was also its beginning, the moment in which our bodies began to glow in the dark like Elizabeth's and Robert's, Pen's, Napoléon's, my mother's, all the pretty little horses. I had become responsible for everything. I had become the penis of everything. Like Pen I had erected a tower. Like Robert I felt an equal propulsion of guilt and of anger. We were none of us Revolutionists. Instead we were, stupendously, the Revolutionized. We had had it written across us ninety ways to Sunday.

(Is it over?)

(Is what over?)

(The Revolution.)

(You mean can we come out?)

(Yes. Is it safe to come out?)

— We wished to be Revolutionists. For what purpose otherwise had we been born angry?

— So what were you doing under the quilt?

(No. Stay where you are.)

(Who is that talking?)

(I don't know. The doorbell rang. I heard it.)

— You mean you had gone back.

— I had returned. I had spoken with them. I had spoken with the gods of Revolution. I had seen the Titans of Anger. I had seen the blocks of marble that fell on them working. I had broken bread with barons and countesses.

— And bishops?

— No. Every research has its boundaries.

— So you had returned.

— Yes, and I had interviewed the Revolutionists of Childhood. They were just as I thought they would be.

— Meaning?

302

— Meaning, they were me. I knew all about it hiding under the bed on Thirty-Ninth Street. It might just as well have been a ditch in Campania with the soldiers going by.

— You understood Revolution and Death?

— No. No, no, no. That was never our problem. I understood Revolution and *Victory*. I understood what it is to fight in a Revolution knowing that even when you win you do not win.

— You lose?

— No, you win but you do not win.

— Who is the priest now?

— You win, that is, according to your capacity. If you are a slave, and then you win the Revolution, you are a slave who has won the Revolution.

— Meaning?

— Meaning very little has changed.

— One thing has changed.

— Yes?

— Now you are free to go if you like.

— Exactly.

And I woke up of course into another dream, realizing at last with a resigned caress of the guidebook, pages by now softer than skin, that the only people who ever really came to grips with our trouble were the Futurists, men of my grandfathers' generation, who wished to blow up the Pope and to shoot paintings with bazookas, at the same time that through a fog of mustard gas I could see that this could never be done that way, for the excellent reason that dreams are the subtlest of essences, finer and more treacherous than incense, it being only anyway too colorfully imaginable what would happen if you were to set about a program of these outrages, how you would make heroes everywhere who slipped away during the siesta, later to die protecting statues from not being allowed to go on dissolving into the grotto, a stalactology of dreams that exists all over the world, people dying of Italy like the plague in Leningrad and Toronto, despite the bracing climate, o no, as I was able from the landing to count the flights above and below me only knowing how delusive a finitude I might compile, since you could walk into one of those walls for ten years without finding an empty room, the crowd of the sound-asleep regulating itself by means of flotation devices to open and close the dependable overflow that levels itself in a field whose gravity is *what wants to be seen*, what wants to be dreamt, what has been carried across the beaten path in a trance cadenza, each raising of a banner or a monstrance marking the stave out of which flutter long roulades of moaning recapitulation tipped in red, under a wall of guarantees where the pedimented windows look down on you like someone else's grandparents, sometimes charming but always firm, always your sadness and their joy, some single perfection frequently lost and found like the clear view of leopard's spots in the black fur of a panther, what you can (in other words) only hold to as a set of faces of dead persons looking out at you unless you prefer the more clinical synchronism that can at least guess how intricately they advertise the selective stare of notaries at you over their writing desks.

What wanted *me* in Rome, I supposed, what I walked around avoiding for three seasons before finally walking in, was the Museo Napoleonico, where you know in advance what you will find, the Bonaparte coat of arms gradually reasserting the mind of the family over the extraordinary gestures of Napoléon, what indeed took place long before he fell, defined itself forever when he declared his brother King of Spain, thus, like the novelist he had been from the start, interweaving tragedy and romance by writing into the script a fatal weakness and a long future as a prototype for ambitious colonels in South America, a move that military historians too readily call the limits of his strategic capacities but one that a more vagrant mind can plainly see as his gardener's neatness that makes plots, as one does, by putting around the growing things a wall or a hedge, since it was recognized at the time that no one else, least of all the pliable Giuseppe, who would much have preferred to remain king in Naples where his name had a profound resonance, could see the use of this dubious new conquest, though it is clear enough by now that it gave the chorus something important to say, a way for them all to have known better and to give evidence, as it were, of how patiently they had waited at the gate for the great planter to emerge. So I was nothing surprised this time. The whole display laid out before the visitor the same funereal luxury I had recognized a year earlier in Paris as my own violence of doubt and insincerity, and exuberantly enough that it opened out like everything else in Italy the spiral clarities and confusions of an acid fingerprint on the onyx, what they publish as the history of the trombone or the anthropology of bleeding statues, carefully observing the women link arms in the procession but not quite catching how it is that they manage not to let go of the dead, or of me, since I just caught how they mime the way I turn my head or trail my hand along the balustrade, so, though I have been locked into a first-class compartment all the way from Venice to Naples with a committee of social engineers, their excellent instruction has been refused entry into the treasure-balls of infancy rolling up and down in the night and the morning, roosters crowing at lunchtime and in the castle a moment to pause over the case of medallions or to show the visitor the miniature of Napoléon's sister's granddaughter, a great beauty, who lived here till the end of the century on a kind of volcanic lip composed of the same long memory and the same long meals

that were making, down in the valley, an inaudible murmur you thought had reached you
when the hilltop winds crossed in the long
grass like riptides and vast flashing silver
schools of tiny fish.

The sun does not travel in a chariot. He
does not come in the morning red as blood
over Austerlitz. He does not handle the golden
bridle of his foaming furious coursers. His
armor is not of beaten brass. His eyes do not
flash long fires. His hair does not stream in the
rushing ether. Nor does he pass through
sphere upon sphere seeking the gifts of
mankind. He has no regard for the buffalo in
the flat fields. He has not stood at the apex of
heaven and singed the thatch of houses. But
you have made his journey nonetheless. You
have risen in order to descend. You have
emerged from deep caves into the brilliant
light of further caves where the same stories
are being told and the same doubts engraved
on the high gray walls. You have seen that you
will kill this Italy this morning in order when
you wake up to build it a monument from
which the need to escape must press just as
hard. And the narrative will spring from the
ground like asparagus Apollo revealing his ma-
jesty over mountains in the usual tears of
blood. We have his picture here. We have his
picture in granite. We have sent you his picture
carefully worked in lacquer. This is my great-
grandmother's enamelled locket with his pic-

ture on the day of Marengo. This is my mother and father at my niece's house. This is a medal of Papa Giovanni with a fragment of his clothing inside. This is the skull of Pope Saint Alexander. This chapel contains the pelvises of five hundred Capuchin monks, arranged like the petals of a rose. This is a postcard of Astoria Square in 1920 with the trolleys and the United Cigar Store, still owned by the same family but much larger. We will go tomorrow to the Catskill Streetcar Museum.

We cannot remember the crimes of the rich long enough to ruin our digestion. My whole trouble, anyhow, is the opposite of Robespierre's. Not an accident. Burial. The French Revolution died of its own coherence, leaving behind its incredibly glassy allegory as a draughtsman's kit with which to plan canals where we have been watching, ever since, the occasional pollution of the water with human blood, and even sometimes the advent of long barges littered with bunting and with refurbished arcana but followed, inevitably, and preceded by the customary drab baboons, our dilemma floating up as a choice between old and new forms of the same fear for what we had hidden under the floor, a problem, however, resolved by Napoléon who changed the one for the other so frequently it amounted to a kind of transubstantiation, the wingtips of dialectic reduced to the radiant glimmer of a portable television set which we carry all over the world without anyone's quite noticing what it really is, not a device but our sense of possibilities. Oh, you say you know him perfectly, the little fellow in the bowler hat, or Mickey Mouse as Steamboat Willie: You have given the correct answer yet have failed the test. This is a grave difficulty.

What might have happened once upon another time I could not say. My mother's way, however, was to help, when her beloved cousin Bill was in a jam, by buying from him a piece of land for which she had no use. Came, five years later, the Long Island Expressway, right in front of it. Ten years after that, she sold it and bought a house in Florida with the proceeds, so that after another fifteen years I finally gave up and went to visit Walt Disney World with her. Like Napoléon's tomb it is so completely insincere that you know it must be honest. Only two things, so far as I can see, are lacking: the Princeton University Library, which induces on another plane a similar euphoria of thorough accessibility, and my mother. My mother showed us Disney World because she owned it. It said almost enough, and she supplied the rest. She called the lights to twinkle on Cinderella's Castle at twilight. In Paris they will have one, too, as they should. But it will be nothing to the one, none of them will, we will build in Italy.

Yes, we must. Not everyone can read so well as you can. Not everyone will have the patience to sit in the gardens of the Quirinale, as I have done, following yet another account of the French Revolution. Somehow before this it always escaped me that on the fourteenth of July, 1789, they went out to Les Invalides to get cannon and shot and that the invalids, just as real on that eerie Monday as ever before or since, joined the crowd and crossed the river to the Bastille. Looking up, I could see, in the rounded pediments and homely wooden shutters of this stateliest of Papal palaces, just why it is that these things never quite happened here, why even the Risorgimento could not make up its mind to go the final distance, because here, at the crucial moment, someone gives way and the bus gets through the narrow street. But this is opaque. We must make it clear. We must put an end to the fruitless debate of the rich and the poor, and begin to talk of who we truly are in our communicating tunnels. Since, if we do so, we may begin to find out what's going on, we must, and boldly, construct this Versailles of the little-middle-class, as the social scientists impatiently call us, Daisy Duck and Ronald Reagan, they think, but you know I know we know they know better, because it was neither of these sadlings that carried himself and his bride in a kerchief down the ice of La Maiella or across the jagged bradyisms of Pozzuoli eighty years ago in order to return last year in a BMW bearing a computer, six hundred books, and an electronic piano, all so that he might sit at his leisure watching the Basilica of Saint Peter turn before his eyes into a bar of perfumed soap. No. That was somebody else. Not especially cuddly he, even if you do find him ridiculous with his scowl, his folded arms, his American tricorne hat. Her Monopoly set, my sister once called it. My uncle Patsy's 1948 black DeSoto had a terrifying gleam. The sentimental communists have tried to make believe we aren't coming or that they themselves, with their praxis of sober restraint and excellent prose, do not in fact belong with the rest of us in the airconditioned bus. L'Astoria does not move, however, except to collapse. It is we who do the moving.

I have given this project a great deal of thought. You must remember that by trade I am among the bureaucrats of theory, riding into the rushing wind taking snapshots in every direction, all exhibits for my proposal. Its principle is very simple: *you cannot leave a place you have not been*. And we have yet to be where we already are. It is not quite there yet, as you see. We need a place where these movements that now only tease our perception can take a lucid form and so die. It must be a garden, but not just any kind of garden. It must be the garden of a myth — which does not mean, in our case, some long recollection suitable for monography but the garden of a movie. Tinkerbell thrills you as a Kennedy can or an Agnelli, because you already know her from the cartoons. In Disneyland, which is my point of departure, you walk around under broad daylight in a collective dream you had imagined only took place in the dark. It is as shameless as a Roman bath and makes for a thoroughly transforming pilgrimage — what theologians call a metanoia. You go home justified to your ranch house. You have been to America. You are inoculated against older creeds. Italy has nothing like it, but the day they invent one will be their millennium, which is my proposition. Of course, they have tried it: there is EUR, where the colonnades without capitals give some hint of what is possible. At first I thought this new garden should be called *Made in Italy*, an apocalyptic parking lot like Disneyland, full of elephantine Pinocchios and Saint Paul carrying a light saber. Then, growing serious, I revised this as *L'Astoria* where the Divine Comedy became an elaborate ride employed to advertise funicular railroads. There was to be a mountain where one fought in Garibaldi's army and was shot by automata dressed as French soldiers. At the end they were to give you a T-shirt bearing the motto *You Aren't Italian Until You Have Died in the Risorgimento*, and you sang the theme song, very funny in Italian, *Mamma, voglio fare l'Astoria*. But I saw this was all wrong. Why try to destroy what already does not exist? Perhaps, I thought, we should make a park called *Europe*, all gnomes and dwarfs in dirndls and lederhosen, Big Ben and the Last Supper fully plastic. But that, really, would be Disney all over again, and we want the next, the current, phase. We want the disappearing future, the naugahyde sofa running into the horizon. That is, we want an Italy consuming all these others, leaving the Popes on the shelf with the dusty milkbottles full of unexploded gasoline. Something might be done in a grand way, yes. Rollerskating in Saint-John Lateran. I would like a great glass mountain range and a great glass ocean, a sort of fountain, on the Gianocolo, with, then, at the other side of it, Hellgate and the Triborough Bridge and l'Astoria itself, all in glass, the whole thing reminiscent of disappearing ice, and there my mother, thirteen years old, beautiful and glass, looking across the water, and glass Bill waving to her as he leaps into the bottomless flood. But we, perhaps, we little people, we don't build that kind of monument. And we don't really need a separate park. Just a wheelchair, fleets of wheelchairs, each with its tank full of drinks and finger food and its talking computer, for rent in every town, rolling you all over, and occasionally, as machines will, taking an independent line, beginning to talk about some other place, Paris in Rome, Antibes in London, Brooklyn in Palermo, a reminder, as the big spoked wheels bounce around the cobbled corner and stop dead before some long facade drooping with saints, that you are still in motion.

• Cap-Saint-Ignace
• Sainte-Marie (Beauce)
Québec, Canada
1996